# Tell Me When It Hurts

For further information, please contact:
chris@whiteheadlegal.com

Printed in the United States of America

Designed by Arbor Books, Inc.
www.arborbooks.com

*Tell Me When It Hurts*
Christine M. Whitehead

1. Title   2. Author   3. Thriller/Romance

Library of Congress Control Number: 2008912044

ISBN-10: 0-9822946-0-3
ISBN-13: ISBN: 978-0-9822946-0-4

# Tell Me When It Hurts

## Christine M. Whitehead

Hadley Press

# CHAPTER
# 1

The assignment was easy enough—the target was the proverbial creature of habit. She watched him get to his New York City parking garage stairwell, mochaccino in hand, *New York Times* tucked under his arm, keys to his fancy BMW Z4 dangling.

What wasn't fancy about him was his lust for little girls. A year ago, he'd beaten a first-degree murder charge when the eyewitness and the forensic evidence proved unreliable. Luck and the devil had been on his side—then. On the eve of trial, the sister of the dead girl had been slated to give the jury a guided tour of her sister's last minutes. After scores of interviews, however, the kid had started to waver. During a pretrial prep session, as the prosecutor played devil's advocate, the eight-year-old began shaking so badly that her mother declared she'd had enough. She wasn't going to lose two daughters in this tragedy.

When the chain of custody of DNA samples—samples that had nailed the man dead to rights—were bungled, the charges had folded. No eyewitness, no DNA, no case. To make matters worse, the accused, buoyed by the botched police work, was threatening a lawsuit for false arrest.

Archer Loh watched him skip down the garage steps, head up, briefcase swinging. Her grip tightened on the rifle. *Go ahead. Enjoy your last moment, pal. This is for Marcie…* Snugging her finger against the trigger of her modified HK G36, she breathed in and let it out slowly. And gently squeezed.

Archer stepped up onto the low wooden porch of her log cabin in the Berkshires, swung the door open, and braced herself for the onslaught. The next instant, a hundred pounds of chocolate lab came bounding into her arms. She stooped, dark auburn hair falling over one eye, and hugged the dog. She stood up. After stowing the rifle case in the front hall closet, she dropped the duffel in the kitchen corner, read the note on the counter from the dog sitter, and opened the refrigerator—empty except for an apple, a dozen eggs, and a stick of butter. She'd been gone for two days, and the sight was uninspiring.

"Hadley, old girl, looks like it's omelets tonight," she said, closing the fridge. The lab wagged at the mention of her name.

Archer glanced around the two-room cabin. The late afternoon sun lit up the floral patterns on the red Heriz rug and fired the distant hills in gold. The cabin consisted of a living area with a kitchen at one end, a bedroom, and a bathroom—simple, uncluttered, all a girl could ever want for living in self-imposed exile.

She flopped down on the sofa and leafed through three days of mail. She got few letters and fewer social invitations. Her family had stopped inviting her to parties years ago. She'd always hated disappointing them by not showing up, but she hated going even more. It was always the same. *Life is for the living,* they'd say. *Annie would have wanted you to go on with your life,* some other well-meaning dolt would always add. Truth was, Archer had no desire to go on with her life. She *had* no life—or rather, what life she did have was a cliché, right in there with the cheesiest movie of the week: *An Eye for an Eye* meets *La Femme Nikita*.

Archer flipped through the letters. She saw the usual generous monthly check from her father's lawyer in New York. Thank God for Daddy's planning and good financial sense. If it had been up to her mother, things would be, well...*different*. But then, her mother had passed on her fluency in Hungarian, for whatever that was worth.

Amid the envelopes addressed to "Resident," she spotted the letter from Connecticut. She didn't want correspondence from them, just the monthly bill, thank you. Archer frowned at the letter for a moment, then slid open the flap and shook out a typed page. She unfolded it and began to read:

*Dear Archer:*

*As you know, we've been boarding Allegra for six years now. Since you have refused to let us lease her out, she is unfit and, frankly, unhappy. You have been a good client, and we appreciate your patronage. However, we again request your permission to either sell Allegra to a child or teen who would love and enjoy her, or at least reconsider leasing her out. Horses need to be used, and Allegra needs to be needed. She is truly wasting away here, and it distresses us, as horsewomen.*

*Please reply with your monthly payment. We hope you understand that our thoughts are expressed out of concern for Allegra. We know that Annie would want her to be loved.*

*Sincerely,*
*Jane Russo*
*Owner, Mad River Farm*

Archer sat back, deep in thought, and scratched behind Hadley's ear. Allegra. One of the most beautiful horses she'd ever seen, with that perfect white heart on her forehead—an Arab/Thoroughbred cross with the temperament of Bambi. The horse to give Annie her own moment, her own passion. Archer slumped inward at the memory. The little mare had delivered in spades. Allegra had been the knockdown, take-your-breath-away love of Annie's life.

Archer stared out the window for a few seconds, not seeing. She then fingered the letter, rereading its polite rebuke, silently accepting its truth, though unable to change it.

She shook her head. How silly and naive her little dream of mother-daughter gallops along Irish pebbled beaches and across English moors had been. Now the dream just mocked her.

Booting up the computer, she wrote:

*Dear Jane:*

*Thank you for your concern about Allegra, but I do not want her leased out or sold. Enclosed please find a check for her monthly board.*

*Sincerely,*
*Archer*

She reread what she'd written. It seemed cold, but it was all she had to say. She folded the crisp white paper in thirds and tucked it in an envelope, to be mailed tomorrow with a check.

Archer walked over to the liquor cabinet, the omelet forgotten, and pulled out the Maker's Mark and filled a tumbler, no ice. She dragged a ladder-back chair over the plank floor to the front hall closet. Standing on it, she reached back to a big, pastel pink box on the top shelf, pulled it out, and brought it carefully down. She lit some candles, then the fire, and then, as if savoring the prospect of opening a special present, sat on the big braided rug, opened the box, and spread out its contents. Hadley came over and plopped down on the corner of a birthday card; Archer slid it from under her and put it with the other treasures.

There was the handprint from kindergarten, a photo from Disney World at age seven, a snapshot from Halloween—their special holiday—at age nine (Annie Oakley), a red show ribbon for equitation from when she was eleven, and a blue ribbon, won on Allegra when she was twelve. Archer opened the report card from second grade—*Annie is a pleasure to have in class, is always prepared, and is a friend to everyone*—and caressed a childish finger painting of their old house with Hadley, as large as the house, standing in front— a big brown oval with a tail. She picked up a pink plastic barrette, clicked it open, snapped it closed, and put it down. Ribbons, a beaded necklace, and a stick of gum. Scores of baby pictures, several school pictures, and a lock of hair, light brown and wavy.

Archer sipped the whiskey slowly, sifted through the contents, and pretended it had all turned out differently. As the country song said, she was having a "night to remember," and it was like ripe melon that, once in your mouth, turns sour.

Jane Russo opened the barn door, rolling it easily to the right, watching the sun creep around the door's edge and blaze up the aisle. She walked into the hay room, leafed apart an open bale, and began tossing hay into each stall. She kept moving, a full day of chores ahead of her. She hesitated in front of the bay mare's stall. The horse nuzzled in between the bars, and Jane stroked the warm, velvety nose. Allegra nickered.

Jane wondered if she would hear from Archer. She'd been one of the few mothers she enjoyed having around the barn. Given Archer's status in her day as first alternate on the U.S. Olympic equestrian team, Jane had braced for a prima donna, but Archer had proved self-effacing and funny.

It must have been awful for her: Annie's murder and all, and then to have her husband—Adam? Andrew?—leave her, remarry, and have two little kids of his own...ugh! Barn gossip had it that Archer had left her big job as a lawyer downtown, that she'd had a breakdown of some sort. Now she lived somewhere out in the Berkshires and, as far as Jane knew, stayed in touch with no one. Since Annie's death, Archer had never returned to the barn or seen Allegra again. She paid her bill but stayed away.

Jane sighed and hoisted two flakes of hay into the stall. The horse needed someone to love—needed a purpose. On the occasions when Jane took pity on the animal and put her in the cross-ties to groom her for a ride, Allegra would shift her weight restlessly, paw the concrete aisle a few times, and then stare steadily at the door, as if wondering what happened to the little girl with the big grin.

# CHAPTER
# 2

Archer woke the next morning hungover. More often than not, she needed a stiff drink—or three—to sleep. But she was a lousy drinker and always paid the price the next day.

She covered her eyes with her arm, then stretched and groaned. Sitting up halfway, leaning on one elbow, she peered at the alarm clock... Ten-something. *Oof.* She rolled over and started to go back to sleep, then heard paws pad over to the bed and stop. Opening one eye, she found Hadley peering at her.

She smiled. "Okay, old girl."

Archer climbed out of bed, slogged into the bathroom, and downed two aspirin with a glass of water. She wrapped a too-bright green terry robe around her, stepped into her black clogs, and pushed open the back door. Hadley was off like a shot into the woods.

Archer turned on the coffeemaker, which she had loaded the night before, and opened *Mansfield Park* where she'd left off.

Almost an hour had flitted by when she heard a knock. She looked up from her book. No one had ever knocked on her door, not once in four years. She got up and pushed aside the curtains on the kitchen window. Standing at the door was a tall, lanky man with thick brown hair, some gray at the edges, glints of red in the morning sun. He wore faded jeans, a worn denim work shirt, real cowboy boots and a hat to match, and was scuffing one boot along the granite step of the back stoop. He was looking down, his hands dug deep into his saddle-colored jacket. He had Hadley tied to the end of a rope, and a black dog sat at his heels. She let the curtain fall back into place.

Archer picked up the .30-30 Winchester she kept in the corner, then pivoted, pressing her back against the solid, windowless door. She called out, "Who is it?"

There was a slight pause, then, "Connor McCall, your neighbor." The voice was deep, friendly.

"I don't think so—I don't have any neighbors," Archer called back through the closed door.

"Well, you sort of do now." He said nothing else for a moment, then filled the silence. "I just inherited the land next to yours and came east to check it out… Been here a few days now. Set up a little camp down the trail a piece." He spoke slowly, as though he had to think about it and had all the time in the world to do it.

Archer absorbed his message for a few seconds, then said, "Well, that's all very interesting, but I'm not catching yet why you're at my door, Mr.… McClure, is it?"

"McCall. McCall, like the magazine," he corrected. "Yeah, I know. Your dog wandered over and, frankly, it seemed like a good excuse to come over and introduce myself. We seem to be the only humans around for fifteen miles in all directions…" He stopped, as if he may have misspoken. "Well, what I meant is, we're way out here, and a neighbor is nice to have sometimes." He paused, then said, "I didn't mean to intrude on you, ma'am, and I sure as hell didn't mean to scare you."

For the first time in a week, Archer almost smiled. *Don't flatter yourself, cowboy.* She was silent for a moment, then pulled the hammer back on the rifle. It made a sound universally understood by those on either side of the law. And still he stood on her porch. Finally, she spoke.

"Well, Mr. McCall, thanks for coming over, but actually, there is no need to introduce yourself. The mountain is big; my dog knows her way home, so no need for an escort the next time she wanders over. There aren't too many cotillions up here, so you and I won't be likely to cross paths much."

She could hear him jingle a few coins in his jacket pocket and could almost see him shaking his head, hands still in his pockets. Randomly, she recalled she'd been voted "friendliest senior" in high school. She bit her lip but stayed with her back against the door, rifle at the ready. The silence stretched on until her new neighbor finally broke it.

"Okay, well, I'll be going, then. We're only a quick walk apart, though, ma'am, so I'd ask that you not shoot me on sight. If you do need a hand in this wilderness, just dial three-o-seven-C-McCall—I'm happy to see, cell phones do work out here."

"Yeah, the people going to Tanglewood like to stay in touch with their brokers. They lobbied hard to get that attractive tower put in down the road." Archer said, wincing. She knew she sounded snide, maybe even bitter.

Silence. Then, "Well, if you need a cup of sugar, neighbor, or lunch, I'm one hell of a cook…three-o-seven-C-McCall. So long, pretty puppy." She could hear him bend down to pet Hadley. "Anyway, see ya."

*Oh, no, you won't,* Archer thought, walking to the kitchen window and peering out just in time to see him amble back into the woods, the black dog on his heel. Once he was out of sight, Archer opened the door.

"Well, aren't you Miss Congeniality!" she grumped at the tail-wagging Lab. "Just remember, we don't need any neighbors, Haddie. We—that's you and me—are loners. We don't need anyone," she said, rubbing the broad head.

It was midafternoon. Archer pulled on a Martha's Vineyard sweat-shirt and took off on her daily run in the woods, with Hadley barreling along ahead of her. Following an old logging path, Archer kept a relaxed pace, enjoying the fall weather. The leaves had just begun to turn. Around Columbus Day, a few weeks from now, the woods would be in their full blazing glory. And by Halloween, the trees would be bare.

The air felt fresh and crisp. A light breeze blew. Archer heard the leaves crunch beneath her feet. Then, rounding a curve that led up a hill, she saw it. In the clearing to the left of the path was a tent and a campfire, and—god*damn*—a paint horse, picketed and grazing peacefully near the tent.

Archer slowed and began to jog in place, taking in the scene. Just then, she saw Connor McCall walking up the path toward her, some kindling in the crook of his arm. He saw Hadley, then her, and his craggy face broke into a smile. "Hey, the voice behind the door, I presume. How you doing?"

Ignoring his question, Archer stopped jogging altogether and stared at him for a few seconds. "What are you, Daniel Boone or something? Did you *ride* that horse up here?"

Looking from her to the horse, then back to her, he shrugged. "Actually, I did. Left my trailer down near the road in a clearing, saddled up, and rode up to the site." He paused, then cocked his head. "You afraid of horses or something? 'Cause if you are, this one's a real sweetheart—'bout as friendly as a golden retriever."

Archer raised an eyebrow. Finally, she murmured, "Hardly."

For a moment, she stood with her arms folded on her chest, appraising the horse again, then looked back at Connor McCall, and spoke more softly, "I just didn't expect to see one loose up here. Aren't you concerned he'll run off on you?"

"It's a she, actually—Millie—and no, she wouldn't do such a rude thing. She ground-ties and pretty much stays where she's put." He tilted his hat back a bit. "So, you a horsewoman? Do you ride?"

"Neither," she said, a little too quickly.

"Oh…" He paused. "I just thought with all the questions…So anyway, how about that lunch we talked about? Or breakfast? I'm out nine, ten every morning on a basic hygiene mission to the Motel Six, but I could do before or after that." Another pause. "What's your name, by the way?"

"*You* talked about lunch; *we* didn't. And no thanks, I'm always busy," Archer replied, turning back to the trail to resume her jog. She stopped for a moment, remembering for the second time that day that she had once possessed social graces. She turned back and stuck out her hand. "Archer Loh." He grasped it, gave one firm shake, and smiled, but she had already turned away.

"Nice to meet you," he said to her back as she started away. "So, what do you do up here, Archer? You a botanist, or a writer, or…something?"

Archer sighed, looked down, and silently counted to five. "Look, I'm sure you're a very nice person and all, but I live here because I really don't want to be with people. So if it's all the same to you, we're not going to be coffee-drinking neighbors. Sorry, Mr. McCall."

"Connor—you can call me Connor. Well, it never hurts to have a neighbor, you know. I have a good first-aid kit, lots of CDs, and a fair number of books," he said. She gave no response, just a steady, unsmiling gaze.

"And…hey, I'm better than nothing," he ended, losing momentum.

"Not really, Mr. McCall," she said. She turned back to the trail and started to run again. She caught his puzzled look and added over her shoulder as she jogged away, "Better than nothing, that is. Let's go, Hadley."

"Well, maybe some other time," he yelled as the distance between them grew.

"No, no other time," she hollered, not looking back.

# CHAPTER
## 3

A rcher sat on the couch reading, legs tucked under her, sipping her second cup of coffee. Hadley snoozed loudly at her feet. A few days had passed since Connor McCall's unasked-for appearance on her doorstep. The day was bright and cool—a good day for riding, she thought reflexively.

She laid down her book and stood up. "Hadley, go for a walk?"

The lab lifted her head, then lumbered off the couch and shook herself. Archer grabbed her cell phone and shoved it into the back pocket of her jeans, hesitated a moment, then stepped over to the refrigerator and pulled out a bag of carrots, and headed out, bag swinging.

As Archer rounded the bend near her neighbor's camp, she saw no one except Millie, the paint horse.

"Hello?" she called. "Anyone home?" No answer. She called again and advanced a few more cautious steps. Silence. Satisfied that no one was around, Archer slowly approached Millie.

The horse, munching lazily on a lush patch of grass and timothy, raised her head. Ears twitching, tail swishing, she eyed the newcomer for a second, then went back to her grazing. Archer moved closer until she could just touch the horse, then reached into the bag and held out a carrot.

The black and white head lifted. Downy lips trembled, then grasped the carrot. The mare began to munch and immediately stretched out her neck for more.

Archer felt warm, moist breath on her hand. "Oh, you like that, don't you, girl?" She ran her palm down the horse's muzzle and stepped closer, offering another carrot.

When the carrots were gone, Archer turned to leave, giving Millie's rump a pat. A little cloud of dust rose. "You need a grooming, girl. You'd shine with a little work."

Before she left, Archer leaned into the mare's neck, inhaling deeply. Then she looked at her watch and pulled away. "Come on, Hadley. Gotta go." She hesitated. "Maybe...maybe I'll see you tomorrow, Millie." And she headed down the path toward home, humming softly.

The next morning at about the same time, Archer found herself back at the camp. Again finding no one around, she plied the mare with molasses treats and three peppermint candies. Then she unrolled an old towel on the ground and started pulling things from a tan canvas bag: a hoof pick, three brushes, a tail comb with wide teeth, and a spray bottle of detangler.

"Here we go, Millie," she murmured. "I'll make you the talk of the mountain."

Then she grabbed the hoof pick and began to work.

For the next hour, Archer cleaned and combed and groomed, talking steadily while she worked. This was the first time since she was thirteen that she didn't have her own horse—unless you counted Allegra, which she didn't.

It had happened quickly, her falling in love with the horses that jumped. When she was eight, at her first horse show, she'd stood, fingers curled around the boards of a rough-hewn fence, and peered through the gaps, watching every move the thoroughbreds made. By the time she went home, she had a goal: to ride open jumpers where only the best rode, wherever that was.

Taittinger's Clique, known outside the show ring as just Clique, was Archer's first horse. At only 16.1 hands, he was small to be a world-class jumper, but he had all the other right stuff: perfect jumping conformation, superb athletic ability, and a "just point me at it" love of taking fences. It was enough; he made it work. While Archer loved him for being a stand-out athlete, she loved him even more for being her best friend at a time when she needed one.

Smiling at the memory, she moved behind Millie and went to work on her tail. She separated a small clump of hair from the rest of the tail, sprayed it, and began teasing out the tangles with the comb tines. Working a small section at a time, she combed through the knots patiently, and within twenty minutes, Millie's tail was silky and loose, floating behind her when the breeze caught it.

Moving in close for the final touches, Archer slid the soft bristles of the finishing brush down the mare's face, whisking away small hairs and debris with long, loving strokes. Millie's ears relaxed and her eyes half closed, as if she were savoring the last minutes of a really heavenly facial.

Millie gleamed, the dapples shining on her dark flanks. Archer stepped back to admire her work and grinned, then scooped the brushes up and put them in the canvas bag. Leaning her head against Millie's neck for a second, she gave the horse a final pat, called Hadley, and headed home.

The next day was raining, but Archer trotted toward the camp at nine o'clock anyway, leaving Hadley home. She approached cautiously, though she was pretty sure that her neighbor—Connor McCall, was it?—was away daily until ten thirty, performing his morning ablutions at the Motel 6. She slowed as the tent came into view. Millie greeted her with a nicker and was rewarded with a few slices of apple. Archer gave her a pat, then looked around.

The tent flap had blown open. She walked over and bent to pull it closed. As she did, she spotted a loose-leaf notebook, lying open on the sleeping bag. She glanced back over her shoulder, then stepped in. Her eyes adjusted to the dimness.

The tent was big, perhaps fourteen by seven feet. It had a mesh vent along the back wall, a skylight, a gear loft for storage, two pockets for more storage, and a mesh window to let the air in but keep the bugs out. Steel poles at the corners held it firm and sturdy. The sleeping bag along the back wall had a patchwork quilt pulled over it, and a portable CD player sat within easy reach. In the front right corner, next to a director's chair, were a radio, a gas lantern, and a big flashlight. On a blanket in the far left corner were piles of books and papers, and a separate pile of folded jeans and T-shirts.

She took another step in, then back out, then in. Gazing to her left, she eyed the tidy pile of books. She knelt down and glanced at some titles. *Fathers and Daughters: In their own words; The Long-Distance Parent: How to Parent from Afar,* by George L. Thoreau; *The Business of Sheep Ranching,* by Duncan Walsh; *The World According to Garp,* by John Irving; *Passages,* by Gail Sheehey.

She then moved to the sleeping bag and flipped through the CDs piled near the portable player: Sinatra, Coltrane, Enya. . . *Enya? He likes Enya?* Brooks and Dunn—eclectic tastes.

Then her eye fell back on the notebook. She sat down on the sleeping bag and glanced at the open page.

*Lauren's birthday is coming up soon. October 1. She'll be nine. I wonder if she'll have a party...*

Archer flipped back to the beginning of the notebook: pages of script, pasted tickets, some photos, a few postcards, more script. On one page she saw a photo of a woman standing in front of a fruit stand, smiling. The sign on the stand read "Rose's Berry Farm." On the opposite page, a teenage boy was beaming at the camera, holding a gray horse on a lead rope. On the bottom, a caption was scrawled in ballpoint: "Sabrina and Me." Turning the page again, she saw a postcard of the Eiffel Tower, with a note under it: *Maybe Lauren would like to see this someday. Is she taking French this year?*

About to turn another page, Archer looked away, feeling guilty. Had she really sunk this low? She closed the notebook with a snap, then, remembering it had been open when she arrived, reopened it. She went outside, and Millie looked up.

"Till tomorrow, Millie," she said, and headed home.

In a fitful Maker's Mark sleep that night, Archer remembered it all again: Clique standing alert, practically on tiptoes, ears pricked forward, shifting his weight from side to side, waiting at the entrance gate for his turn, the glint of bit at the edges of his mouth, the sound of him champing it between his teeth, the scent of lanolin and saddle soap on soft oiled leather. Madison Square Garden on a June night. *The Garden*—the place she had dreamed of long ago, not even knowing its name. The place where only the best rode.

It was all there, clear as yesterday, from the quick pat on Clique's neck to her own little shiver as she squeezed him lightly. The horse moving under her, gaining momentum, the customary canter in a perfect circle before starting the course…Some murmuring in the background as horse and rider set off at a steady pace…the acceleration as she pressed him forward into the bit…the building impulsion…

As Archer took her first jump, the Garden quieted. The crowd watched the girl and her beautiful horse move in unison over jumps taller than she was. They went over with no hesitation. *Now,* she thought, squeezing with her calves just behind the girth...*now*...The coiled spring released in an upward sweep of energy as they jumped the five-and-a-half-foot wall. *Jump, stride, stride, jump, jump, stride, stride, jump, stride, jump, jump, and jump.* When they completed the last jump with no faults at breakneck speed, the moment was captured, distilled—timeless.

It was all there. In that dreamy softness between sleep and almost sleep, Archer summoned the exquisite triumph again. At twenty-one, a senior at Smith College, she had lived her one spectacular moment, the moment that would carry her through a lifetime of ordinary, the one that would be retrieved for sustenance when life fell short. The floating canter around the outer edge of the arena; her gloved hand caressing Clique's neck; Adam's cheers, identifiable above all others; her father, catching her eye, wiping away a tear as he sat anonymous and proud in the stands, tweed jacket across his lap, felt hat resting on one knee; her own wide smile; and the feel of the horse beneath her making her strong.

# CHAPTER
# 4

A dam MacKenzie sat on his front porch, watching the rain pour down in sheets. He liked Colorado; it was where he had met Allison. The evening was cool, but Adam was comfortable with just a sweatshirt. He propped one foot up on the railing and struck a wooden match to light his pipe, puffing until the coal glowed evenly. He thought about Archer—and Annie, of course. Archer's birthday was yesterday, September 5, though he doubted that she had bothered to acknowledge it even to herself.

Archer...From the day he met her, he'd known she was something. She'd been so sassy then, always teasing, always tossing that head of dark hair—and laughing. His best memories were of Archer doubled over laughing.

"Hey, Minnehaha, this is a serious legal issue," he'd say after describing to her one of his new criminal cases only to find her limp with laughter.

"But it *is* funny," she had insisted, gasping for breath. "I mean, they steal a police car and then stop for coffee at Dunkin' Donuts—

the quintessential cop hangout—and are picked up with lattes in hand." He started to laugh, too.

From their first meeting, on a bus heading back to college, to their wedding four years later, he'd never once doubted their cosmic rightness for each other. But for one twist of fate—his Karmann Ghia being in the shop that week—he would never have been on the lumbering behemoth, grinding north to Dartmouth and passing through Northampton, Massachusetts, home of Smith College. The thought of the near miss still made him wince, decades later.

It came back to him easily, that first glimpse of Archer. He'd been engrossed in *Sports Illustrated* as the bus clunked to a stop in Hartford, Connecticut. Glancing out the grimy window, he saw a gamine girl with a book bag slung over her shoulder come bouncing up the steps of the bus after turning to wave to a stylish blond woman in a black Mercedes. His gaze followed the wave and he caught sight of the woman waving back wanly.

As his eyes turned back to the girl, Adam lost interest in the magazine. She had thick auburn hair falling straight to her shoulders, green or maybe blue eyes, high cheekbones, full lips, pale skin. Neither tall nor short, she had a slight figure and was wearing gray riding pants, paddock boots, and a deep-green parka. Audrey Hepburn, in place of Elizabeth Taylor, as National Velvet, he thought as the girl grinned at the bus driver, her book bag falling forward. She shifted it back, tucked a wayward lock of hair behind her ear, and headed for a seat. As she sat down, he glimpsed "Smith Equestrian Team" in white block letters on the back of her parka.

Adam felt as if he were on a Ferris wheel that had just crested the top and dropped. He knew, with the fervor and certainty of a born-again Baptist, that he was meant to be hers.

The girl took a seat across the aisle, a row in front of him, plopped her book bag on the seat next to her, and pulled out *The Sun Also Rises.* Then she reached back in the bag and fished out a leather case to put on a pair of wire-rimmed glasses.

Adam flipped through the mental Rolodex of the great loves of his life—well, more like a list of three: Jackie the rower, Joan the artist, Kate the scientist. Or was it Kate the rower, Jackie the artist, and Joan the scientist? He glanced at the girl across the aisle—no chance of ever mixing *her* up with anyone else. Watching her read, he yearned to slip into the seat behind her and lean forward just enough to read over her shoulder and breathe in her scent.

Adam nudged his duffel forward with his foot and slid into the seat in front of him. Taking a deep breath and wishing his long suit were a James Dean devilish charm instead of a Jimmy Stewart nervous sincerity, Adam leaned over and cleared his throat. "Um...is that seat taken?"

She looked up from her book, eyes wide, and gave a slight smile and a shake of her head. She moved her bag to the floor and went back to her book. Adam kicked his duffel over, and hopped in beside her.

He glanced over at her open book, maintaining a respectful distance but stealing occasional peeks, happy to be sharing this slight familiarity. He glanced left and read:

> *"Isn't it rotten? There isn't any use my telling you I*
> *love you."*
> *"You know I love you."*
> *"Let's not talk. Talking's all bilge. I'm going away from*
> *you, and then Michael's coming back."*
> *"Why are you going away?"*
> *"Better for you. Better for me."*

Adam looked away. Fascinating stuff, that Lady Brett Ashley and her cohorts, he supposed. Better than striking up a conversation with the dull shlub sitting next to her.

Finally as they entered the city limit of Northampton, he blurted, "So, you go to Smith?"

She looked up, eying him curiously as if for the first time. "Yes."

"What year are you in?"

"Junior."

"Ah," he said, as if this were a most revealing bit of information. "I go to Dartmouth—junior, too."

"Oh, do you like it?"

"Yes, I love it."

"Hmm, I always thought the guys from Dartmouth were smart jocks who drank too much on weekends."

Adam thought fast. "Oh, not me. Well, I mean I am kind of a jock, but at least I'm not smart, and I'm always the designated driver... Oh, right, I'm the exception that proves the rule," he rushed on.

She broke into a grin. She had straight, white teeth. "I was just teasing you. Everyone I know from Dartmouth is great." She seemed about to comment further when the bus slowed. She glanced out the window.

"Northampton," called the bus driver.

"That's me," she said, rising and gathering up her things.

"Hey," said Adam, "I'm Adam Mackenzie." He held out his hand.

"Oh, I'm Archer Loh. Nice to meet you," she said, grasping his hand firmly. Hers was slim and cool. She turned and began moving down the aisle toward the door.

"Well, maybe I can call you sometime, do you think?" Adam called out.

Stepping down from the bus, she turned and called over her right shoulder, "Oh, sure! Gillette House—" The rest was drowned out as the wind swept in and her words swirled up and away.

Needless to say, he'd found her. They were married right after both graduated from Columbia Law School several years later. Adam had proposed six months earlier, on a snowy day just after Christmas, as he and Archer strolled arm in arm along Fifth Avenue, the Christmas lights haloed in a van Gogh blur in the icy air. They had just had the least expensive dinner in town: tacos and beer at Margaritaville on Forty-first and Fifth Avenue.

"Hey, MacKenzie, you think I'm some cheap date you can get into bed after just a chintzy taco?" she teased, looking up at him.

"Well, if the riding boot fits…" She punched him on the arm.

In front of Tiffany's, Adam stopped and turned Archer toward him, both hands on her shoulders.

"Arch, I may not be able to come up with a Tiffany ring right now, but I can offer you a lifetime of love, law, and laughter," he said nervously. *And alliteration*, he might have added. "I really, truly love you, and I can't imagine going through life without you. Will you marry me, Arch? I'll never make you regret it."

Grinning, she pulled her ski cap down tighter over her ears and gave him a mittened thumbs-up, then stood on tiptoes and squeezed him with all her strength. "Yes, yes, yes, I will marry you, Adam. Anywhere, anytime."

Adam stood still, then threw back his head and laughed at the gods, returning the hug for all he was worth. He had planned this uncountable times. It was to be a grand gesture their grandchildren would beg to hear retold again and again—perhaps on bended knee some April morning among the lilacs in the Cloisters. Or on ice skates in Rockefeller Center on a February afternoon. Or at the top of the Empire State Building some sultry July evening, just like in *An Affair to Remember*, one of Archer's all-time favorite flicks. Still, the unchoreographed proposal couldn't have been more perfect.

Now, more than twenty years later, on this porch outside Denver, mountains in the distance, Adam puffed on his pipe and felt again the heartbreak of a dream gone wrong. Archer. She was the love of his life, and he had lost her, and he had lost Annie. Yes, he had Allison and the boys, and he loved them. He was luckier than Archer in that way. He'd taken a second chance. But there can only ever be one first love, the one love that makes you ache with the knowledge that you can never survive its loss and still be who you are meant to be.

In his own dreams that night, Adam could still see her victory lap at Madison Square Garden, the reins in one hand while the other stroked Clique's neck; her endless smile, and the cocky confidence that comes from being twenty-one and feeling as though you had the world in your pocket.

# CHAPTER
## 5

Archer ran a comb through her hair. The sun was shining after the morning rain and her illicit tour of Connor McCall's tent. She glanced in the mirror at the door, grabbed her car keys, and headed out. Hadley trotted around the side of the cabin and jumped into the back of the old Jeep. Archer buckled up and cranked the engine.

She headed down the driveway, steering clear of the deepest ruts. Fully three-quarters of a mile long, that driveway had been one of the cabin's main attractions when, four years ago, she was looking for a place to call home.

She had known that the suburbs no longer suited her. The thought was laughable—the grieving assassin next door. *Oh, going out of town again, Archer? Want us to walk Hadley? Take in the paper? Watch over your arsenal?* No, the cabin was perfect: no questions, no neighbors—a place just to park herself until...well, whatever.

The Jeep lurched through a rut near the end of the driveway, jolting her back to the present. Hadley swayed on the seat and lost her footing but scrambled back up easily. At the end of the driveway, Archer got out and opened the locked iron gate, hopped back in and edged toward the road just far enough to clear the gate, then hopped out again, relocked the gate, and pulled into the traffic.

She hummed as she drove to the local Stop & Shop. To her surprise, she had found that she liked to cook. In her old life, meals were brief, no-frills affairs or they were takeout—there was just no time between her practice and Annie's schedule. Now, though, she had some fifty cookbooks arranged in alphabetical order in the bookcases lining the kitchen walls. She now had time to burn. She cooked meals daily, setting the table with the "good silver," as her mother called it, a starched linen tablecloth, and taper candles, all for a party of one.

Her last dinner in an elegant restaurant with tablecloths and candles had been in Washington, D.C., when she and Adam were awaiting the trial of Annie's killer, the day the bombshell was dropped on them: the DA's office was not going to prosecute.

"I'm sorry, Ms. Loh, Mr. MacKenzie. We're just not going to be able to prosecute this one. I'm really sorry," the prosecuting attorney had said, eyes downcast, mouth drawn tight, his words hanging in the air like a bad smell. He'd been the picture of confidence a few weeks ago. Now he looked defeated, slumping in his leather chair, looking small and ineffectual.

Archer stared, mute, waiting for him to take the words back, to say he was thinking of another case, but he didn't. Everything in her tightened. Her hands closed into fists; her jaw clenched; her eyes squeezed shut in denial. She leaned into Adam, dizzy, unable to right herself under her own power. She knew that the killer had hired the top criminal defense lawyer in D.C., but even so, they had evidence. They had an eyewitness. *What happened?*

She hadn't waited to hear the maddening, incomprehensible details. Everything she'd done for nine months—her assemblage of a parallel evidence folder, her analysis of the inconsistencies in defense witness statements, her notations on the medical examiner's report— my God, he was saying it was all of no use. It was all a fraud. There would be no trial, no justice, no satisfaction of even the meanest sort. *Stop!* she had told herself then. *Stop thinking about that.*

But she couldn't. Then it happened as she sat rocking on a graffiti-covered oak bench outside the district attorney's office, wringing a handkerchief, wadding it up, then releasing it, her eyes rimmed red. Adam was still in with the lawyers, trying to make sense of it. She'd run out, choking down the rising bile, unable to bear the sudden, sickening realization of their impotence. Archer already knew it was over. Adam was still arguing the point, but she could see it clearly enough. It was all over but the crying.

Archer had raised her hand to her mouth and clamped down hard to stifle a howl of protest at the injustice of it all. Annie—her Annie—meant nothing to these people. It was just another case that had been botched. *It happens,* she knew they would say among themselves. *It happens sometimes. Things get fucked up. We're only human. What can you do?* Then they'd shake their heads and leave the office for a drink at the pub next door.

As she sat stunned, nails digging into the palms of her hands, arms hugging her body, one of the assistant DAs, who had sat in on several of their meetings, passed her. About thirty-five, she was pretty, her long blond hair held back in a barrette, low at the nape of her neck. She wore a chocolate wool pantsuit. She paused, pivoted back, then perched lightly on the bench next to Archer. She placed a smooth, finely manicured hand on her shoulder.

The woman hesitated, then said, "There is a way to get justice. Wait a week. Then call this number." She handed Archer a small pink square of paper. Archer took it mechanically, then stared dully at the woman. The woman smiled sadly, squeezed Archer's arm in a gesture of solidarity, got up, and left. The statement barely registered, but she thrust the scrap of paper into her jacket pocket.

The next week, as she prowled her West Hartford home, unable to eat or sleep, Archer had gone into the kitchen closet and yanked the jacket off its hanger. She dug into the jacket pocket, pulled out the pink piece of paper, stared at it, then put it back in the pocket, and hung the jacket back up.

The next day she pulled it out again. The numbers seemed fainter today than yesterday. *Disappearing ink? Jesus, Loh, get a grip.* She stared, but this time she dialed the numbers. She was transferred twice via automated voice mail until she heard the voice of a real person.

"Can I help you?" asked a brisk male voice.

"I…I was given this number to call for help," stammered Archer.

"And what kind of help do you need, ma'am?" asked the voice, formal but not unkindly.

"My daughter was murdered and they let him go. They just let him go," she said. "I don't know how you can help, but…but I can't live…I can't go on. I just…This can't be right. It can't be right," she said, shaking her head though no one could see.

"Ah, I see," he said. "I need your name, address, courthouse and docket number, Social Security number, child's name and birth date, and phone number. Someone will be in touch if your information checks out."

While the man waited, Archer jerked open desk drawers, quickly assembling it. Most of it was in just one file. The man hung up after taking her particulars. Archer shook her head, expecting nothing. Was this what it was like? Like ordering a fleece jacket from L.L. Bean?

But she did hear something. About two weeks later, on a sunny day in June, just over a year after Annie's death and just after Adam left for his office, there was a knock on her front door. Archer peered out the sidelight window. There on the stoop was a handsome, slender young man in a business suit and sunglasses, and beside him an even younger woman with long dark hair, in tight jeans and a T-shirt decorated with Mick Jagger's smirking open mouth. Archer opened the door.

"Hello. May I help you?" she asked through the locked screen door.

"Archer Loh?" the man asked, looking down at a sheet of paper he had just taken out of his inner jacket pocket.

"Yes."

"Mother of Hannah MacKenzie?"

"Well, yes. What is it? Has there been a development?" asked Archer, eyes eager, thinking that perhaps the district attorney had changed his mind. But she realized instantly, he would have called on the phone if that were the case; he wouldn't have sent two members of the Mod Squad to inform her. The young man didn't give his name or the name of the woman with him.

"We're here from a private group that tries to see that justice is done when the legal system fails. We take action only if you request it. We got your call and felt, after a review of your case, that our involvement is appropriate—if you want it, that is. We do need to know now, however," he added, and Jagger Girl nodded.

The man spoke with authority. He appeared calm, but there was also a warmth about him. He smiled, and his eyes did, too.

"We know. We understand, but this is your choice."

"Well, what exactly *do* you do? And what does it cost?" Archer asked.

"No cost. We do an eye for an eye," he said simply.

Archer made her decision immediately. "Yes—*absolutely* yes."

The young man nodded. "Okay, then. For Hannah."

It was her first meeting with Gavin Kennelly. Although Gavin did not personally do the hit, he saw to it that their top urban sharpshooter took out Annie's murderer three weeks later. The man was leaving a D.C. movie theater by himself at 11:05 p.m. No one was ever charged. One consequence of the meeting was that Gavin and Archer became fast friends, ultimately leading to Archer's becoming the forty-second member of the Group.

Adam had gotten a call the following week from the district attorney's office, noting the coincidence. He told Archer that night. She stared at him a moment, then said, "Well, what goes around comes around." They never discussed it again.

They separated a year later, civilly but sadly. Archer recalled it all and sighed deeply, tears filling her eyes. Regrets enough to go around, Archer thought, biting her lip and willing herself to think only "blue-sky thoughts," as her group therapy leader called them. Not the memories that take you to the "bad place." *Ugh.* She hated group therapy. Within the space of six years, the Group—and not the therapy group—had become her family, her friends, her career, her religion.

The Group comprised forty-five people from seventeen countries, allied by grief and horror, each a survivor of personal tragedy and of paralyzing impotence at the hands of the justice system. With each member contributing as his or her resources permitted, they were an impressive collective of strengths. One was a physics professor at an Ivy League university, with an encyclopedic knowledge of explosives and how to trigger them; another, an English heiress who committed her personal fortune to the cause; and the newest member, a technology genius who had masterminded cutting-edge encryption technologies used by various Fortune 500 companies to secure their e-mail communications. Taking the technology three steps further for his own use, member forty-five guaranteed the impenetrability of the Group's infrequent communiqués.

The Group's rules of engagement were simple: It took on cases with at least one reliable eyewitness or, better yet, conclusive DNA findings, where the damage was irremediable and the accused had gotten off for other than substantive reasons. If the justice system worked, wonderful, but if it failed, they stepped in—though only with an invitation. Although assignments were routinely handed out in reverse order of geographic convenience to minimize the chances of an operative's connection to the hit, Archer's last job, the man in the parking garage, was an exception—the Group had such loyal and long-standing ties in New York City that there was less need to go through the customary subterfuge of using an operative from across the country.

Apprehension and arrest were always possible, but being in the

Group made the possibility remote. Given its staunch sympathizers in every major U.S., European, and Asian city, its serious financial backing, and the steadfast cooperation of key members of big-city police forces and certain district attorneys, the Group had had only one arrest in its fifty-six-year history. And even then, the charges had been dropped within two weeks after seven pillars of the New Orleans community swore that the accused was at a black-tie dinner with them on the night in question. Photos were produced commemorating the event, and further inquiry ended.

Archer shook her head and moved back to the here and now. She wheeled her cart past the dairy case. Enough woolgathering—there was dinner to fix. At the seafood counter, she pointed to pink shrimp and fresh clams in the glass display case, then added a box of linguine, a big bulb of garlic, virgin olive oil, arugula. Oh, and some apples for tarte tatin.

She pulled into her driveway a half hour later, just far enough for the Jeep to clear the road, then went through her ritual with the gate. Anxious to get the shrimp scampi going, Archer speeded up the steep driveway, trees lining both sides, wheels flinging up bits of mud behind her until she pulled up by the house and hopped out. Lifting the back of the Jeep, she looked up and saw a redtail hawk wheeling high overhead.

"Look, Haddie, Gus is back!" she said, hoisting the two bags of groceries in her arms.

Hadley barked in reply and bounded ahead as Archer trotted to the front porch, but in her haste, she caught her toe on a root. She fell fully onto the bags and immediately wailed in frustration. Pain shot up from her ankle.

"Damn, damn, *damn!*" she moaned. "Great, just great."

She pushed up onto her knees and, leaning on the porch step rail, tried to weight the leg. She winced and sat back down. She rolled up her pant leg, probing the ankle with her fingers and palm. *Ugh.* Just a sprain, but a bad one. Still, it hurt like hell, and it was her *right* ankle, damn it, her driving leg.

As Archer mentally calculated how long it would be before she could resume her routine, she heard whistling, then approaching footsteps. Connor McCall turned the corner of her cabin, stopped, stared, and sized up the damage at a glance. Archer looked up at him. From down on the ground, he seemed really tall.

"I…I just tripped. I was looking at Gus, our hawk, and didn't see the root," she stammered, craning her neck to look up at him.

"Well, nice to see you again. I was coming over to see if your cell phone was charged up. My battery's almost dead, and I need to call my ranch by the end of business today. I can charge up in my truck, but you're closer, so…" He eyed the mess. "Yeah, I can see you tripped on something. Too bad about the shrimp," he said, surveying the torn packet, the garlic cloves strewn next to it, and a box of pasta, apparently intact. "I do love shrimp scampi over pasta," he sighed.

Connor looked at Archer again and paused a second, as if wondering how to fix things. Then, in one graceful movement, he bent down, scooped her up, and carried her up the front steps onto the porch. Automatically, her arms went around his neck. Balancing Archer on one bent knee, he pushed the wooden door open, walked across the room, and eased her down onto her sofa, the end near the fireplace.

"I could have walked with a little help," Archer muttered.

"No big deal. You're no harder to carry than one of my small ewes, and you weren't exactly hopping up. Sorry if I offended. Anyway, can I wrap that ankle or something? I have first aid stuff at my camp."

"No, no, it'll be okay. I've twisted it more times than I care to remember. A little ice, and it'll be great in a week or so."

Connor walked into the kitchen, opened the freezer compartment, and removed a handful of ice cubes. He placed the cubes in a towel lying on the counter and folded the corners. He walked back to Archer and gave her the ice pack.

"For the ankle."

"Thanks."

Archer pulled up the leg of her jeans and peeled back the navy blue sock. It was already swelling. She snugged the ice pack around it and, in spite of herself, sighed with relief.

As Archer examined her foot, Connor gathered up the scattered groceries. On the second trip in, he brought the rebundled shrimp packet and the box of linguine while, unaccountably, whistling "Winchester Cathedral." Without asking for direction, he put everything away.

As he finished putting some lemons in the basket on the counter, Archer recalled that she owed him a favor. "Uh, my cell phone's always charged up. It's on the kitchen counter. You can use it if you want."

"Thanks. I appreciate it."

Connor turned to the counter and picked up the phone, fiddled with it for a few moments to see how it worked, then managed to punch in a number. A pause, and he spoke, apparently to an answering machine.

"Uh, Felix, it's me, Connor. Just calling to see if things are going okay. It's payday tomorrow for the summer guys, so just have Jim Betts sign the checks, and be sure the guys get paid before the banks close on Friday or there'll be hell to pay. Say hi to Susie and tell her she's still my favorite. Okay, that's it. Talk to you soon."

Connor found the Off button. An awkward silence settled.

"So…then, is Susie that lucky girl back home who's waiting for you?" Archer asked in a half-sincere effort to be sociable.

Connor cocked his head and studied her for a moment as if weighing whether he could joke with her. He jingled a few coins in his pocket, then shook his head. "Not really. Susie's my foundation ewe, and although sheep are not the smartest animals, Susie knows me and, I think, knows that she's key to the whole operation." He grinned. "You might say Susie made me what I am today."

More silence.

"Ah," said Archer, unable to think of anything else to add.

"You know, I realize you aren't exactly rarin' to be friendly, and God knows I'm not much good at it myself, but do you need any help till you can get around better?" he asked, arms folded on his chest.

"Oh, no, thanks. We're fine, really."

There was a moment of silence while he looked at her.

"No," he finally said, shaking his head, "I don't think you're fine, at least not for a few days. I hate to be the one to break it to you, but this isn't exactly the neighborhood for ordering takeout. I'll be back with Alice to make you dinner. I think I can salvage that shrimp scampi; nothing actually hit the ground, and I snatched it up pretty quick. I'm a good cook, by the way—did I already tell you that?"

Not waiting for an answer, he checked the ice pack, then nodded and left by the front door. She heard him go down the front steps, and his melodic whistling receded into the woods.

# CHAPTER
# 6

Looking back, Archer always thought of the year after graduating from Smith as "the lost year." Planned as a year of work in the real world before starting Columbia Law School, the "tween year" for her and Adam was to be altruistic by design, probably low-paying as a result, and fun, if at all possible.

Adam's job fit the bill. After graduating from Dartmouth, he effortlessly got a job teaching geography in a magnet school in Harlem, to start in September. He rented a tiny apartment with two other teachers: Cody Geronomo, a gay art teacher, and Travis James, a black mathematician who had grown up three blocks from the school where they would teach. Adam rode his bike to the school each morning, hoped it would be there when he came back for it at four, and trusted that he would make a difference for someone. The job was definitely low-paying, somewhat altruistic, and fun enough if defiant teens happened to be your idea of fun.

Archer's job was another story. Her honors history advisor, John Vilardi, had steered her to apply for a job with the Justice Department. He suggested that her fluency in Hungarian, and her knack for languages in general, combined with her perspective as a history major, could prove useful in an internship. The job was as a "liaison specialist" and was slated to begin in mid-August. The job title puzzled her some—with whom was she to liaise? And about what exactly? The job paid adequately and promised exposure to the legislative and judicial processes, and though it had no obviously fun part, who knew?

"Hey, Arch, you're gonna miss me when I'm gone," Adam had teased as they strolled along Main Street in Litchfield in July.

Archer smiled her best Mona Lisa smile, aware that he took comfort in knowing that they both had been accepted at Columbia Law School and that both had deferred for a year only.

"Oh, sure," she said with a toss of her head. "Of course, I'll be so busy going to diplomatic balls with foreign dignitaries, I may not notice you're gone until April or so."

Archer had moved south in early August with everything she owned slung into the back of her mother's old Volvo wagon. She'd rented a studio apartment in a "transitional neighborhood," as the realtor called it. The transition looked to be off to a slow start, she reflected, staring at the crumbling front of her brick apartment building, and the blighted tenement house next door. Her second-floor walk-up's only charm was the vaguely rustic wooden deck off the kitchen, overlooking an interior community garden of flowers and vegetables. The charm wore off when Archer spied a rat feasting on the produce.

Her father drove the wagon, and Archer hauled the horse trailer behind the old Ford pickup to a stable in Alexandria, Virginia, where Clique would be quartered for the year. She'd kept the old Volvo to get around in and left the truck at the stable. As she said good-bye to her father at the airport, she clung to him.

"Oh, Dad, I don't tell you anywhere near enough, but you are the best. I couldn't do any of this"—she gestured feebly—"without you. Thanks for everything, Daddy."

Porter Loh had hugged his daughter tight. "And you, my dear Archer, are worth any trifling little inconvenience in my life. There isn't a thing I wouldn't do for you."

Assigned to a group operating in the basement of the Justice Department Building, Archer spent her first two months organizing data collected by security personnel on candidates for federal jobs on the lowest rung of the career ladder. She worked in a stark room with shiny yellow walls and a long Formica table, setting out pages of background data on each candidate in neat piles. Then she prepared a summary page to place on top of each profile so lazy or harried members of Congress could grab the gist at a glance while walking down a hallway.

For variety, she compiled dull dossiers on visiting dignitaries. Her work area was drab and dim, and lonely, to boot. At times, Archer rued her decision to defer law school. At least Adam actually was helping someone.

When Archer's boss decided to make use of her fluency in Hungarian by sending her to Budapest to deliver some classified papers, she jumped at the chance to get out of her monotonous routine and that grim basement. She picked up her tourist-class plane ticket from her boss's assistant, Cassie, the day before the flight.

Cassie was about sixty, with a tight perm in her blue-gray hair. She had the serene confidence of a lifetime federal employee who had made herself indispensable to her boss. "So, off to Budapest, I hear, Archer," Cassie said, smiling and handing her the ticket, her itinerary, an enlarged map of Budapest with key streets highlighted, and directions to her hotel.

"Yes," replied Archer. "I've never been. I can't wait."

"Well, judging from your schedule, you won't have much time for sightseeing, dear, but still, it will be an experience, I'm sure."

"I know. It's a short turnaround, but still I can practice my Hungarian on real people—not much call for it over here," Archer said, nodding. "Thanks, Cassie."

"Bon voyage, Archer."

Upon her return, Archer was startled to find five thousand dollars in cash in an envelope tucked under the blotter on her desk. She studied the envelope: white, plain, heavy bond. Her name was typed in the middle, but there was no return address, no indication of the agency. There was no note enclosed, just the cash in crisp new hundred-dollar bills. Assuming it was a mistake, she went to see her boss, a grandfatherly-looking man with the bland, generic name of Peter Bennett. He was decidedly *not* grandfatherly in demeanor or bland in affect. She knocked on his office door.

"Come in if you must," Bennett called out.

Archer entered tentatively. Bennett sat at his desk reading from a fat loose-leaf notebook, short white hair carefully combed straight back, horn-rimmed glasses low on his nose. He wore a brown tweed jacket with a yellow and green paisley tie over a cream-colored shirt. He looked up over his glasses as Archer entered.

"Well, hello, Ms. Archer Loh, my favorite intern. What can I do for you? How was Budapest, by the way? Lovely city, isn't it?"

"Yes, it is. I loved it. But, Mr. Bennett, when I got back, I found this envelope of cash on my desk with my name on it. I think it must be for someone else," Archer said, holding out the packet.

He didn't take it. "Hmm, no, I think it's for you. You did that courier thing over there, didn't you? Went okay, didn't it? Well, we always pay an incentive fee for such services. Lucky you on this one. And call me Peter, would you? 'Mr. Bennett' seems rather formal. We're a small office, and everyone gets to know everyone pretty well." Bennett smiled quickly, then looked back down at his notebook as if their business were concluded.

Archer stood there a moment.

"But I didn't do anything really…uh, Peter. I just went to the address you gave me, and gave the packet to the man who answered the door."

"Well, that was all this particular job required. Don't look a gift horse in the mouth, Archer. That was the job; the envelope is the incentive. This boat doesn't need rocking, so there it is. Have a lovely day." Bennett finished with a wave of his hand.

Archer turned and left, confused but cautiously thrilled, feeling as if she had won a small lottery. How lucky she'd been to be chosen for such a simple assignment with such a windfall! She'd bank it for a rainy day.

Several days later, Peter Bennett called her into his office. She arrived as he was shoving papers into a battered brown leather briefcase, hurrying to catch a plane at Dulles.

Barely looking up, and without any preamble, he said, "Oh, yes, Archer. I'm a bit concerned about you. Dodgy neighborhood you're in. I love D.C., but we are the murder capital of the nation, you know. Far cry from my hometown of Des Moines. Far cry even from Oxford, my alma mater. Go to our little class on self-defense, why don't you? Humor an old man in his dotage. Hate to see my favorite intern stabbed to death while I'm in Beijing," he finished with a wink. He closed the clasp on the case, grabbed his coat, and moved briskly out the door, looking anything but the picture of an "old man in his dotage." The "my favorite intern" thing had become a tired joke, but Archer supposed he thought it was cute.

"See Cassie. She'll set you up. Little school we run up in New York State. Go up for a month or whatever. I'll be back in a week or two. Have fun," Bennett said, sprinting for the elevator.

When Archer stopped by Cassie's office, Cassie seemed fully apprised of the situation.

"Oh, yes," she said. "Peter mentioned that. Your ticket to Syracuse will be here this afternoon. Just drop by any time after three, Archer."

"What is this place, Cassie?" Archer asked.

"I only know we do some training up there. Routine self-protection stuff, I think. You'll have fun, I'm sure, if Peter's sending you," said Cassie, as if Peter would never dream of sending an intern anywhere that was not a guaranteed fun-fest.

Archer left for Syracuse the next day, where she found herself the only woman among a dozen men, all from either West Point or Annapolis and all about six or seven years older than she. The "self-defense" curriculum was narrow: basic weaponry, scoping tactics, ammunition alternatives, and stalking the target. That was it. The minimum stay was six months, though a year was preferred. *Six months!* Archer thought with alarm. *This can't be right.*

She had expected basic karate moves for fending off the average mugger, evasive driving maneuvers for outwitting the random carjacker, and strategies for responding to a potential rapist. What she got was a program light years beyond that. The contrast between her expectations and the real thing was actually laughable. This program, if completed, would fully prepare her to launch a revolution in a modest-sized developing country and defend herself against anything short of a nuclear attack. Archer's fellow students looked capable of it already. Though they were obviously curious, Archer sensed no animosity or testosterone-fueled hostility. They were generous with their help and seemed perfectly comfortable with the idea that someone, somewhere, felt she needed to be there. That was enough for them.

At the end of the second week, Archer had had enough. She drove down to Washington on a Sunday night to confront Peter Bennett on Monday morning. The Volvo chugged steadily south, with Archer sipping coffee to stay alert on the night drive. She stopped only for gas and coffee refills. Once in Washington, she sat in her car outside the Justice Department, waiting for the doors to open at 8:30.

When they did, she ran a comb through her hair, walked inside, and headed straight to Bennett's office on the second floor.

Cassie looked up, surprised to see her. "Oh, Archer, how are you? Back already? Peter will be in this morning, but he's booked pretty tight. Do you need to see him?" she asked. When Archer nodded, she replied, "Then have a seat. He should be in soon, but don't count on more than a few minutes with him."

Archer sat outside Bennett's office until he arrived at 9:10.

"What the hell is going on?" she asked, hopping up from her metal seat in the waiting area and walking alongside him into his office.

"Well, good morning to you, too," Bennett said as she stepped along with him. He slipped off his light overcoat and hung it on a hook on the door, closing the door behind him. "Have a seat, Archer. I thought you were up in Syracuse. Now, what seems to be the problem?"

Bennett sat heavily on his green leather desk chair and hit the intercom, holding up a finger to delay Archer's response.

"Cassie, a coffee, please, pronto." Pause. "Right, thanks."

He looked up at Archer. "Okay, shoot. What's the problem?"

"The problem is Syracuse. I'm in training for a hell of a lot more than self-defense around the old neighborhood. Assault weapons, silencers, stalking tactics. What *is* that training center you sent me to? I'm a nobody, a little intern here for a year, and you're sending me to training for six months? For my own *self-defense*? Come on!"

Bennett hesitated, uncharacteristically reticent for a moment, then said quietly, "Well, Archer, I have to admit, we do hope you'll stay on a few years. We feel there is a place for you here. We have many needs and programs to fill, and there is one highly specialized program that we think would be an especially good fit for you."

"What are you talking about, Peter?" she interrupted. "I'm going to law school next year. I'm a one-year gofer—you know, see how the halls of Justice work, then move on?"

Bennett sighed patiently. He was fiddling with a paper clip while leaning back in his chair. He closed his eyes for a moment, then said, "You see, Archer, you are an interesting combination, all in all. Quite interesting. You're small and rather wholesome-looking, which makes you less likely to arouse suspicion at airports, or wandering around a foreign city, or…what have you. The Israelis always have these Amazon women you can spot a mile away. So obvious…" He sniffed with disdain. "You're also smart. Your grade point average at Smith made you a summa and a junior Phi Beta Kappa, and your IQ puts you into Mensa territory."

Bennett was now studying the ceiling, speaking without pause, an adman rattling off the virtues of a new product.

"Further, you're good with languages and are already fluent in Hungarian—a rare language and, just coincidentally, the very one used in some of our confidential communiqués. Not quite as rare as Navajo wind talker language, it's true, but it takes a while to figure out. Not Slavic, not Indo-European. Only Estonian and Finnish are even close, and barely at that. You'd be surprised how many linguists are stumped by it—at least for a half hour, maybe an hour, which is usually all we need. With limited resources, most intelligence training is going into Chinese, Arabic, Middle Eastern languages—nothing European. Strangely, Hungarian has worked very well for us of late."

Bennett paused as his secretary knocked and then entered with his coffee.

"Thank you, Cassie," he said as she placed a mug on a coaster on his big mahogany desk.

"Anytime," she said with a smile. "Anything else, Peter?"

"Not at the moment, thank you."

Cassie turned and left, closing the door quietly behind her. Archer sat stunned, her heart speeding up with each comment Bennett made. Her fingers were clenched in a tight knot in her lap. She wondered what else Peter Bennett knew about her. As it turned out, she didn't have long to wait.

"Where was I? Oh, yes. You ride horses like an Apache, which, could prove useful in certain circumstances. And you have steady nerves, judging from the video I saw of you jumping a six-foot wall. Quite impressive, by the way. I liked watching you. Very elegant, you and that horse you had there.

"But I digress. You're heterosexual—not that we care, but it keeps things simple. Our testing shows that you are resourceful and rather creative when backed into a corner, and tend not to be bound by traditional rules, although in many ways you are quite traditional—conservative, even." Peter looked up for a moment and, seeing the confusion on Archer's face, added, "Oh, right, when you took your law school entrance exam—you know, the LSATs—we added a little segment to the test that...er, no one else got. Just you. We've found it quite helpful in homing in on the characteristics we require. John Vilardi thought you might be a potential fit for us, and we are opportunistic in that way," he continued matter-of-factly, without apology.

"We'd really like to have you for at least two years, Archer. Preferably longer, but we're not the Mafia. You're free to leave anytime. We hope that if you leave, though, you care enough about this country to keep your own counsel about the things you do and see."

Bennett paused and looked at Archer as if to gauge her reaction. She sat silently staring at him, then spoke. "Want me for what?"

"An operative."

Archer waved her hand in the air dismissively. "Speak English, not CIA mumbo jumbo. What kind of work do you want me to do—exactly?"

Bennett hesitated, then said, "We're not CIA. We're—how shall I put it?—a semiautonomous joint arm of the Justice Department and the Pentagon. A little cusp agency, shall we say, all but invisible to the naked eye." He paused to sip his coffee, then continued. "We want you to be a sniper—for the good guys, of course," he added hastily. "Archer, this is an opportunity—a tremendous opportunity." He was leaning forward now, eyes bright. "Your country needs you. Your mother's family came here from Hungary in 'fifty-six and found safe haven from a tyrannical regime. Can't *you* give two years to your country? Just two. Reagan is going to make a sweep of it in November, and we'll have even more latitude and superb resources, financial and otherwise. You've seen the quality of our training facility."

Archer said nothing.

"The money is good. It's cash—tax free."

Archer stared at her hands for a minute, then looked back into those eager eyes. "You want me to kill certain people—people I don't know—just because someone somewhere thinks they should die?"

"Archer, Archer. Don't be naive. You may not know the reason for the assignment, but I can assure you there is a reason, and a good one. Look, just give it a chance. Do the training, and if, at the end of it, you decline, well, we'll shake hands and you can finish out your little internship and return to your other life, if that's what you want. Hey, look at the perks—after our training, you won't have to be afraid in a dark alley. You see, you really are my favorite intern," he concluded with a wink.

Archer was unmoved. "Tell me, Peter, if I ever got caught, would you or the Agency or whatever you are get me out, go to bat for me, or am I hanging out there on my own?"

"Well, that would be a bit of a sticky wicket. You see, we are unofficial, and if…that ever came to pass, we would have to, uh, deny any knowledge of your operations. Surely, you can see why that would be necessary."

"Sure," she said with a wry smile. "Sure. That's the story, then."

"Look, finish the training, Archer. What else do you have to do for the next seven months? Write thank-you notes for some bauble from the Ambassador of Ceylon or Sri Lanka or whatever the hell they're calling it these days? Review boring foreign student visas? Come on, that's not for you," he cajoled. "You'll die of boredom."

Archer felt a strange combination of repulsion and attraction. Bennett's agenda repulsed her, and she felt violated, as if he had just ransacked her personal desk and read her journal. *Maybe he had.* Moreover, she hated being "handled." Still, she hated being bored even more. She hated preparing tea for visiting heads of state and being window dressing. He was right on that point: she wasn't cut out to be an office worker bee. In truth, some aspects of the "program" intrigued and attracted her, and in spite of herself, Peter Bennett's zeal was intoxicating, and the man himself was inspiring. Spending another six or seven months at the training center would at least be interesting—maybe even useful.

She made up her mind. "I'll finish the training, but then I decide."

"Absolutely," Bennett said, putting out his hand. She shook it firmly, then turned to go. As she grasped the doorknob to leave, he added, "Oh, and, Archer, I'd suggest you keep this little assignment to yourself. No need to tell Adam. Easier for everyone, you know. We can help you with the cover, if you like." He picked up the phone.

Archer stopped and turned around, finally nodding. She was at her old table in the basement before she realized she had never mentioned Adam's name to him or anyone else at the job.

For the first time in her life, Archer couldn't make it home for Christmas. Her father said he understood that her career had to come first. She would miss seeing his eager face peering out as she pulled into the driveway on Christmas Eve. Adam was disappointed, too, but seemed to revel vicariously in her trip to Paris on government business. He told her the best places for a Christmas Eve dinner on the Left Bank, having gotten the scoop from Cody Geronomo.

In fact, Archer was in Syracuse, not Paris, mastering the cleaning, assembling, and loading of various firearms in the dark, while on her knees in a forest blanketed with ten inches of snow. On Christmas day, Archer and her colleagues ate turkey while sitting on benches at a long table. Archer put a bouquet of wildflowers in a glass, and three candles on the table—for "atmosphere," as she put it. The rest of the group teased her.

"Oh, yeah, Arch, now, *that* makes all the difference."

"Hey, Arch. Are you sure those flowers aren't wired, Arch? Everything else around here is."

"Oh, yeah, I never noticed what a gorgeous place this is by candlelight, Arch. Thanks for making all this possible. You've opened my eyes. In fact, I think I love you, Loh."

Archer gave him a mock sneer. "Shut up, Dobbs, or I'll forget it's Christmas and give you the finger."

"Oooh, no, not the finger."

"Yeah, Arch, when we run into the bad guys, be sure to give them the finger. That should scare them to death."

"Just be sure, Arch, that some finger, any finger, is on the trigger of your Uzi."

Everyone hooted, including Dobbs.

"She's got your number, Dobbs."

"Hey, Dobbs, even in the dark, you're stump ugly."

Banter aside, they were touched by Archer's gesture and pleased they weren't alone on Christmas on this dreary Syracuse afternoon. One of the West Point guys, Davis Jones, sat down at the spinet piano wedged haphazardly into one corner of the dining room. To Archer's surprise, he was a more than competent player.

"Man, I loved Christmas as a kid," said Davis, getting up from the piano to eat with the others. "My brothers and I lived for it. My mother could get us to do anything just by saying, 'Just wait till Christmas.' We were poor as church mice then, but we remember a really happy childhood, and Christmas was the happiest day of the year."

"That's funny, I always hated Christmas," said Deke Curran, taking a bite of stuffing but not before scrutinizing its lumpy texture. "So many expectations, and then my father would get drunk by five on Christmas Eve, my mother would end up crying and yelling at us kids, and we would cry and yell at our father for hurting our mother. I couldn't wait for it all to be over and go back to school. How about you, Archer? *Bleak House* or *It's a Wonderful Life*?"

"Hmm. Well, I had a pretty happy childhood, guys. No dark stuff, and I loved Christmas. Still do. But it's different now. When you're a kid, it's about the stuff. Now it's more about getting together with family, since we're all going in different directions the rest of the year and don't live together," she said thoughtfully. "Guess we're each other's family this year." She paused. "And come to think of it, I barely even like you guys."

"Hey, it *is* just like family. I hate my sister Sherrie; what an asshole *she* is. And I'm not too crazy about my brother, either. This *is* just like Christmas at home, now that I think of it. I hate you guys, I really do!" Harrison Dobbs exclaimed, grinning and helping himself to more turkey and gravy.

Everyone laughed, and Davis uncorked the champagne, provided courtesy of Uncle Sam, and they toasted one another and the future. They even sang a few Christmas carols; then Davis played ragtime tunes into the wee hours.

On Valentine's Day, when Adam thought Archer was in Rome attending a midlevel diplomatic conference on global warming, she was in El Salvador, collecting intelligence on a guerrilla group in the mountains after the military's assassination of Archbishop Romero. When her six months of training ended in March, Archer stayed on. She spent Easter in Baghdad, observing the movements of one Mohamed Al Jahad for future targeting if necessary. Memorial Day found her in Israel, learning advanced scope shooting and escape options.

Peter Bennett showed up monthly to give a pep talk and observe the day's maneuvers. Although he never made notes, Archer knew he was sorting them, evaluating them, planning their futures for them. Still, when Bennett grabbed a long-range sniper rife to illustrate the optimal stance for executing a shot from a vertical position, strong wind at the shooter's back, Archer was impressed. Not just a suit, then.

Archer saw Adam once every six weeks or so, in New York City. Her work and home phones were rigged to forward calls to a line in Syracuse, where the home phone rang in Archer's barrack room and the work phone went to an office at the main training building, where it was answered, "Justice Department." Archer felt bad about the deception but rationalized it as a short-term expedient.

When Adam suggested visiting her in Washington, she protested that New York was the only city in the world worth living in, and she wanted to be there. It was a schizophrenic existence. While she was in New York with Adam, her other life seemed preposterous and unreal. She ate in restaurants on Fifth Avenue, wore clothes from Barney's, and laughed with Adam's friends, drinking beer at a brasserie. Then, when she was back in Syracuse or on assignment, New York was barely a memory.

Archer got out at the end of her year. She hadn't had to do a hit, but she could. When she told Peter Bennett of her decision, he took his glasses off and rubbed his forehead.

"Archer, Archer. You don't know what you're saying. All the reports I've had on you have been superb. Everything I've seen has been as close to perfect as it gets," he said as he flipped through a manila file on his desk. "Look at this," he said, stabbing at the page with his finger. "You're the number one shot in your class. Think about it: *number one*. Better than every guy from West Point and Annapolis. My instructor says there are two Marines who can match you in the right conditions, but still, it's nothing short of remarkable…and priceless."

He got up and walked over to the big freestanding globe. "Christ, Archer, you can't possibly find more important work than what you're doing now, here, for us. After two years you'll have a fantastic start on financial security, at the age of twenty-three or -four. And you want to quit—have you lost all *reason*? What's the matter with you, girl?"

"What happened to 'It's your choice; we're not the Mafia'?" she asked coolly.

He gave the globe a spin. "Of course it's your choice, Archer, but no one leaves. No one *wants* to leave," Peter sounded uncharacteristically angry, dismissive.

"Look, Peter, I finished the training—did the full year and then some. I gave a lot of thought to this, but this is someone else's agenda, someone else's decisions about what's fair, who lives, who dies. And they may be well qualified to make those decisions, but I'm not in on them. I'm just doing someone else's wet work, with no explanation. It's not for me, Peter."

Stopping the globe with his hand, he looked at her and said, "Bullshit, Archer. All you need to know is that someone else further up—someone eminently qualified—decided it was right for this country. That's all you have to know. You're a perfect candidate, and you're throwing it all away."

"I'm going to law school. Columbia deferred me for only one year, and I'm taking them up on their acceptance. I start in two weeks." Archer hesitated. "I'm…sorry, Peter. I hate being a disappointment to you."

"You'll never be as happy as you would be working here. You know it and I know it," Bennett said.

"Getting your ego stroked and making good money isn't the same as being happy."

"That's *not* what this is about, Archer. You think about this. And when you're ready, you call me. Joke or not, you *are* special to me. You *are* my favorite intern. There will always be a place for you here. You will be our finest shooter. I *feel* it."

"Good-bye, Peter."

Archer left Peter Bennett's office without looking back.

Straight through law school, Archer received contacts regularly, urging
her to reconsider. Some were subtle, some not so subtle. There were
phone calls from Peter Bennett, casually asking how she was doing,
and letters from a trainer in Syracuse, suggesting she visit them
sometime. On the one year anniversary of leaving the program, she
received flowers with a note saying only, "Miss you. —the Syracuse
crowd." Adam asked who the Syracuse crowd was.

"Oh, a bunch of kids in Washington who went to Syracuse. I told
you about them, remember?"

"Oh, right," he said, absently.

Once she had Annie, the calls and letters slowed to just a card on
her birthday. The year of Annie's death, Peter's card just said, "Still
waiting for you. Peter."

Each time she opened one, Archer felt apprehensive. She would let
it sit for a day or two, then sigh, slip her finger under the edge of the
flap, and slide the card out to read the annual sentiment. What she
disliked most was that she opened the cards at all and didn't just throw
them away. She liked hearing from Peter.

In truth, she had felt challenged by the work. She had enjoyed the
camaraderie with the guys. She had liked being needed. What she
didn't like was death and almost death, and anxiety and fear. El
Salvador had been one of those near-death experiences, she recalled
with a shudder. At the time, U.S. support was on the fence, and either
side, the *muchachos* or the military forces, would have killed Archer
and her five colleagues if they'd been discovered crouching in a
jungled ravine outside a small town.

Her six-man unit survived only because they had pushed out of
the mountains forty, maybe fifty minutes before the military moved
back in to kill anyone they missed the first time around. A helicopter
picked them up with no time to spare.

Archer had been scared, no question about it. She would have
killed if necessary—no question about that, either. She had felt hyper-
alert, quick, ready, but also dead-bang scared. And then in one of the

villages, when she saw her first dead body up close, she'd felt sick and weak. It was a woman of about sixty, skirt hiked above her hips, legs splayed, shot mid abdomen, blood staining her thin cotton floral blouse. She still wore a little hat, just a slip of white lace bobby-pinned to her graying curls.

The hat got to her. *Poor soul,* Archer groaned silently, *poor soul.* She'd never get home again. Someone would wait and wait, then go looking, then find her, then scream, then dissolve. Archer couldn't stop thinking about it. This was someone's mother, or grandmother, or maybe sister, with her legs splayed in public. She would have been humiliated if she knew. Archer bent down and pushed the woman's hair from her eyes, secured the bobby pins to the hat, and closed her eyelids. Then she pulled the skirt down over her knees, gently folded her legs together, and tucked them under her. At least when killing, you weren't the victim. That was something.

"Let's go, Arch," called Dobbs, grabbing her arm and pulling her up. "No time to waste—they're getting way too close."

Wiping away a tear, Archer bounced up and ran beside Dobbs as the shots from the government forces drew closer.

# CHAPTER
# 7

Connor sat on a blanket in front of the fire at his camp. It was early evening; the sun was low in the sky but still warm and bright. By now he'd been in the Berkshires almost a week. He had originally driven out to see if the land left to him by his uncle George was marketable. It had some frontage out to the road, and its sale prospects were good. Now, however, after six days of walking every hill and swale of its three hundred acres, he found himself less and less inclined just to sell to the highest bidder.

It was a lovely piece of land: part meadowland, part wooded rolling hills, and wonderfully isolated. The only resident for miles was the reclusive lady who lived a short walk-away, through the woods, along an old logging trail.

Connor poked the fire. His original plan for the evening had been to cook the chicken he'd bought this morning in town. Just getting it had been a trek. He'd ridden Millie down to the clearing, a good mile from his camp, where the trailer and pickup were parked, some two hundred feet off the main road into Lenox.

Connor had tied Millie securely to the trailer, unhitched it from the truck, and started into town, a twenty-minute trip each way. But then he fretted that some random passerby might poke around Millie or even try to take her. So he had turned back, hitched the trailer back up to the truck, put her in the trailer, and taken her along. Now he'd committed himself to getting dinner for the hermit next door—an attractive woman, to be sure, but so grim it was wasted.

Connor sighed and poked the fire again. He had planned on staying here only long enough to get a break from Tara—that's what he sometimes called his stark, dusty Wyoming ranch, in an ironic nod to his mother, Colleen, who hadn't lived to see it. Its actual name was Three Chimneys Ranch. All the local ranchers guffawed at that one.

*Hey, Connor, you took a real wrong turn, son. This isn't Lexington, Kin-tucky. Just what do you think you're raising there, thoroughbreds? Three Chimneys? What in hell does that even mean? Bad luck, that name . . .*

The area spreads had names like Giant Bars Ranch, Twin Oaks, and Big Sky. Connor would just laugh. "The sheep don't seem to mind," he would say.

He knew the ranch was doing fine—Christ, it probably functioned better without him always double-checking everything and driving everyone else crazy. No need to rush back. Felix was a topnotch manager, and, for the past three years, the herd had grown at a good pace and cash flow had been robust, thank God.

Connor had always been afraid of being poor. His family had been solidly middle-class—his mother was a librarian at the Boston Public Library, his father a PE teacher at Milton Academy outside Boston— but it was middle-class basics only. There was never much in the bank for a "pamper," as his mother put it. That was no longer true for him, yet here he was in the New England woods, living in a tent and trying to figure out if it was time to reinvent himself—again.

The tent living was no big deal. Connor and the hands often camped out for weeks at a time when tagging or moving a herd. On his arrival at the Massachusetts property, he'd made an arrangement with the motel two miles down the road. For the princely sum of sixty dollars a week, he had full use of a motel room between nine and ten thirty each morning. So far, it had worked fine for basic hygiene. The solitude, however, was trying. Sometimes he found himself longing for a beer and some good conversation with Jordan Hayes, his vet and best friend back in Wyoming.

He glanced at his watch. It was getting late; he'd better get moving if he was going to make dinner for his crabby neighbor. He wondered if she ever smiled or lightened up. He sighed, grabbed his lantern for the walk back, and headed for the logging path.

When Connor arrived at Archer's front porch, the sky had turned navy blue, with fingers of pink reaching through it. He knocked on the door. "It's Connor McCall."

He heard movement inside, and the inner door opened. Archer leaned on a walking stick, but she looked alert. She peered out at him without opening the screen door.

Seeing him standing alone, she asked, "Where's Alice?"

"This is Alice," he said, pointing down.

Archer looked down—though not too far down—at the black, bearlike creature standing next to Connor. The dog was wide and woolly, eyes hardly visible, and she lowered her head suspiciously, looking out through long ropes of hair at Archer as Archer studied her. Alice's stump of a tail was not wagging.

"God, what *is* that?" Archer asked.

"Hey, don't say it like that. She's very sensitive. She's a Bouvier des Flandres, a Belgian herding dog. She goes where I go; that's a nonnegotiable."

"Fine by me," Archer shrugged. "I generally prefer dogs to people. Hello, Alice. How are you this evening?" Archer pushed the screen door open and leaned forward to scratch behind Alice's pointy ears. Her tail began to wag a little.

"Yes, Alice, you are a lovely, big girl, aren't you?" Archer crooned to the Bouvier, whose stump now wagged as if it had been switched on. Archer looked up at Connor. "Is she basically friendly?"

"Depends what you mean by 'friendly.' If she takes to you, she can be. Just watch the sudden moves toward me. She views protecting me as her mission in life, and she's been known to misinterpret things," he said, as he and Alice stepped in.

"Don't worry, I'll control myself." And for just an instant, a smile played on the edge of her full mouth.

"Good idea."

Connor replenished the ice pack and then began assembling ingredients. After a sprint around the little cabin's great room, the dogs settled down together on an old sofa near the front window. Archer pulled a rocker from the living room to the edge of the kitchen to watch Connor cook, and soon the scent of sizzling garlic and herbs filled the cabin.

A half hour later, he put on an Ella Fitzgerald CD and set the pine table with cutlery, candles, and napkins. He lit the candles and served dinner.

"I see you've got gobs of linens and candles," he said as he sat down at the table. "Do you use candles and cloth napkins when it's just you?"

"Yeah," she admitted. "When I moved out here I got into the habit of making a nice meal most days. Gives my day a little focus." She gave a sheepish shrug. "Soon I'll graduate to setting a place at the table for Hadley, and from there it's only a short step to getting a party hat for her and adopting seven cats, I suppose."

Connor gave her a puzzled smile, not sure how much of this was self-effacing humor and how much cut to the truth of her life.

"So, who are you actually, and what are you doing up here?" she asked, changing the subject and taking a bite of pasta.

He pulled out his wallet and handed her his driver's license. Archer pulled her glasses from her shirt pocket and read aloud:

"Connor McCall, Rural Route Twenty-two, Three Chimneys Ranch, Little Tempest, Wyoming."

"This is who I am, and I'm here ostensibly to decide whether to keep or sell the three hundred acres next to you. I planned to come here for a few weeks and turn around, but I'm liking it and may stay a few more weeks."

"Were you born in Wyoming, then?" Archer asked, handing back his license and taking her glasses off to lay them on the table.

"God, no! Boston originally," he replied, pivoting slightly in his chair to put the wallet back in his hip pocket.

"How did you end up in Wyoming, then?"

"Long story, but the short version is, I was a displaced businessman looking for a new beginning, and I'd always wanted to be a cowboy. I went out there seven years ago to start over. I have a two-thousand-acre ranch—small by Wyoming standards, but it's big enough for my needs at the moment."

"Hmmm. And what exactly do you do on this little two-thousand-acre ranch?" asked Archer, stabbing a shrimp.

"I raise sheep."

"Ah, you mentioned that. So you slaughter animals for a living, then?"

Connor shot her a half-annoyed, half-exasperated glance. "Not exactly. I raise Rambouillet sheep for their wool. It's the softest wool in the world, and I have one of the best herds in the West. Lots of people who are allergic to other wool can wear ours. Shetland's good, but Rambouillet is the Tiffany of wool. We sell a lot to European markets, and I go to Scotland once a year to sell to one of our agents there."

Archer had the grace to redden and looked genuinely embarrassed. "Oh...sorry."

"No big deal." He took a bite of shrimp. "Needs some salt...So are you one of those fish-eating vegetarians?"

"No. Actually, I'm one of those fish-eating assholes." She paused and bit her lip. "I…seem to have lost any semblance of conversational skills over the past few years."

"Oh." Connor wiped his mouth. "How come?"

"Long soap opera of a story."

"That's okay. I've always kind of liked soap operas myself."

"No." She shook her head, then, to lighten the sting of her answer, added, "I warned you that I'm up here because I'm not good at being with people."

"No, actually you said you're up here because you don't *want* to be with people. That's different from being here because you're not good at it."

Archer didn't reply. The cordial energy circulating when Connor was cooking had been sucked out of the room, and her ashen face suggested that she knew she'd done it.

After a few feeble efforts at small talk, they finished dinner in silence. Connor cleaned up hastily. After putting the last dish away, he asked, "So, you okay for tonight?"

"Fine. And thanks. It was…nice of you. And I like Alice." She almost smiled. Connor grabbed his jacket, thinking that this evening couldn't end soon enough.

"Well, okay, good night."

"Good night."

He ambled into the woods toward his camp, black dog a few steps ahead of him, lantern lighting the path. Looking back over his shoulder, he saw Archer watching him from behind the kitchen window.

Archer woke at 3:30 in the morning to the sound of Hadley panting loudly. She propped herself up on one elbow and clicked on the lamp on her bedside table. She squinted, then found Hadley standing in the doorway. The sight revved her to full alert.

"What's the matter, Haddie?"

The dog stood staring dully, her breathing labored, drool stringing down from both sides of her mouth. Grabbing her cane, Archer hopped to the kitchen and grabbed her cell phone before collapsing onto a kitchen chair to dial the vet's emergency service.

"Berkshire Emergency Animal Clinic. May I help you?"

"Yes. This is Archer Loh. My lab, Hadley, is a patient. She has Jordan disease and gets shots every six months. She isn't due for another month, but she's panting and can't seem to get comfortable. She had something like this about a year ago. If you look at her chart, you'll see it there."

"Can you hold, please?"

*Do I have a choice?* "Sure."

Hadley stood in front of Archer, tongue out, head hanging. She walked to the back door, sat, struggled back up, and shuffled awkwardly back to Archer, still panting.

"It'll be fine, girl, just fine." She stroked the dog's head, then scratched above her tail. She was rewarded with a slight wag.

"Archer?"

"Yes, I'm here."

"Hadley needs to come in. Dr. Jensen looked at her records, and it's the Jordan, for sure. A shot should fix her up, but he said the sooner the better, given her age."

"Uh, do you think it can wait for a few hours? I need a ride and I'm not sure…"

"No. If she's already panting, that's not good. He said she has to come in now."

"Okay, I'll have to…see about a cab, I guess. Well, thanks. I'll get her there."

Archer clicked off. She held the phone to her mouth for a minute, then gazed at Hadley. For a cab to get up here, she'd have to unlock the gate—all well and good if she could *drive* to the gate, in which case she could as easily drive to the vet. But with a sprained right ankle, she could barely hobble with a cane, much less use the gas and brake pedals.

"Damn it. I can't believe this," she sputtered to herself, rubbing her forehead.

Then she remembered. *Glad to hear cell phones work up here… Just dial c mccall.* Staring at the phone keypad, she decoded the number from the letters of his name. *Got it!* 262-2255. But the area code? What area code? Then she remembered his driver's license. Little Tempest, Wyoming. Who could forget that name? She quickly called information, got the Wyoming area code for Little Tempest, and hoped he had enough cell phone battery left to pick up one quick call.

Archer hesitated, remembering dinner's chilly end. She glanced at Hadley, then tapped out the numbers. *Please answer.* The phone rang four times. She slumped, losing hope of reaching a live person. Then a voice broke in.

"Hello?"

"Uh, is this Connor McCall?"

"Yup."

"This is Archer Loh." Dead silence. "You know…uh, your neighbor."

More dead silence.

"Hello? Hello? Are you…

"I'm here. I've been told I don't have any neighbors, and I'm pretty sure I don't *want* any neighbors at three thirty in the morning…" He stopped and asked, almost as an afterthought, "Are you okay?"

"Um…not really. My dog has to go to the vet, and I can't drive yet. She's got this condition, and I know it's terrible calling you like this, but I didn't know…"

"I'll be right over." The line went dead.

Connor was at her door in fifteen minutes.

"What's wrong with her?" He bent to pet Hadley, who was now lying down but still panting and drooling. "It's okay, Hadley. We'll fix you up."

"She's got this endocrine condition that's treated with shots every six months, but I guess it didn't last, or something. When I woke up, she was like this. The vet said she needs the shot now."

"Okay, well, I better take your car. My truck's down by the road on my property. It would take at least a half hour to walk down to it, and I know you have a locked gate—I can see it from the road—so I couldn't get up here anyway. You'll need to give me the combination."

"I can come with you," she said, struggling up. "Just need to throw on some jeans."

"No offense, but I think I'd move faster without you."

Startled but realizing it was true, Archer nodded. She wondered, though, if perhaps he just didn't want her company.

"Right…you're right." Archer limped to the basket on the kitchen counter where she kept her keys. She handed them to Connor. "Here. The combination to the gate is nine one two three three. Turn to the right first. The vet is down on Route…"

He cut her off. "I know where the vet is. Berkshire Clinic, right?" She nodded. "The first thing I do when I go anywhere with Alice and Millie is find out where the closest vet is, just in case. You have a leash?" Archer pointed to a flowered leash hanging from a peg on the wall. Connor grabbed it and clipped it to Hadley's collar. "Come on, puppy. Let's get you fixed up." Hadley looked back at Archer, then walked out slowly with Connor.

"I'll be back as soon as I can." He turned and left.

Archer watched them head down the driveway. She wished she'd said more. She wished she'd had more to say.

Two hours later, Connor returned with Hadley, who had stopped panting. She took over her end of the couch and promptly fell asleep.

"Thanks so much. I really appreciate what you did. Can I make you some coffee?" Archer offered.

"It's okay. No problem. Animals and kids get to me. Take care." He tipped his hat, gave a thin smile, and left.

# CHAPTER
# 8

Early that evening, Connor McCall showed up at the cabin door with Alice and a sack of groceries. He knocked, then called out, "It's me."

Archer limped over and opened the door to find him there grinning.

"Let's start over. Hi, I'm Connor McCall, your new neighbor, come to cook you dinner in light of your unfortunate plight."

Archer smiled, hesitated for an instant, then unlatched the screen door. She held out her hand. "Archer Loh, uncouth mountain woman."

Connor shook her hand. "Pleased to meet you, ma'am."

In twenty-five minutes, sautéed lamb chops, a tomato salad, and pasta were on the table. As he sat down, Connor looked meaningfully at the chops. "These aren't part of my herd, by the way."

Archer reddened. "I'm sorry, I just…"

"Forget it. I was teasing you, not fishing for another apology."

Archer smiled and cut her chop.

"Actually, Jordan Hayes, my best friend and vet, tried to convince me to raise cattle like everyone else out there—skip the wool thing. He thought we'd die on the vine the first winter." Connor paused, took a sip of wine, and hoped he was putting her at ease. "'Boston Bean and his little lambs,' he called us." Laughing, he shook his head, and was rewarded with a faint smile.

"You said you were a businessman before Wyoming. Did you know a lot about ranching before moving out there?" Archer asked between bites of lamb chop.

Connor shook his head again. "Hardly. I grew up in south Boston. I did work summers picking berries at a farm, but there wasn't a sheep in sight. After I lost my corporate job, I decided to try something completely different. Between the Internet and the library, you can learn almost anything, given patience and time. Well, I had lots of time and a decent amount of patience. By the time I bought my ranch, I was darned knowledgeable about the industry—book-wise, anyway. You name it, I studied it: soil types, sheep breeds, fleece microns, the marketplace. Decided to try this French breed. Turned out the books were right, too. Rambouillet sheep are tough, and they adjusted beautifully to everything about Wyoming."

"Still, it sounds like a lot more work than the lamb chop game."

"Well, it is, in a way. I mean, isn't it always harder to keep something alive than kill it? Totally different investment in the outcome. But if there is one thing I know, it's me. When push came to shove, I just couldn't see myself spending twelve hours a day raising some animals just to kill them off." He paused reflectively, then said, "Hey, I love a steak or a chop as much as the next guy, but, hypocritical as it is, I like it all cellophaned over at the grocery store. I'd rather work with my animals and get to know them than kill them off each season." Looking a little embarrassed, he twirled some pasta onto his fork. He saw her looking at him and said with a shrug, "It's one of my Colleenisms."

Archer raised an inquiring eyebrow.

"'Colleenism,' after my mother. She was a great dreamer. Always hoping for drama and romance in our little south Boston hovel. She read a lot of Thomas Hardy, that sort of thing. She had these notions that fate would always make things come out the way they were meant to, that man and animal are partners in life, valiantly facing nature together—totally unrealistic stuff like that. My crazy notion, courtesy of Mom, is that my little crew and I are working as a team with these dopey sheep to provide the best wool around, for the good of mankind. Must be my destiny, right?"

Now it was Archer's turn to shrug. "There are worse ways to spend your days. It sounds as if you like what you do and you do it well." She took another bite of tomato salad.

"I do like it in a lot of ways. Sheep aren't as dumb as most people think—at least, my sheep aren't. They have personalities, and I like the life. It's simple. I mean, we're always busy, between foot trimming, tail docking, ear tagging, and shearing. And except for lambing season, my days are pretty predictable, and I'm only answerable to me. Before the ranch, I worked for a bunch of corporations, traveled a lot, put mergers together, things like that. I had stockholders, comptrollers, everyone and his brother with their hands in my pockets, ready to pounce if profits weren't good enough, and ready to see if I could sustain the growth if they were. I can tell you, I don't miss it."

"Yeah," Archer said, nodding, "I practiced law for a while, and it was pretty dog-eat-dog. I was into it myself at the time, just as bad as everyone else. It's only since I moved away that I can see what it was doing to me—and what it does to everyone who's part of it."

"So what do you do now if you're not practicing law?" Connor asked. "Or are you doing mountain law out here?"

She stiffened. "I don't do much, I guess. My daughter died six years ago, and I needed to get away. I found this place, quit my job in Connecticut, and moved here." She seemed a little surprised and added, "I...I don't usually talk about that. It's something of a conversation stopper, as I guess you can imagine. It's customarily followed by an awkward silence, an unwanted question, and then a comment about the weather."

Connor looked up. "Well, I'm not silent a lot and I won't ask you any questions. I'm just real sorry. That must have been horrible. You must have had the mean reds bad for a long time then."

Archer glanced up, holding a forkful of pasta. "*Breakfast at Tiffany's,*" she said, smiling just a little. "Yeah, you could say I had the mean reds real bad for quite a while. And how do you know the film so well that you remember that bit of trivia—Holly calling her black moods the 'mean reds,' I mean?"

"Well, for about twenty years the only way I escaped my work was by going to the movies. It was the only way I could stop my mind from racing, at least for a few hours. I became a real movie buff. I saw my favorites over and over—can quote whole passages of dialogue from them. Weird, huh?"

"Not really," Archer replied. "I did the same thing after Annie died. I'd go just so I wasn't alone with my head—spent hours at the movies. "Sometimes I'd go in at two o'clock and go from theater to theater until they closed. And the ones I liked, I saw again and again, too. I guess there was some comfort in knowing what's going to happen next."

For a few minutes, they ate in comfortable silence.

"Do you know how to use that thing?" Connor asked, nodding toward the Winchester propped behind the kitchen back door.

Archer's eyes followed his gaze. "Yeah, I do. I took some self-defense after Annie died, and learned to shoot a bit." No need to add that she was such a crack shot that when the Group had gotten an appeal for help and the client asked for the best man available, Gavin chuckled and replied that the best man was a woman. Archer had flown to Hong Kong and returned four days later, mission accomplished.

Archer looked down and quickly changed the subject. "So, do you have any children?"

Connor hesitated. For years he'd answered yes or no to this question, depending on the circumstances. No outnumbered yes by a huge margin, since a yes required a hell of a lot more explanation. "Yes, a daughter—Lauren. She's…uh, nine, I guess. I've never met her."

Archer looked up. "Come again?"

Connor swallowed a bite of pasta and took a sip of Merlot. "Just that: I've never met her."

"Okay, you've got to explain that."

"Oh, God. The whole dreary soap opera, or can we just do the synopsis here?"

"I've always liked soap operas, myself," Archer said, settling back into her chair, wineglass in hand, eyes wide.

"Hah! Guess I asked for that one." He sighed. She was watching him expectantly. "Okay, well, I guess that's fair. So, here it comes. I already told you I ran different companies over the years. At one of them, GenTech in Chicago, I met a really great woman—Sarah. We dated on and off for a few years, but to tell you the truth, I never wanted the picket fence thing with anyone. I went to Harvard Business School so I could run the world, or a little part of it. I didn't want a wife and brood of kids tying me down."

He looked up from his plate to see Archer looking quizzically at him. He waved a hand. "I know, I know. It sounds selfish, even to me, but frankly, I *was* selfish. I was young and ambitious, knew where I wanted to go, and didn't want any detours to my plan. My parents never had more than necessities. We ate out at a good restaurant maybe once a year, if that. I wanted to have money and success and a penthouse on Fifth Avenue by the time I was thirty-five, not a house in the burbs with a Volvo wagon in the driveway."

"Hmm, I thought that's what Harvard guys were *supposed* to do: marry a smart but conventional girl and raise the next generation of exceptionally brilliant overachievers to start the whole thing over again."

Connor grimaced. "Some do, but it sure as hell felt to me like it would be a death sentence. At least, that's how I felt then. But anyway,

Sarah got pregnant, and she knew I wasn't cut out to be Ozzie Nelson. She did want that house and the picket fence, and the husband coming through the door at six every night, saying, 'Honey, I'm home.' Even if I'd been of a mind to get married, it wouldn't have been to someone like Sarah."

Archer interrupted. "And just what, pray tell, was so unmarriageable about poor Sarah?"

Connor sat back, and his smile bordered on sardonic. "Ah, well, here it is, since you asked. I've always been attracted to difficult, complex women who have lots of their own things going on and not much time or patience for me. You see, it creates great angst and makes my ultimate failure preordained, so I never have to deal with a real relationship. It works for me."

Archer was watching him, head tilted, an amused look in her eyes. "Go on. I'm still waiting to hear how you screwed this up so badly that you've never met your own daughter."

"Yeah, that's coming. Well, we agreed I would help Sarah financially, and I did. When I moved to New York, she stayed in Chicago. Next thing I knew, I got a little card and photo in the mail of Lauren— that's my daughter. Born in Chicago on October 1, 1992. I still have that picture." Connor pulled out his wallet and dug out a tattered photo of a baby in pink, peeking out of a frilly bonnet. He handed it to Archer.

"She's adorable," said Archer, reaching for her glasses again. "Do you write to her or anything? Any more recent photos?"

"You'd think so, wouldn't you?" Connor said with a shake of his head. "About a year after Lauren was born, Sarah got married and wanted her new husband to adopt Lauren. There was a lot of legal stuff, and I didn't like the idea. Sarah was gentle about the whole thing but pretty firm. She felt the adoption would be the best thing for Lauren.

"I couldn't deny her that. Even I knew I was just being selfish on that one. I didn't want to be a father to Lauren, but I wanted to keep this guy, this Donald Giordano, from taking on the job. So finally, I agreed as long as I could still contact Lauren.

"So I send a monthly check, something at Christmas, and little gifts when I travel. And that's it. I have a daughter named Lauren Giordano, who doesn't know me from the postman. And no, I don't have any more recent pictures, because apparently *Donald* prefers it that way." He finished with a rueful smile after slapping out the name.

Archer shook her head, put down her wineglass, and leaned forward. "Well, McCall, I'll tell you a little secret: you've got to get to know that girl. She needs you, and you'll regret it forever if you don't. Even if you're not in her life day-to-day, she wonders. Don't kid yourself that this Donald is enough for her. He may be a terrific guy and a great father, but she wonders, and she needs to know why you left her. Till then, it'll torture her."

Connor looked at her, now his turn to be amused. "Please, don't hold back. Stop sugarcoating it and just say what you really think."

"Yeah, I know. I'm opinionated. Sorry. But seriously, you have to do this." She looked intense and beautiful, her green eyes steady, that luxuriant auburn hair framing her face.

He hesitated. "I'm afraid."

"Afraid of what?"

"That it's too late," Connor said. Then, noticing her still-questioning look, he added, "You know how you forget someone's name, and then, for whatever reason, you don't ask right away? And then so much time goes by that it's weird to ask. And then, even later, it's just an embarrassment and you *can't* ask, because they'll know that all the times you've met, you never knew who they were. Well, magnify that feeling, and the magnitude of your little faux pas, oh…say, about a billionfold. Well, I feel like each year that's gone by has made it harder to try to introduce myself. And by now, it might mess her up for me to enter her life. You know, that's a possibility, too."

"Well, you could ask Sarah. She sounds grounded and fair."

"She is. I don't know. Sometimes I'm just dying to know about

Lauren, you know—how she's doing, what she looks like, what she likes to do. But I suspect she's done okay without me so far."

"And what about you? How have you done so far without her?"

# CHAPTER
# 9

The next evening, Connor showed up at the cabin at dinnertime with a chicken, a box of rice, and a bundle of crisp asparagus in a yellow plastic grocery bag. He knocked on the door. No answer. He knocked again with more vigor.

"Is it you again?"

"Yup. Please try to control your eagerness."

He heard movement inside the cabin, and in a few seconds, Archer opened the door. She was still leaning on the cane, with Hadley peeking out behind her. She looked surprised but not displeased. She was wearing a long faded denim skirt with a cream-colored Irish cable-knit sweater. Her hair was pulled back with a tortoiseshell barrette, and she was barefoot, her pale ankle still wrapped neatly in white gauze. She cocked her head and stared at him. "Lost, are we? Look, Wyoming's out thataway." She pointed in the direction of the setting sun. "You can make it by sundown if you hurry, cowboy." She smiled, though, and unlatched the screen door.

"Most amusing"

Archer opened the door and motioned him in, and he set the

yellow bag on the counter. After pulling out the contents, he took off his jacket and tossed it on the arm of the sofa.

He took over the kitchen. Chopping, braising, stirring, tasting, seasoning, he checked the recipe, then deviated from it, all while listening to Frank Sinatra croon away about the lady being a tramp. Sometimes he sang along off-key for a few bars.

For a few minutes Archer sat on her chair near the fire, reading *National Geographic.* Then she moved to a chair in the kitchen, where she could watch and talk while he worked.

"Don't add salt to the rice," Archer called from her seat. "Oh, and cook the asparagus standing up in the extra coffeepot, over there near the sink—it stays crisper.

Connor shot her a sidelong glance. "Are you always so, uh, instructive?" he asked as he added herbs to the rice.

"Pretty much."

"I see." He paused and tested the rice. "It's okay, though. I'm pretty good at taking direction from women—I've had a lot of practice."

"Really? Do you want to elaborate on that, McCall?"

"No, not at the moment," he said over his shoulder. "I need to keep my last shred of mystery to hold your interest a few days longer after last night's seriously excessive true confession. Hope I didn't bore you too badly."

"No, I found it interesting, actually," she said, then paused. "I…I had a nice time."

Connor nodded and said, "Yeah, me, too."

A few minutes later, the meal was served. They ate silently for a few moments; then Archer looked up, remembering a stray thought. "So, did you ever get that penthouse on Fifth Avenue?" She got up and limped to the sink to get a glass of water.

"Hey, I would have gotten that for you."

"Don't worry. I'm from a long line of 'don't baby it' Yankees, at least on my father's side." She limped back with the glass. "So…?"

"You don't forget a whole lot, do you? That was from last night's tragic discourse."

"Nope, I never forget anything—mind like a steel trap. I'm one of those complex, difficult women you find so irresistible."

He chuckled. "So you *do* understand the principle of a joke."

"Of course I do. I'm just selective," Archer said. "So, did you?"

Connor sighed. "I was hoping you'd forget about my saga. How come you're going to know my whole story after three dinners, and I know nothing about you?"

Archer shrugged. "There's not that much to know about me. And don't change the subject. Did you ever get your penthouse?"

"Yes. It's where I lived when it all caved in, so to speak. I sold it to get the Wyoming ranch."

Archer waved her hand for him to continue.

Connor paused, recalling the year of his professional downfall. At forty-three years old and at the height of his career, he had thought he was happy. Yet, when he sat alone that Christmas Eve in his designer-decorated Fifth Avenue co-op, he'd wondered. People were hurrying for trains home or celebrating with family and friends down below in Manhattan's restaurants. Yet there he was, looking out over Central Park without even a Christmas tree. He'd always thought he'd have to be dead not to put up a Christmas tree, but…well, who had time for Christmas?

"Hello?" said Archer.

He came up from the pit of memory. "Oh, right. Okay, my illustrious career, such as it was, came to a crashing halt in 1994. I was working for North American Financial, the largest real estate management firm on the East Coast. The real estate market took a really bad dive in 1988, and then in '94 the other shoe dropped. Everyone from middle management up was let go, including yours truly. As part of the top management, I carried the stench of North American's failure. Companies that had once begged me to work for them were now cold, to put it mildly."

"That hurts."

"It did and it didn't. I hadn't been really happy for years. This just forced me to do something about it. I missed the big income and the perks, but I had enough money. When you come from modest beginnings, you learn to save—or at least I did. I didn't have enough to stay in a New York penthouse indefinitely, but I had enough so my next meal wasn't a worry. I just had to decide what my next step was."

Connor paused as he buttered the last piece of bread and took a bite. "First thing I did was get this big map of the United States and set it out on my kitchen table. For four months, that thing sat there next to a few travel books. I studied that map and those books like I used to study the Dow Jones averages. I read everything, cross-referenced towns and local economies, checked property values, and basically put together a grid comparing the three or four locales that came up as my finalists.

"After that, it was almost a toss of the dice, and I finally decided on Wyoming because it was so darn beautiful. *Well, there it is,* I thought. Just like the Dow Jones: forty percent logic and sixty percent emotion. I sold my Beemer, bought a pickup, and headed out. And that was the end of the penthouse. Once I bought the ranch, I was about as far from Fifth Avenue as you can get in the continental forty-nine."

"But it was good in the long run, right? You got off the speeding train?" Archer asked, leaning forward with her arms resting on the table.

"Well, I got six of the things I love most in the world, so I guess it was good," replied Connor, dabbing at his mouth with his big yellow napkin.

Archer cocked her head. "Those things being…?"

"Millie, Alice, and the city girls."

"The *city girls*? Assuming they're not four hookers from Laramie, they are…?"

"My sheepdogs. My first purchase after the ranch and Millie. They're Great Pyrenees, and I've only lost two sheep to coyotes since I started up, which is unheard of. Most ranchers lose one percent of their herd yearly to local varmints. Dallas, Savannah, Boston, and Tallahassee, I call them."

"Ergo, the city girls. Cute," commented Archer. "How about Millie? Did you ride as a kid?"

"Yeah, right. As if the McCalls had access to a stable." Connor smiled at the impossibility of it. "No, I started riding when I was fifteen. I worked at that berry farm I told you about. It was just north of Boston. They kept six or seven horses just for fun. I worked there every summer through high school, and it became almost a second home to me.

"Mrs. Rose, the owner, treated me like family. She let me ride anytime I wanted. I had a favorite—Sabrina—and I rode her every free minute. Man, I loved that horse. Pretty little gray mare. For whatever reason, I loved riding and everything about horses. My father thought it was stupid—you know, that I would do that when I could be playing baseball. No chip off the old block. Another disappointment for him. But anyway, that's how I started."

Connor stopped and took a sip of his wine, feeling a bit melancholy at the mention of Mrs. Rose's farm. "Anyway, when I moved to Wyoming, I got Millie from the rancher next door. He was trimming down his herd and had too many horses. She was only five at the time, and I loved her sweetness, I really did, and she adjusted to the ranch like she'd always been there. After working cattle, she probably found the sheep pretty easy. They don't kick or charge at you and are pretty docile compared to an angry steer. Yeah, old Millie and I bonded, and the rest is history."

Archer nodded. "I know what that's like. And Alice?"

"Alice. Alice is the love of my life—to date, anyway. She'd give her life for me without blinking, and I just might do the same. I never had a dog as a kid. Never had a dog when I was moving and traveling, and now I have this canine partner who lets me control things—and God knows, I'm controlling—but who's always interested in what I have to say, is always loyal and accepting of me without wanting to change me, and loves me unconditionally. It doesn't get much better than that, does it?"

Archer looked at him and said quietly, "No, it doesn't."

# CHAPTER
# 10

By the fourth night, when Archer knew that help was not strictly essential, Connor showed up with fresh flounder, two potatoes, broccoli, and an apple pie. Archer devoured her share.

"Soon you'll be sprinting again," Connor said as they sat down at the table, plates in hand. "You and that chubby Lab of yours."

"Hey, that's not chub—she's got big bones."

"Hah! I've heard that one before."

Hadley lay flat on the floor next to Archer's chair, as if attempting to conceal her "chub," tail thumping, eyes cast upward.

As Archer took her first sip of crisp white Chardonnay, she leaned forward and looked at Connor, eyes narrowing. "So tell me, McCall, are you just showing up here to get free use of my major appliances, or what?"

Connor smiled. "Well, that was the second draw, I must admit. The first was that cordial welcome you gave me. Yeah, that first chat we had at your back door—actually, *through* your back door, since you never did open it—made me feel real warm and fuzzy all over. I was drawn back here like a moth to a flame. Yup, I knew I'd come to the right place to regroup." He masked his grin by taking another bite of flounder.

"Very funny. I get it. But you know, your style could use some work. That 'Aw, shucks, ma'am, howdy neighbor' thing was kind of hokey, you know. I don't get any company up here, and for all I knew, you were some freakoid escapee from an asylum for the criminally insane."

"Jesus, I looked that bad?"

Archer stopped eating and peered at him longer than necessary. "Well, now that you mention it, you do have a kind of crazed look in your eyes. In fact, you sort of remind me of that guy—"

"Okay, okay. But don't you get lonely up here?"

"Nope," she lied. As she spoke, she remembered dinner parties at the long claw-footed dining table in West Hartford, friends laughing and glasses clinking. She remembered setting the table, picking just the right tablecloth and napkins for the occasion, the right flowers. She remembered the hugs at the end of the evening, and lovemaking with Adam after the dishes were done.

"So, are you ever going to call me by my Christian name?"

Archer looked at him. "Hm-m, I don't know, McCall. It's an old habit. I call a fair number of the men in my life by their last names. Think of it as a term of endearment." She tossed a napkin at him. He caught it and laughed.

In reality, her defenses had crumbled under the onslaught of his disarming presence. Fighting against his entreaties was like warding off a friendly golden retriever who, despite repeated stern rebukes, refused to take offense and go away. She liked the way he told a story straight, even when it cast him in a bad light. She liked his self-effacing jokes and the way he stopped to stroke Hadley just because she was there.

Archer had to admit, a man who kept a scrapbook with a picture of his boyhood horse, who read about father-daughter relationships though he'd never met his daughter, and who listened to Enya had to have *something* going for him. If this Wyoming sheep rancher turned out to be an ax murderer, so be it. There were worse things in life than being killed by an ax murderer posing as a Wyoming sheep rancher.

After the fourth evening, getting together for dinner was part of their day. When Archer got back on her routine of errands to the store and fetching the mail, she'd look at her watch as the afternoon shadows lengthened. Even her weekly trips to the movie theater had become the two-o'clock show instead of the four thirty show—it seemed important to be home for dinner.

They had had this de facto arrangement for three weeks and two days. Archer now closed the bathroom door in case Connor should poke his head in the front door unexpectedly, and she moved her "personal items" from the open metal shelf above the toilet to the cabinet under the sink. Her laundry was folded and stacked in her drawer promptly, instead of sitting for days in a pile at the end of her bed.

She kept expecting Connor to ask more of her—more conversation, more intimacy, even—but he remained undemanding and seemed to look to her for clues to their daily pace. Most nights, while making dinner, he was quiet when she was, chatty when she wanted to be, as he worked around the kitchen in a methodical, unhurried way. He would leave at night the same way: just tip his hat, whistle for Alice, pick up his lantern, and close the door gently behind him.

It was early Wednesday evening when Connor, with Alice at his heels, walked into the front yard just as Archer was coming up the driveway. She turned off the engine, opened the driver's door, and bounced out of the car. Her dark straight hair hung to her shoulders. Usually she pulled it back in a big tortoiseshell barrette, but today it swung loosely from side to side. She wore blue jeans, black clogs, a navy blue T-shirt, and an oatmeal-colored cardigan sweater.

When she smiled at him, with the flaming red and orange leaves of the Berkshires as a backdrop, Connor thought she looked beautiful. He moved closer and felt a sudden weakening as she smiled up at him, eyes shining. He wished mightily for the first time in his life that he were a spontaneous, damn-the-consequences kind of guy who could sweep her up into his arms and carry her to the bedroom. *Steady, old man,* he thought to himself, *you're a bit long in the tooth for the Rhett Butler routine.*

"Hey, where've you been?" he asked, strolling up to the Jeep, noting that Hadley was sitting on the porch. Hadley usually went everywhere with Archer.

"To the movies," she replied. "I go once a week—Wednesdays, matinee. I told you, I'm a movie freak."

"No kidding! You've been holding out on me. Where is there a theater around here?"

"You know, McCall, the Berkshires aren't the end of the earth. We have theaters. You just have to drive thirty minutes to Pittsfield."

"A revelation. What did you see?"

"*Return to Me.* It's about a man whose wife dies, and he donates her heart to a woman who needs a heart, and…" She stopped and laughed. "I know it sounds stupid, but it was terrific. I loved it. Minnie Driver and David Duchovny. By the way, I only see things with happy endings. It's my one requirement," she said as they walked side by side up the path to her cabin. "And the wife had been training a gorilla in sign language at the time of her death, and the girl gets the heart, and they meet. And she has this grandfather who's played by Carroll O'Connor…and then…" She broke off, laughing, and pulled the screen door open and went in, with Connor two steps behind her, holding the door for the two dogs.

The next week, they started matinee Wednesdays. Selecting a movie became a serious project for Tuesday night dinners, with a full debate ensuing over the contenders. Connor and Archer would open the morning paper to the theater page, spreading it across the pine table.

As it turned out, they had similar taste in movies. They loved *Miss*

*Congeniality,* thought *A Beautiful Mind* was terrific, and found *Training Day* a bit overrated, although Denzel was great.

"I heard that one is really violent," said Archer.

"No, it's not supposed to be that bad. I heard Bruce Willis is really good in it."

"Ebert and Roeper hated that one, and I usually agree with them."

"Yeah, but I read an article about Uma Thurman and how they made this movie. It sounded really good—happy ending, too."

They saw every good movie that came along, sometimes twice, and a great many forgettable others. They loved the classics and shared a weakness for sentimentality.

"I love every cliché in the book, especially when good wins out," Archer admitted.

"Yeah, me, too. And I have to admit, I love a good love story—the more sentimental, the better." Then, catching her look of surprise, he added, "Hey, I'm sharing deep feelings here. Just go with it."

She looked down and smiled. "Fine. As long as you don't have to kill me now."

He chuckled.

On the way home, they debated whether the movie had any quotes that would become timeless. By accident, a word game developed between them: slipping a movie quote into conversation to see if it got by unnoticed. Both were sharp, and both were cutthroat competitors. Points were tallied at the end of the week, and the loser cooked dinner the following week.

"I think when Jack Nicholson says, 'What if this is as good as it gets?' will be a classic," commented Archer after they saw *As Good as It Gets*—second time for both—at a theater in South Hadley.

"Hmmm, maybe, but it's kind of bland, you know. A really good one has to stand on its own, be totally unique. You know, like when Lauren Bacall says to Bogie, 'You know how to whistle, don't you, Steve? Just put your lips together and blow.' Now, *that's* a memorable line."

Invariably, when they got there the theater would be almost empty, except for a handful of seniors. They always ended up sitting off to the right on the aisle, ten rows back. Occasionally, Archer would throw a kernel of popcorn at Connor when he was engrossed in the movie. He would ignore it until a scene held her rapt, then throw a kernel back at her. That would then start them each tossing popcorn and shushing the other.

On occasion, they leaned together conspiratorially to share a comment or a joke, or Connor would brush Archer's hair back to whisper a witty observation that wouldn't hold until the ride home. Archer would shiver and lean in closer, sometimes giggling like a tenth-grader on a date. Sometimes she took Connor's arm to emphasize a point.

One day, on the way home from seeing *On Golden Pond* at a classics theater in Springfield, Connor grew quiet.

"Hey, anything wrong, McCall? You're unusually morose, even for you," Archer joked.

He said nothing for a few seconds, then shook his head. "Nah, it's stupid, but that movie got me thinking about Lauren. You know, in almost every movie I've ever seen, the estranged child softens at the end and is happy to see the creepy, absent parent. I mean, in *The Rock,* Sean Connery's daughter wants to see him even after, what was it, twenty years? In *My Favorite Year,* Peter O'Toole finally gets up the courage to see Tess, and it goes well, or so we're led to believe. Even in *Absolute Power,* Clint Eastwood's daughter forgives him his life of crime and his abandonment of her.

"But maybe, in real life, a kid is just mad and cuts you out forever for leaving them." He looked at her, then refocused on the road. "Maybe sometimes it *is* too late."

Archer put her hand on his arm and said gently, "No, that's not true. It's never too late if you really want something. Wasn't it your mother who said it's never too late to be who you might have been?"

He was quiet for a moment, then drawled in his best Wyoming twang, "Yeah, but what did my mother know, anyway? She was a librarian in south Boston, who expected Heathcliff to stop in some afternoon for tea." Still, he smiled as he drove on.

# CHAPTER
# 11

The dream started again. This was the bad one, not like the dream of Clique in Madison Square Garden. *Everyone remembers her first time,* Archer thought wryly as her midnight mind went again where it willed, *and it's never quite what you expected, is it?* Four-plus years had not blunted the force of the dream that recorded in accurate detail every moment of her first time—her first solo assignment for the Group.

Miami Beach was no one's destination of choice in August. Archer arrived at Miami International from Boston's Logan Airport on a steamy afternoon, her itinerary memorized, no incriminating notes to lose, just one sheet of paper with a neighborhood map.

She glanced around, but no one appeared interested in her. Walking briskly past the window of a dark bar and restaurant, she caught her reflection in the glass. She drew in her breath, startled by her own appearance. With gray curly hair, owlish wire-rimmed spectacles, realistic-looking face lines, a denim wraparound skirt to midcalf, a plain yellow T-shirt, and blue Keds, she looked every day of sixty-two. "Frumpy" didn't begin to do the look justice, she thought, satisfied. Turning away, she headed to the Hertz counter, dragging a medium-size overnight bag behind her.

Ford Taurus—that was her car. No one ever remembered someone renting the most popular, most vanilla car in America. Arriving at the counter, she pulled out her wallet.

"Reservation for Miriam Hayes, please," she said evenly.

"Welcome to Miami, Ms. Hayes," beamed a young woman with dark hair and eyes, identified by her name tag as Maria. Thumbing through a stack of reservations, she found Archer/Miriam's.

"Everything seems to be in order. May I please see your driver's license and a credit card?" she asked, glancing at the form.

"Oh, certainly," Archer replied, and presented an Illinois license and a MasterCard, both identifying her as Miriam Hayes of Chicago. Maria examined them and handed them back with a cheery smile.

"Just sign here, please." She handed Archer a pen.

Archer smiled and held up a pen from her purse. "My lucky pen," she joked, and Maria nodded.

"I see you're from Chicago, Ms. Hayes. Are you here in Miami for business or pleasure, may I ask?"

Archer hesitated an instant, then replied, "Pleasure. To visit my grandchildren. My daughter moved down here last winter, and I'm dying to see her new home." She smiled fondly.

"Yeah, I figured it wasn't a vacation. Not many tourists here in August. Is it your first visit, Ms. Hayes?"

"Yes," she lied smoothly. "And I sure like what I see."

"Well, we do hope you enjoy your visit," said Maria, handing her the keys. "I know it's hot, but don't let that get to you. Everything is air-conditioned. And don't miss the aquarium, if you've never been."

Archer smiled, taking the keys. "Thank you for the suggestion, dear. That's a lovely idea."

The woman nodded and smiled. Archer gave a small wave and stuffed the keys in her pocketbook, then turned away and walked slowly, hoping she looked like the sixty-something Miriam. As she headed toward the ladies' room, she was already reviewing her itinerary in her head: Check into the motel; get to the post office: Confirm the route and the discard spots; get some sleep…do the job. Then report the completion and get out of town.

The ladies' room was crowded. *Good,* she thought, *the more the merrier.* Archer went to the farthest stall, pushed the door open, and walked in, luggage in tow, latching the door behind her. Unzipping the central compartment of her suitcase, she pulled out faded blue jeans, a white tank top, and black mules with wooden wedge high heels.

Hurriedly, she pulled off the gray wig, yanked the T-shirt up over her head, unwrapped the skirt, and kicked off her Keds. She folded the shirt and skirt, tucked them neatly into her open bag, shoved the Keds in along the edge of the suitcase, and tucked the wig into a corner. Then she pulled on the jeans and tank top and slipped on the black leather mules. From a side compartment she pulled a small silk pouch and shook a pair of pink-feathered pierced earrings into her palm. She slipped these through her ears. Then, from the same pouch, she took a premoistened makeup removal tissue and wiped her face clean of the powder and the lines drawn in for the morning flight. Going back into the suitcase once more, she pulled out a spiky medium-brown wig. It rolled easily over the beige stocking cap, hiding her real hair. She shook her head to fluff out the wig, ran her fingers through it, and sat down on the toilet.

She was breathing fast. *Focus, now…breathe deep.* Feeling slightly more relaxed, she reached in her pocketbook and flipped open the compact. Hardly her style, but not bad. Miriam Hayes from Chicago, here in Miami to visit the little ones, was no more. She pulled out a black eye pencil and rimmed her eyes, then finished the look with red lip gloss, a swipe of pink blush, and a pair of oversize sunglasses.

Before stepping out of the stall, she snatched her leather wallet from her purse and slid the tip of her pen along a slim, credit cardsize sleeve inside. A fine Velcro closure yielded, and from the narrow opening she grasped her new ID with a pair of tweezers and slipped Miriam Hayes's license back in its place. In less than eight minutes, she had become Michelle Danaher from Cincinnati, here for the party.

Archer left the stall, paused for a second at the mirror to take in her new look, smiled myseriously, and moved out to the parking lot to find her Ford Taurus.

The afternoon traffic on the interstate was moderate. Archer stayed to the right and never exceeded the speed limit. Her ID was in order, but no need to put it to the test. She had reviewed the maps repeatedly on her first visit to scope out the job. She knew her highway exit, the neighborhood, and her street of interest as well as she knew her own hometown.

At Exit 33, she turned off the highway and drove to the Daisy Inn, a modest motel with no security cameras and a preference for payment in cash. She parked away from the front entrance. Registration at the Daisy Inn was still done manually, and the recordkeeping was slipshod at best. The motel was two blocks from her target's home. She had made no reservation.

Archer sauntered in, chomping a piece of gum. The clerk, a young South Asian Muslim woman, looked up from the television with little interest. She shoved a form toward Archer, who filled it out using her fictitious Cincinnati address and a fake Ohio car license number. No need to put down the rental car tag. The more the trail was muddied, and the more dead ends inserted into the mix, the better her chances if worse came to worst. She chided herself for thinking of worse coming to worst. That had already happened.

Archer paid for one night in cash, all small bills. Nothing to draw attention to herself. If anyone remembered the girl from Cincinnati, all that could be said was, she had brown hair, was cute, and wore tight jeans. No relationship to the dowdy grandma from the airport, and certainly no relationship to Archer Loh of Lenox, Massachusetts.

As the desk clerk turned to get a key, Archer leaned forward. "Listen," she said, "do you mind giving me a room away from the main street? I'll be out late and I'll want to sleep late, so something away from the noise would be wonderful." She smiled conspiratorially. No need to be in front, where one's comings and goings were more noticeable.

For the first time, the desk clerk showed signs of life—she understood. She nodded and smiled, then moved her hand along the board to another row of keys.

"Here you go. You won't hear a thing in this room."

"Thanks. You're a doll," Michelle said, turning her three-hundred-watt smile on the desk clerk.

At her room, she unlocked the door, pushed it open, and looked around. Tacky, with a dreadful harbor scene print over the headboard— screwed to the wall, as if someone might actually be tempted to steal such a thing. But the place was clean enough, and private. With a relieved sigh, she pulled off the short brown wig and the skullcap and, opening her suitcase, tucked both next to the Miriam hairdo, and shook out her own reddish-brown shoulder-length hair. Then she took off the earrings, removed the eye makeup, slipped into white cotton shorts and a white T-shirt, and lay down on the bed for a half-hour nap. That left plenty of time to get to the post office before closing and pick up the package she'd mailed to herself a week ago.

Two hours later, having run her errands, she was back in her room. With a big pair of scissors from a local drugstore, she cut through the thick packing tape on a package addressed to Michelle Danaher—

nineteen inches by five by five, weighing a little over three and a half pounds. She had packed it well and addressed it in large print in black indelible marker, with fake return name and address in the upper left corner, before taking it to the post office window in Pittsfield, where she was not known, and sending it by priority mail with the correct postage. It was labeled "Fragile: Glassware."

Inside the cardboard box was a smaller cardboard box, with three pairs of beige latex gloves, a disassembled Armalite AR-7 rifle, a variable-powered scope, disposable plastic silencer, and ammunition. The AR-7's serial number was filed off. Putting on the gloves, she laid the gun parts out on a dry cleaner's bag on the bed—all there. Methodically, she wiped each part and assembled the weapon, then swabbed each bullet clean of prints before loading the clip.

After reviewing the street layout one more time, she burned it in the bathroom sink and washed the ashes down the drain.

Her target was Julián Baca. Baca had beaten his wife, Maricela, to death when she tried to leave him after enduring years of abuse. His record of drug dealing and violent assaults on women, both before and after his marriage to Maricela, was long and grim. Two neighbors had seen virtually the entire murder and had been more than willing to come forward.

But Baca was released because the police had not given him his full Miranda warnings on the scene, before his confession. The confession was thrown out, and without it, the case against him collapsed, leaving him at liberty to continue his personal reign of terror.

Maricela's parents, Cuban immigrants, were devastated to learn that this madman had been freed—and then he petitioned the court for a return of custody of their granddaughter, Lucero, whom they had been raising since their daughter's murder. They were told, "Florida law supports the rights of the biological parent above all others." It was just a matter of time before Lucero would be returned to him.

Julián Baca lived alone in a duplex on the south side of Miami. Archer had come down a month ago for a few days to settle her strategy and learn his routines. Although the Group's advance arm typically provided the legwork, Archer preferred to do her own. Everything must go perfectly on this, her first solo assignment.

Like most people, Baca kept a predictable routine. Each morning around seven, he appeared on his back patio, wrapped in a blue robe, to smoke and drink coffee from a red ceramic mug. He was tall and muscular, with curly, black hair and a black, full mustache. He would sit for at least an hour, smoking, reading the newspaper left at the front porch, and talking on a cell phone.

Around eleven, Baca's house became a hive of activity. Cars would pull up, usually with two people, one of whom would get out and knock on the door. Baca would open the door with a smile, wave the visitor in, glance around, and close the door. In a few minutes, the passenger would return to the car, and the car drove away. This went on until around four in the afternoon.

Around seven in the evening, Baca left home on foot, in a clean shirt and cutoff jeans, for a café a block away. He had dinner alone, drinking three glasses of red wine with a plate of pasta, and ending each meal with a glass of sambuca and an espresso. He always paid in cash and was home by nine. He watched television until eleven, when he went outside for a last cigar of the day. He would sit on the patio in the dark, the end of his cigar brightening with each puff. That was the moment, the vulnerability.

With her gear stowed in a new canvas duffel, she sat back on the couch. She thought about Maricela and her daughter, Lucero. Had Maricela, during those last moments of life, thought about Lucero, about the hopes and plans she had for her little girl?

Archer remembered when she and Adam had learned they were having a daughter.

When they debated whether to ask for the ultrasound results showing gender, she had said to Adam, "Hey, I want to know, what's the point of all these scientific advances if not to get the big surprise early? It's still a surprise, just sooner." Adam was persuaded.

"It's a girl," the doctor had pronounced. "Get ready for sleepless nights until she's, oh, about twenty-five."

*A girl.* Her spirits soared. Boys were a wonderful mystery to her, but girls...she knew girls. And for days after learning the news, she had hummed stupid girl songs—"Thank Heaven for Little Girls," "Brown-Eyed Girl," "It's You, Girl"—until Adam started doing it, too.

"We're becoming insufferable, you know," Archer said, beaming as she handed him a strip of pink and yellow flowered wallpaper for the baby's room border.

"I know, I know. Maybe we're gonna be one of those couples who can't talk about anything but their kid. You know, someone says, 'What did you think of that Supreme Court decision?' and we say, 'Oh, I don't know but my daughter used the potty today.' Scary, Arch, really scary," Adam said, laughing as he smoothed a strip of paper onto the wall.

"So did we settle on a name then?" Archer asked.

"Hannah, wasn't it? Hannah MacKenzie sounds nice."

"Hannah." She paused, sat back on her heels, and relaxed against the wall. As a test run, she called, "Hannah, time for dinner... Hannah, if I've told you once, I've told you a thousand times..."

Adam laughed. "Hey, if you slop any more glue on that wallpaper, I'm gonna need a squeegee."

Archer closed her eyes. Had Maricela thought about her little Lucero there at the end?

She ate the apple and an orange from her suitcase and glanced at her watch. It was time.

She donned fresh clothes from her suitcase: black cotton pants, T-shirt, and sneakers. Then the beige skullcap and the Michelle Danaher wig. She put on the latex gloves and wiped down the motel room and luggage for good measure. Compulsively, she checked to be sure nothing in her luggage pointed to her real identity, in case she didn't make it back. Then, after cinching the duffel with her killing tools and equipment, she peeled off the gloves and stuffed them in her pant pocket, and slipped out of the room.

She walked a block south, turned left, then right, bringing her to a street parallel to the street where Baca lived. She looked like any fit young woman going to the gym for an evening workout, athletic bag slung over her shoulder.

The street was dark but for a streetlamp on the corner. Most houses had few lights on. Archer walked in the dark to a vacant house backing up diagonally to Baca's duplex.

Archer had made this happy discovery on her first trip to the area. Crawling through an easily jimmied basement window, she had sighted in the shot to Baca's patio from the second-floor window: urban shot in low light—piece of cake. The alternative would be a confrontation in Baca's house, using a revolver at close range. She preferred the rifle shot, mostly because it multiplied exponentially the confusion for investigators. Moreover, there was no chance of leaving forensic evidence at the scene.

Archer slipped on the latex gloves from her pocket and slid feetfirst through the basement window, for once appreciating her small size. She dropped four feet to the concrete floor, reached out the window, and pulled the duffel in. The basement was dank and smelled musty, but it was empty. Pulling out a small flashlight, she climbed two flights of stairs to the second floor and hunkered down by an upstairs bedroom in back. She opened the window, removed the screen, and sighted in the patio through her scope. She had a few minutes before her quarry arrived.

Still on her knees, Archer mounted the barrel to the Armalite's plastic stock, then took the silencer from the open gym bag and spun it onto the barrel. She stood up, raised the rifle to her eye, and aimed it out the open window. Her heart was pounding, and her scalp was sweaty and itched under the wig. *Focus,* she reminded herself. *Breathe.*

The glass door slid open, and there he stood on the patio. Settling into the chair, he lit his cigar and puffed two, three times, the picture of contentment. *Thank God for creatures of habit.*

From this point on, everything happened fast. Sitting on one buttock, one knee up, left hand resting on the windowsill, she breathed in and, on the exhale, squeezed the trigger twice, and heard the *zip, zip* of the muted rounds. For a moment, Baca still sat up in his chair. Archer scowled in disbelief. Could she possibly have missed? Then, she saw the cigar tumble and spark on the concrete patio, and Baca crumpled and fell forward off the chair. Archer knew he was dead. Her aim was true, and the hollow-point rounds would have found their mark at this distance and pureed a large portion of his chest cavity.

Archer glanced around the bedroom, collected the two spent cartridge casings, and made sure she had left nothing on the floor. The shoes would be discarded. She had touched nothing but the insides of the gloves, which she would also discard, and the wig and cap had kept her hair tucked away. She turned and closed the window. It was time to go.

Archer hurried down the stairs and crawled out the basement window. Baca would not likely be found until morning. Resisting the urge to run, she crept along the edge of the property, then out to the street, crossed over the road, and strolled back to her motel room in the rear of the building. She unlocked her door, closed it behind her, and leaned against it, breathing heavily. Walking over to the bed, she slumped onto it, shaking, and took three deep breaths. She still had work to do.

With a fresh pair of gloves on, she disassembled the weapon, wiping it down, then crushed the plastic silencer into bits with a hard shoe heel and put the pieces into six separate plastic bags, sealed with twist ties. She cut up the latex gloves with the scissors and put the pieces in six other small plastic bags. Then she took off the black T-shirt and pants and black running shoes and the Michelle Danaher wig, putting these in a plastic trash bag and knotting it. By the time she finished, it was two a.m. Archer lay on top of the made bed, staring at the ceiling and feeling sick.

She pulled out of the motel at six a.m. On her way to the airport, she pulled into the back of a convenience store ten miles out of town and tossed the large trash bag with the clothes and wig into the Dumpster. The timing worked well—too late to run into the four a.m. delivery trucks and too early for the regular staff to be sneaking out back for a smoke. She then stopped at four other strip malls, dropping the smaller plastic bags in various trash bins at each stop, never putting two in the same bin.

Archer glanced at her map and, at the next stop light, turned right onto a twisting wooded road. Every few miles, she stopped and walked deep into brush, discarding a piece of the AR-7. She made six stops in all.

Before reaching the airport, she pulled into a rest area to wipe the car free of prints, then donned a pair of leather gloves for the rest of the drive. What was it Peter Bennett had said about her? That she looked wholesome, that she was unlikely to draw unwanted attention wandering around an airport. She hoped to hell he was right.

Archer drove into the airport rental lot and returned the car with no drama at the automatic drop-off. She took her bag from the trunk and headed for the ladies' room, to emerge ten minutes later as Miriam Hayes of Chicago, flying to Boston to visit her old college roomie.

Archer looked around. Businessmen were hustling past her to catch their connections, cell phones to their ears. Families were shuffling forward with too many bags, trying to escape to the cool breezes of Camden, Maine, or the temperate shores of Lake Michigan. She headed to a coffee shop for an espresso to jolt her awake for the flight home. First, though, she had to make a call. She stopped and sat down on her travel bag and dialed a number on her cell phone. A man picked up on the first ring.

"Good morning."

"This is Miriam. I'm heading home. It was a successful trip."

"Well done, Miriam."

The bad dream ended, and then it started all over again.

# CHAPTER
# 12

"So," Connor said, rinsing a dish off in the sink, "I have to ask, and you don't have to answer—how did Annie die?"

*Yes, how did Annie die?* Archer thought to herself, wondering if she could embark on that memory without falling apart.

They were cleaning up after a dinner of burgers, salad, and potato chips. The weather had started to cool, but tonight was almost balmy—unusual for early October.

Archer savored the breeze that drifted through the front screen door. Without answering Connor, she dried the last plate and set it in the open cupboard. Then she folded the dish towel, went over to the cabinet, and took down the Maker's Mark. She got out a glass and poured. "You want one?" she said, holding the glass out to him.

"Sure."

She gave it to him, then poured a double for herself, took it to the sofa, sat, and gulped down almost half. *How did Annie die?* As they said in court, *that was the question pending.*

"I'm surprised you never asked before, and it's not something I bring up," she said, grasping her glass with both hands.

"I...didn't know if you could tell it, and I didn't want to make you sad, I guess."

She nodded, then shook her head, and said, "I think I can tell it—to you, anyway."

Taking another slug, she began. "Annie was twelve. Her actual name was Hannah, but we always called her Annie. She had just turned twelve on May fifteenth. We lived in West Hartford then. It's a really nice town—safe, upper-middle class. You know, tree-lined streets with nice neighbors, sidewalks, Starbucks. Annie was used to being friendly. She thought everyone was like the people she saw every day." Archer hesitated, staring at her hands, then continued.

"Anyway, there was a class trip to Washington, D.C., for the seventh grade. It was June, the end of the school year. Everyone was going; it wasn't even a question. The kids were leaving by bus from the school on a Thursday morning and returning home on Sunday. Routine. Adam took Annie to the bus that morning. I had an early court case, so I was already gone when they left the house. Annie had her little travel bag—she'd packed it herself the night before and was really excited. It was her first real trip away from home except for some nights with grandparents or sleepovers with one of her girlfriends. She was sharing a room with her best friend, Sophie. I was going to pick the girls up from the school on Sunday afternoon around five—all very normal, you know."

She took another gulp of the bourbon. "I guess everything was fine until Saturday night. I mean, most of what I know came from Sophie or from Mrs. Dennis, the class chaperone. The class was going to see a live performance of *Grease* downtown. They had just finished dinner at a Mexican restaurant and were going to get back on the bus. Annie went to the back of the restaurant to use the ladies' room. When she came out, everyone apparently had already left to get on the bus. Annie went out front to get on the bus, too, but it wasn't there, and none of the kids were there, either. She probably got a little bit scared. At least, that's what Sophie thinks happened.

"Then, we think, Annie went over to one of the side streets, thinking maybe the bus was parked there. This guy came up to her—a well-dressed man—and asked if something was wrong. She said she was looking for her school bus, and he said, oh, he knew where it was. Just follow him; he had just seen it. He knew a shortcut to the other side of the building—she'd better follow him or it might leave without her. That's what a local cabbie who had been waiting nearby for his fare said he overheard. He said he never gave it a second thought, just thought the guy was associated with the school kids somehow."

Connor nodded as Archer began to cry—not big, heaving sobs, just quiet tears. Connor got up and grabbed a tissue from the bathroom and handed it to her. Archer took it and dabbed at her eyes.

"They found her a few hours later, raped and strangled in that little dirty alley. They realized Annie was missing as soon as the kids filled the bus. Sophie told them, and they all started to search, but they started inside the restaurant, and by the time they got to the streets around it, it was too late."

Archer felt dazed; her voice was flat with little inflection, as if this was a story she had thought about too many times. She just kept shaking her head, oblivious of the tears running down her face. "She was only twelve…just twelve years old. The bus *was* on a side street, just the other side of the one that Annie went to. Jesus…Jesus…she was just a *kid*." She began to sob now, shoulders trembling, head in her hands.

Connor sat dead still, leaning forward, elbows on his knees, his head in his hands. "God, Archer. I'm so sorry. I had no idea. I'm so sorry I made you tell it. I thought it was some illness, or an accident or something. I didn't know it was some hideous, monstrous thing. I'm so sorry." It was all he could say. He moved to her on the sofa and wrapped his arms around her.

She cried quietly into his shoulder. "They didn't call me. Nobody called me. I got to the school to pick up Annie and Sophie, and then they took me aside and told me. Nobody called us. I could have been there."

"Oh, Archer, I am so sorry. So sorry. My God…" He released her, and she sat back on the sofa. He shook his head, eyes stinging. "Did they ever get the guy?"

"Oh, yeah, they got the guy. An accountant for the Justice Department. How's that for irony? And there was even an eyewitness to the actual attack—an old woman who lived in a rooming house that overlooked the alley—and they had DNA matches. They had his clothes from that night, with Annie's blood and hair all over them. But when the trial came up, the old lady couldn't be found, and the police had no search warrant when they seized the guy's clothing, so all that evidence was worthless. The monster's wife had signed a consent to search the house while he was at work, but the house was in *his* name and *he* hadn't consented to the search. The wife thought there was just some big mistake, and a search would clear her husband, but when the detectives got to the laundry room, they found what they were looking for—his clothes from that night.

"Adam and I lived in D.C. for almost two months after it happened. I went down a few times every month after that, following every move, every lead. Then, when they had us in and said there had been a screw-up, that the appellate court said the search was illegal, that they couldn't believe the wife's consent hadn't held up, that they had to let him go, that they couldn't hold him any longer, it was too much.

"My sanity had been hanging by a thread, and I mean a thread. I had been so focused on getting that horror of a human being that it was my sole reason for getting up in the morning. That was how I got through each day. Then when they let him go—the man who everyone knew did it—I just lost it. Knives, scissors, anything sharp, I began to cut on myself. Day after day, sometimes several times a day, I'd cut. At first, I cut where no one could see—you know, my legs, my upper arms, and then any part of my arm. I began wearing long sleeves all the time, even in ninety-degree heat. Soon I didn't care. When I began to cut my face, Adam did begin to notice.

"Adam tried to understand. He tried to be patient; he really did. I know he did. He's a good man, and he hurt as much as I did, but we handled all of it differently. He needed to get back to work, back to a routine, or he would have gone crazy. That helped him not think about it twenty-four hours a day. For me, I guess I would have gone mad getting back to a routine. I mean, *what* routine? Without Annie, I was lost. I became obsessed with getting the guy. I plotted all day; I went over the evidence all night; I stopped seeing family, friends. While I wasn't exactly *fired* from my firm, it was suggested I might want to take a leave of absence. That was no sacrifice, since I hadn't been to the office in nine months."

Archer paused to rub her eyes with the damp tissue, tossed it on the table, and continued. "Daddy was the only one who really seemed to understand me in those days. He could always find something to say that I could accept or that helped, at least a little. I think he stayed strong for me. We had always been close, and I felt terrible burdening him with this. He was almost seventy years old when it happened, and he was getting frailer each year. But we sagged—he and I—almost in unison after they let the guy go. We were diminished by…well, we were just diminished.

"Adam and I tried to keep the marriage together—you know, sometimes a tragedy brings people closer. Maybe if we'd had other kids…but for us, every time we looked at each other, there was no Annie.

"We never blamed each other, but…but I was so ill mentally that I had nothing to give Adam or the marriage. And everything I did reminded me she was gone. That there would be no more Christmas mornings, no more Easter egg hunts, no more pancake breakfasts, no more Halloween skits. Adam could take only so much. I resented that he could go on, and he resented—no, that's not right—he, he ached for me that I couldn't go on. Our marriage ended that day in Washington, with Annie.

"And so, we quietly divorced. I got my fair share of the assets, and my father, my dear father, left me—and Sharon, my sister—money in a trust that sends me a check every month. So much for independence," she said ruefully.

"So you don't do any legal work at all now?" Connor asked.

"Well, I do a little work for an international firm once in a while, some research and writing, you know, but it's sporadic. Sometimes I have to go out of town to see the client in person, you know," she said quickly.

They sat quietly for a minute. Then Connor got up to make tea. "Want some?" he asked.

"Sure."

As he filled the kettle with water and put it on the stove, he asked, "Did you ever want more children?"

"No, not really. I'm not exactly a well-balanced person, in case you hadn't noticed." Archer started drying her tears with her T-shirt sleeve now. "I worry all the time, and I need to be in control all the time. I thought, with only one child to worry about, I could handle it and actually be a good mother. One daughter was perfect for me, just perfect, and I felt so lucky to have her. I'm not a religious person, but I thanked God every night for Annie. When she would ask us if she was ever going to have a brother or sister, we would say we'd done so well the first time, we didn't want to tempt the gods. You know, bad rice and all that."

Connor nodded, acknowledging the reference to *Love Is a Many-Splendored Thing*. The kettle began to sing, and he poured the hot water into two mugs. He dipped the bags up and down a few times, then brought the mugs to the living room, where he set one in front of Archer and kept one for himself.

Archer continued, "Annie would laugh, but I knew she was pleased, you know, that she was enough for us."

"Did your ex-husband stay around Connecticut?"

"No, he looked for a job out west and got one with a firm in Denver. He moved a year after our divorce, met another lawyer in his firm that same year, got married, and now has two boys—they're around two and three years old, I think."

Connor was quiet for a while, just sipping his tea. Then he said, "I wish I had something really pithy to say now, Arch, but I don't. And I'm sure you've heard every cliché in the book: 'life is for the living'; 'this too shall pass'; 'she would want you to go on.' How does anyone *know* what she would want? But I will say this. Unless you're going to kill yourself, you have no real choice but to go on. And given that you have to keep going, I wish I could help you think of a way to keep something of Annie alive in a happy way, incorporate it into your day-to-day life and kind of, somehow, just strip the horror from what happened—sift through it and let the bad parts filter out and be left with only the good parts at the bottom of the colander."

"Good trick if you can pull it off," said Archer. "I could barely eat for almost a year, and when I did, nothing stayed down. Between that and the cutting, I was not a lot of fun to be around. It's just that I've always had this thing about fairness. Things should be fair. If you follow the rules, you should be rewarded, or at least not punished. I mean, I return library books on time; I drive the speed limit; I wait my turn in lines. I always figured you couldn't come to any harm if you colored inside the lines, you know.

"We taught Annie to be responsible, not talk to strangers, but in one instant, one slight mistake, which in most circumstances would have been fine, but in this one freak instance wasn't fine…it's just so *unfair*…" Archer's voice trailed off.

"You bet it is," Connor affirmed.

They both were quiet for a few minutes. Connor glanced down at his watch. It was nine—his usual time to head to his camp.

"About time for me to go," he said, looking at his watch. He stood up. "So what did Annie like?"

Archer paused, then said quietly and firmly, "Horses. She liked horses. No, she loved horses."

"Oh, yeah? Did she take riding lessons?" Connor asked, interested.

"Yeah. She had her own horse. I did, too. We thought...I mean, we always meant for it to be our thing together. We always said that when she graduated from high school we would take a riding vacation in England."

"You mean you ride, too?" Connor asked.

"Yes, I ride, too."

"No wonder you were interested in old Millie. How well do you ride?"

Pause.

"Pretty well, McCall."

Connor grinned. "Coming from you, that means you're probably practically an Olympian, I reckon."

Archer's mouth made a little cryptic smile, but she said nothing.

"So come over tomorrow and ride Millie. She's getting fat and lazy."

"Maybe," Archer said, smiling a little and downing the last dram of bourbon, chased with a sip of tea. "But I don't think Millie would like you talking about her that way."

"I better get going—it's late," said Connor, smiling, too, and picking up his lantern. "I'll see you tomorrow for your ride. Let's go, Alice."

The Bouvier jumped up, showing a lot of agility for a big dog. Connor opened the door, turned to tip his hat, and set off for his camp.

Archer watched until he disappeared into the woods. She got up to pour herself another drink, then stopped. Maybe she didn't need a second drink—or a third—to sleep tonight. She'd thought she would feel wretched after talking about Annie. Usually, when someone asked if she had children, she just said, *No, I haven't been that lucky,* thus avoiding the obvious next question that would follow a "yes" answer.

Still, Archer slept soundly without the second dose of Maker's Mark's helping hand, with no shrieking banshees tearing after her in her dreams for one night.

# CHAPTER
# 13

Archer showed up at Connor's camp at midmorning, just as he was trudging up the path from the road, returning from the motel.

"Hey, you live pretty rugged, McCall," Archer commented. Despite her observations during her morning trysts with Millie, she had never thought through the logistics of living in a tent. Today she did.

He shrugged. "No worse than when we bring in the herd from the far pastures at the end of the summer, and it's a lot warmer here. Plus, I do have my little arrangement with the innkeeper down the road."

Archer plopped down on the big, lichen-speckled granite boulder next to the tent and began eating the apple she had brought for Millie. She watched Connor soap up Millie's bridle and polish it with a clean, dry cloth.

Munching on the apple and watching him, Archer was reminded what a damned attractive man this was: tall, broad-shouldered, lean, with a great smile, dark hair with just a hint of gray at the edges, clean-shaven, dark blue eyes…and beautiful *forearms*. It was crazy, but she loved strong, sinewy forearms, tan from a day's work. And he was clean, always squeaky clean.

As Connor worked on the saddle, she thought of yesterday, when they went swimming at a pond not far from Connor's campsite. She had christened the pond "tiny tempest," in dubious tribute to Connor's Wyoming hometown, Little Tempest.

It had been a hot day for October. Archer had felt Connor's eyes on her as she emerged from under the little waterfall, sputtering and laughing, in her white T-shirt and denim shorts. He had steadied her as she stumbled on the rocky bottom. He'd held her hand, his left hand on her hip, her wet shirt clinging to her, concealing nothing.

Connor gazed at her not so much lustfully as admiringly, she thought. Or maybe it was just her imagination. He'd become almost shy for a moment, then bridged the awkwardness with a lame joke about it being a good thing he was there, lest she drown and leave Hadley orphaned.

She had laughed and shoveled water at him as he ducked and weaved out of her way. Finally he succumbed to her grabs as she pulled him with her under the waterfall. No question, Archer had felt the heat of desire.

Connor had clowned a little as they walked back to the cabin, hair dripping, towels draped over their shoulders. Not that she wanted things to escalate—God, no, that would just complicate things.

Snapping back to the present, Archer asked, "So, how long do you think you'll be staying here?"

After closing the can of saddle soap, he looked up. "Don't know. I have to be back at the farm by lambing time...maybe sooner."

"When's that?"

"Oh, end of February, early March, I'd say. But by rights, I should get back before Christmas to prep the ranch for spring shearing and then lambing."

"Oh," Archer replied, still munching on the apple. "But don't you miss Boston? I mean, do you *really* like Wyoming?"

"*Really* like Wyoming?" Connor mimicked, laughing. "Sometimes you do talk like a girl, Archer. Yeah, I do *really* like Wyoming, but I've gotta say, it took a while. There's a vastness to everything out there that can be exhilarating or bleak, depending. And then the winters— they were even colder than I expected." He shook his head. "But then, spring suddenly comes on you, and the sky gets real high and as blue as blue gets, and then I wonder how anyone could live anywhere else."

"It sounds beautiful," Archer sighed. "I'd like to see it someday."

"Well, then I'm sure you will. So…let's get this show on the road, shall we?" he said, handing her Millie's tack. "You already have a passing acquaintance with this stuff—and with my horse, as I recall."

Last night, over burgers, Archer had confessed to visiting Millie daily, though she omitted her invasion of the tent. Now deciding that the best defense was a good offense, she said, "Well, didn't you notice Millie looked a lot nicer? I never heard any thank-yous, now that you mention it."

Connor shot her a sidelong glance. "Uh, not really. We kind of use our horses in a functional way in Wyoming, much as we love 'em. I don't inspect her daily for dust, since *everything's* dusty. I did think she was getting a bit vain, though, staring at herself in the brook all the time, but I couldn't for the life of me figure out where that was coming from. Now I know."

"Hah! Very amusing. You should do stand-up."

He didn't look at her, but he smiled. "You could have just asked to play with my horsey, you know. I don't bite."

"That remains to be seen."

He laughed and tossed a halter to her, with a lead rope attached. She caught it in one hand. Archer stepped over to Millie, fastened the halter, and then just let the rope hang. She began brushing the mare, who kept grazing.

With Millie brushed and her hooves picked out, Archer grabbed a fresh saddle pad from Connor's tack pile and threw it over Millie's back. It fell smoothly into place. Then she settled a heavy brown western saddle on her back and nestled it into the gentle swale between withers and rump. Archer stared at all the leather loops and ties on the saddle.

"Hey, McCall, what goes where? This is a big mess—too many strings and hangy things," she protested, glaring at the saddle and grabbing various ties and thongs, trying to make sense of it all. Millie stood patiently waiting.

Connor was repacking dry goods in the hanging satchels. He turned, looked amused, and ambled over.

"Still need me, huh?" With a couple of tugs on the girth, the saddle was snug.

"I ride English. It's not like this," she murmured, a little defensively.

"Uh-huh."

As Archer stood next to Millie, her heart began to race with excitement. Then it slowed. She hadn't ridden since she gave away her own horse, Half Moon Bay, just after Annie's death. Half Moon was the horse she'd bought after Clique's death. He'd proved honest, talented, and sweet. But now her hands began to tremble.

*I can't get on this horse,* she thought. *It's not fair to Annie.* But almost as quickly, she thought: *You're being crazy as a bat. Annie loved horses. She wouldn't want them gone from your life any more than she'd want them gone from hers. Stop being such a drama queen.*

Archer shoved her quaking hands into her jacket pockets and leaned into Millie to steady herself. Millie stood her ground, then bent her neck and looked back at Archer.

Archer blinked, then took a deep breath. She grabbed the saddle horn, put the toe of her left boot in the wide western stirrup, took a quick bounce, and swung her right leg up and over. Settling in, she breathed a sigh of contentment. It felt like opening the front door of her cabin after a long trip.

She sat up and squeezed lightly with her calves, and Millie immediately started away from the camp in a relaxed stride. Connor looked up and waved. Archer grinned and waved back.

When she was ten minutes away and out of earshot, she stopped and bent low to wrap her arms around Millie's neck. Then she straightened and stood up in her stirrups, raised both arms, and opened her hands to the sky in a silent gesture of thanks. After a minute, she lowered herself back into the saddle and pressed with her calves, moving into a walk.

For more than two hours, Archer and Millie walked down hills, trotted up slopes, and cantered along level open stretches where the footing was firm. On one long gallop, Archer imagined herself on Clique—a team again, tearing up the countryside, jumping logs and stone walls and fences just because they were there. While Millie was no Grand Prix jumper, she easily took the fallen logs on the paths, and even jumped a stone wall with grace, her black mane and tail flying. *Millie, my dear, you've been holding out on me,* thought Archer, delighted, stroking the little mare's neck on the walk back to the camp.

When she got there, Archer couldn't stop grinning. "It was beyond wonderful, McCall! I don't know how to thank you," she said, swinging out of the saddle and handing him the reins. Connor smiled back and said, "Well, I can see that Millie enjoyed the ride."

# CHAPTER
# 14

Archer stood at the kitchen counter, peeling potatoes for dinner and reflecting on her morning with Millie. It was getting dark earlier. Next week they would turn back the clocks. Hadley sat near her bowl, waiting less than stoically for her evening kibble. Archer finished the potatoes and put a pot of water on to boil.

Hearing three raps at the back door, she looked out to see Connor and Alice. She smiled and opened the door.

"Hi. What's cooking?" he asked.

"Mashed potatoes, flounder, and salad."

Archer's cell phone rang, and she followed the sound to the jacket hanging by the back door.

"Hello?" she said. Her smile broadened. "Gavin! How the hell are you?"

Pause.

"That's terrific—it's quite a feather in your cap to get that kind of a commission!"

Pause.

"Oh, gee, Gavin, I just did a job last month. I'm in the midst of a project here, so I think I'll pass on this one, if you don't mind."

Pause.

"Oh, I see. New York? Well, if there's no one else... Wait just a sec." She opened a drawer and pulled out a pad of brightly colored paper and a pen. "Okay, go." She took a few notes. "Okay, fine. You'll send me the itinerary and specifics by overnight mail tomorrow?"..."Okay, yeah, I think so."..."Got it."..."When do you need it done?"..."This week's okay, then?"..."Okay...I'll get it done... Good-bye, Gavin. See you soon."

Archer hung up, lost in thought. Connor looked at her, took off his saddle-colored jacket, and hung it on the peg over her jacket.

"So?" he asked.

"Huh? Oh, sorry, I was off somewhere else."

"So, who's Gavin? Your secret lover?" he asked, moving his eyebrows up and down in a credible Groucho Marx imitation.

Archer laughed. "Hardly. He's an old friend—an architect in Boston. He's only thirty-four—way too young for me."

She said the words, knowing that Gavin had been in love with her for years. He'd joined the Group nine years ago, after the murder of his wife and two-year-old son, and had since become the East Coast coordinator. He and Archer had become close confidants and best friends after Annie's death. He admired Archer's directness, energy, and passion—to him, not letting go was a plus. They spoke at least weekly and met at least once a month for informal dinners in Springfield or Sturbridge.

She came up from her thoughts to hear Connor saying, "Hey, don't knock it. The older woman younger man thing is very hot, you know. How old are you, anyway?" He was looking in the cabinet for the corkscrew.

"I turned forty-three a month ago, September fifth," Archer said.

"Really? I would have pegged you for ten years younger than that."

"Clean living, McCall, clean living. And since we're getting personal, how old are you, pray tell?"

"I turned forty-nine last August. And don't tell me you pegged me for ten years *older* than that—I couldn't take it," he said, testing the boiling potatoes. "So, what led your young friend to call?"

"Legal work—a quick research project."

"Ah…"

Archer retook her territory in the kitchen, and Connor set the table, then sat reading a British magazine, *The Field,* on Archer's coffee table. Archer checked the flounder, and Alice fell asleep on one end of the sofa as Hadley fussed around the kitchen. Archer opened the door, and the Lab scooted out.

An hour passed. They were just clearing the table when they heard the howl. Archer dropped the dish of potatoes; it shattered on the floor.

"Hadley!" she cried.

Grabbing Connor's xenide lantern from the counter, Archer flung open the back door and bolted in the direction of the howl.

"Archer! Wait a minute—you don't know what's out there!" shouted Connor, chasing her.

She speeded up, flashing the light up ahead, then close, ahead, then close. Then she saw. Five hundred yards ahead, three coyotes had encircled Hadley. One lunged at her flanks just as Archer flashed the light that way. Hadley was turning in frantic circles. Archer could see that her slow old Lab was terrified.

In an instant, Archer also could see that she couldn't get to Hadley in time to make a difference. She turned and raced back into the cabin, straight to the closet in the front hall. Out of the corner of her eye, she saw that Connor had grabbed a smaller flashlight from the kitchen utility drawer, then had snatched up a four-foot maple branch, and was running toward Hadley.

"Wait!" she yelled to him over her shoulder as she dragged a flattish box from the bottom of the closet, opened it, and pulled out the parts of her assault rifle and night vision scope. She had it assembled and loaded in eighteen seconds. She ran past Connor.

Connor tried to grab her arm. "Archer, you can't—you'll shoot Hadley."

Without pausing, she ran toward Hadley and the coyotes, then stopped. She brought the rifle up and sighted through the scope. She could see one of the coyotes clinging to Hadley's flank. Another had the side of her fleshy neck in its mouth. Hadley was staggering. The third coyote was closing in.

Her training ran through her head. *Sight...focus...steady... squeeze...* The rifle cracked, and the coyote on Hadley's flank fell away. A second later, its yelp drifted back to her on the still night air.

"Archer, stop. Please. No way can you make that shot," Connor pleaded from a dozen steps behind her.

Without lowering the rifle, Archer sighted again and fired. The coyote at Hadley's neck dropped, and then she heard the yip. The third coyote ran into the darkness.

Archer engaged the safety and laid the rifle down on a grassy hummock, and she and Connor raced toward Hadley. Without a word, they lifted the mauled Lab onto Connor's jacket and carried her swiftly but gently to the Jeep. Archer got her jacket and car keys and hopped in, while Connor got in the backseat with Hadley. She lay there motionless but for her labored breathing.

"You're gonna be fine, old girl," he crooned to her, smoothing her wrinkled brow. "Just fine. Such a good, brave girl you are."

At the end of the driveway, Archer jumped out, unlocked the gate, and pulled out of the driveway, wheels skidding in the wet dirt. For the first time in memory, she didn't relock the gate. She called the veterinary clinic from her cell phone. The vet on call, a Dr. Tulloch, assured her they would be ready. When Archer pulled into the parking lot, the staff was in gear.

Two assistants got Hadley onto a stretcher. Twenty minutes later, she was in surgery. Archer and Connor waited in silence in the little waiting room. Unable to sit still, Archer began to pace.

"So, Arch, why'd you name her Hadley?" Connor asked in an effort to distract her.

Archer sat down on a bench and leaned forward, head in hand, staring straight ahead. Finally, she looked at Connor, as if realizing for the first time that he was there.

"Sorry. Did you say something?"

He repeated his question.

"Oh, right. Hadley Richardson was Hemingway's first wife. He loved her best."

"Really? How many wives did he have?"

"Four."

"Didn't know you were a Hemingway fan."

"I shouldn't be. I hate war, hunting, fishing, bullfights, boxing—most of the stuff he wrote about and loved. But I love the way he tells a story: direct, simple…and always about love, or dignity, or courage. You know, winning even in defeat because you fought for something true, something that mattered. In two sentences, he made you feel exactly the way he wanted you to feel."

"I've only read a little Hemingway. I've read more of Fitzgerald."

"Well, you can't like Hemingway and Fitzgerald both. It's impossible—they're mutually exclusive."

"Oh, really? Says who?" asked Connor, sounding both puzzled and amused.

"Just my opinion," she said, uncharacteristically declining the challenge. Silence. "We got her for Annie when Annie was eight. She was cute as all get-out. We all went to pick her out. Adam and I were playing with the lively, funny ones, but Hadley walked over to Annie, sat at her feet, and just stared at her. Annie picked her up and put her in her lap. Hadley lay there, happy, and Annie kept saying, 'This one, Mommy. This is the one.'"

Just then Dr. Tulloch came out.

"Hadley's going to make it," he said with a smile. "She lost a lot of blood, and we want to keep her here for a few days for observation. But she's a tough old gal. Strangely, all that extra flesh that she...um, carries around her neck protected the artery. That chunkiness probably saved her. Two more bites and...well, anyway, I'm just glad we could save her. She's a sweetheart."

Archer laughed out loud and hugged Dr. Tulloch. Then she turned and hugged Connor. He looked surprised and pleased.

"Can we see her, Doctor?" Archer asked.

"Yeah, sure, but she's pretty sedated. She's sleeping in room four. Come on along."

Archer and Connor stepped softly into the room. Hadley was lying on her good side, eyelids fluttering. Archer touched her broad head lightly, bent forward, and kissed her brow.

"Dear old Haddie, we love you, and you'll be home soon, eating everything you see," Archer whispered. She gave the dog one last nuzzle and moved away.

"Thank you, Doctor. Thank you so much." She kept turning to thank him as they moved toward the outside door.

"You looked like one of those Japanese dolls that just keeps bowing once it gets going," Connor teased her when they got outside.

She punched his arm, and they both jumped into the Jeep. It was just after one a.m. The shift from high adrenaline to relief had left them drained. Archer guided the car out of the parking lot and onto the highway toward the cabin. The night was quiet.

"So do you want to tell me about that?" Connor asked after a few moments of silence.

"About what?" asked Archer, not looking at him.

"Uh, the high-speed assault rifle that you keep in your closet. Oh, and which you just happen to be able to assemble in the dark in under twenty seconds, and which you keep with night vision goggles and scope, too—like all of us do, just in case of the random invasion. And then there's the little matter of you making two shots—*standing*—that even the best shot in a crack SWAT team could only dream of making. That's what I thought you might give me some background on."

"Oh, that," she said, with a little wave. "No big deal. I told you I took a self-defense class after Annie died, and that's some of the stuff I got."

Connor looked at her, amazed and shaking his head. "Huh. I took a self-defense course myself. I don't remember assault rifles and night vision scope being part of the equipment. I guess you took the advanced class." He tipped the brim of his Stetson forward, leaning his head back on the headrest. He closed his eyes. "Yeah, right. And in my self-defense course, they handed out grenades to those of us who completed the class. Fine—if that's how you want to leave it."

"Well, don't get mad."

"I'm not mad. I'm just sorry you don't trust me enough to be honest."

Archer made no reply.

When they pulled into the driveway fifteen minutes later, Connor hopped out to lock the gate once Archer had pulled in. Alice wagged her tail in greeting at the cabin, and Connor petted her without a word. He turned to Archer, cocked his head as if about to say something, then shook it. He gave her a hug, holding her head in the hollow of his shoulder for a moment. Then, giving her a little smile, he backed away and grabbed his lantern, whistling for Alice. And with a tip of his hat, he walked out the door.

Archer stood silently at her kitchen sink, deep in thought. She shook her head and began to clean up pieces of the shattered baking dish. When she finished, she went out the back door with her flashlight to retrieve the specially outfitted rifle she'd left in the grass at the edge of the woods.

It wasn't until a few minutes later that she realized she hated deceiving Connor. She wanted them to be on the same side of the fence, with no secrets between them.

Connor arrived at the cabin with his few possessions and dropped them on the floor. He plopped down on the chair and watched in amusement as Archer hurried from room to room, gathering her things. She was going away for two days to do Gavin's project, and Connor had agreed to stay in the cabin with Alice, pick up Hadley from the clinic when she was ready, and take care of her until Archer returned.

Archer was in a good mood, running around the cabin, leaving sticky notes about heat, plumbing, and old-dog idiosyncrasies. She wore a new black and white tweed sweater, cropped at the hip and buttoned down the front, black gabardine slacks, and low black boots.

"Hey, fashion plate, you better snip that tag hanging off the back of your sweater before you hit the Big Apple."

"Yikes! Thanks. Could you grab the scissors from my sewing box on the table next to my bed? I'm just calling to see when Hadley gets out." She spun around, cell phone in hand.

"Sure, whatever it takes," said Connor, ambling into the little square bedroom. He saw the mahogany sewing box, shiny and compact, sitting on the bedside table. Archer's suitcase lay on the bed, lid open, but bulging and unlatched. Connor leaned over and opened the sewing box, taking out the scissors.

"Hey, Arch, want me to close your suitcase and put it in the car?" he called to her.

No answer.

He walked to the bedroom door and leaned out, holding on to the doorjamb with his left hand and balancing on one leg. She waved but was still talking on the phone. He walked back into the bedroom and tried to latch the suitcase, pushing the top down to compress the bulky contents. As he did, he saw a glint of metal in the front corner. Not really thinking, he opened the top to resettle a sweater with a protruding sleeve.

Then he saw it: an HK Tactical, cocked and locked, with two spare clips and a sound suppressor. He blinked as if not quite believing what he saw. He looked again, his eye falling on an open piece of paper next to the weapon. He read, "Wayne Bremmer. Child molester and murderer. Opportunity: leaving the gym."

Stunned, he closed the suitcase and carried it to the front door. Archer mouthed a thank-you, finished her call, and grabbed her coat. She stood on tiptoe to kiss him on the cheek, then left for two days of "legal research" in New York.

# CHAPTER
# 15

When Archer returned from New York, the fall days fell into a routine. Around midmorning she would jog down the logging path with Hadley. Connor and Alice would be ready at the camp, and they would all set off on a two-mile run: Archer in front, followed by Connor, with the dogs weaving behind them, surging ahead, snuffling for interesting smells in the grasses and the forest duff.

One morning, just before the end of October, Archer arrived to find Connor on his knees with a small gardening trowel, making holes in a circular pattern around his camp. He was wearing black sweatpants and a faded navy sweatshirt.

"Hey, what's with the gopher holes, McCall?" she yelled out as she approached the campsite.

"Daffodil bulbs, you philistine," he called back. "Feel free to join in."

"I didn't know you liked flowers," she said, jogging in place, then stopping.

"Well, now it's out: I do. Nothing better than seeing a field of daffodils in the spring. Rain's due this afternoon, and I want to get these in before it hits."

Archer knelt down and began dropping bulbs into the holes, covering them with the little piles of dirt, patting each spot firmly. They moved along in assembly line fashion. Within ten minutes, the forty remaining holes were covered.

"How many did you plant in all?" asked Archer, patting down her last two.

"Hm-m. I started with three hundred. I've been at it for hours while you were sipping decent coffee, woman!"

"So, you'll be here in the spring, then?"

"Don't know. But *they* will be. There—last one. Three hundred bulbs, all set."

Connor shook off his hands and then dipped them into a bucket of water near the tent door before drying them on a clean towel.

They began their jog. Archer was in her usual navy blue and red print running shorts, with a white sweatshirt over a white tank top. The sweatshirt always came off at the top of the first hill and was tied around her waist for the rest of the run. They ran uphill and down, around, and up again to the highest point of their little corner of the Berkshires. As close to heaven on earth as they could ever hope to get, Archer always said when they got there.

"This is the only way you're getting to heaven, McCall," she would say, panting and leaning forward, hands on knees, catching her breath after the uphill grind.

"Oh, yeah? How little you know about my secret good works! Anyway, I'm sure I'll have lots of company where I'm going."

"Hm-m, how true."

The clearing was perhaps a hundred feet square, with a granite ledge overhanging one side and thick forest bordering the other, but the view was spectacular: green hills in every direction, caramel-colored canyon, under a dome of pale blue sky. They called it "the Cloisters" after the monastery and sanctuary at Manhattan's upper edge.

Sunday afternoon, weather permitting, was their time to picnic there. Archer and Hadley would show up at Connor's camp in the early afternoon, a basket dangling from Archer's arm. Connor would look up when he spotted them, grab a book and a blanket, and take the basket from Archer, and they would head up the steep hill, chatting.

At the summit, the two would sit cross-legged on the big cotton blanket, eating and laughing, periodically feeding a morsel of chicken or cheese to the closest dog. Sometimes they stretched out on their stomachs, side by side, sharing an apple or a slice of baguette, joking about their present lack of gainful contribution to, oh, pretty much anything.

"I went from Type double-A to type G," Connor commented.

"That's not too bad—I fell off the whole chart."

By the second picnic, they each started bringing a book. Connor had brought Pearl Buck today, but he was ignoring it, just resting with his eyes closed. Archer had picked it up and started reading aloud. She read a paragraph and stopped.

"That's good. Keep going," Connor said without opening his eyes. She read, and when she tired, he took over. Though at first it seemed a little corny, it quickly proved to be a luxury just to listen, with nothing more required.

"This is like kindergarten, McCall," Archer said one balmy afternoon. "And I *loved* kindergarten. School went downhill from there, if you ask me."

"Yup. I always loved story hour, too. My favorite was the Hardy Boys."

"Where'd you go to school? We never got anything like that. We got *Winnie-the-Pooh* and Dr. Seuss."

"We were advanced in South Boston, unlike you kids off in the hinterlands of Litchfield, Connecticut," he said, winking.

Archer threw a handful of leaves at him, but they fell short of their mark. They were more than halfway through *The Good Earth*, with Connor reading. Archer lay back, using a yellow cotton sweater folded to make a pillow. She was popping grapes into her mouth. They were just the way she liked them: really crisp, seedless, red. Connor read another page.

"I don't get it," she interrupted, shaking her head, still lying down. "Now, why don't they see it was the land that got them where they are? Why would they jeopardize their whole way of life by even *considering* selling off some land?" she asked accusingly. "And why would he take on that tart when he has such a loyal, hardworking wife? People can be so blind to what really matters."

"I'm just reading it, not writing it, Archer," said Connor drily.

"Yeah, but what about that? I would see it. I would…" She went on; then, seeing him looking at her over the top of his glasses, she stopped. "Okay, okay, you're just reading. Go on. You're doing a fine job, I might add."

Later, with the chapter done, they just lay on their backs. Connor chewed on a blade of glass. Archer watched a long V of geese overhead. It was quiet and peaceful.

She broke the silence. "So, why do you think we haven't become lovers?" Without looking at him, she quickly added, "I mean, we're both free and over the age of consent, as they say. We like each other. We're here. Why do you think it hasn't happened?"

Dead silence.

Connor flushed, but Archer was still on her back and couldn't see him. He turned to his side. Putting a hand on her shoulder, he pulled her to her side to face him. They were looking at each other, but neither spoke for several minutes. Finally, Connor said, "Well, *that* was a surprise."

He waited for her to comment, but she said nothing.

"Uh, just for the record, was that a pass?"

She looked down, then away.

"No. I was just curious—you know, from a sort of academic point of view."

Connor gazed at her and said, "Academic interest, huh? Okay, well, fine. Look, in case you were wondering but didn't want to ask—

although that's hard to imagine—and just for the *academic* record that we're setting straight here, I'm not gay, or impotent, or infirm, or taken." Connor paused, weighing his words.

"And…since I think you are the most maddeningly attractive woman I've met since, oh…puberty, it's not for lack of wanting on my part, either, in case you wondered *that*. You are my type, after all: complex and difficult," he said, aiming for a joke and coming up lame.

Archer rose up on her elbow. "But you've never *said* anything."

Connor sighed, then said in almost a whisper, "To what end, Arch? How does it help either of us for you to know that…that every time I touch your hand, I want to take you in my arms and never let you go; that every time I see you in those crazy psychedelic running shorts of yours, I want to pull you into my tent for the rest of the day; that every time you whisper in my ear, I feel like I'm sixteen again? You aren't in the market for that, as far as I can see, and I won't risk what we have by pressing the point."

Archer was still up on one elbow, listening silently, eyes lowered.

Pausing as if trying to select just the right words, Connor went on. "But I think if it ever happens, if we ever make love—hypothetically and academically speaking, that is, of course—I want it to be not by default, not because I'm the only man you've seen in five years up here in the wilds on Mount Loh, but because…because I'm the only one you can ever imagine making love with again."

Connor paused again, looked away for a second, and seemed again to be trying to put feelings into words—words that were not coming easily.

"I want to be a *choice*, Archer, not some convenience born of proximity. I'm not looking for a quick fix—I've done that and have no interest in it. I want you to choose me. Out of all your options, I want you to choose *me*."

Silence.

"I see," Archer finally said, her voice low. She raised a hand and gently brushed back a lock of hair from his forehead, saying nothing for a minute. Then, looking straight at him, she said in a steady voice, no smile, "You, Connor McCall, are an exquisite man, truly exquisite, and if I ever could love anyone, I *would* choose you. No question."

Then she turned away, rolled onto her back, and closed her eyes.

# CHAPTER
# 16

It was Halloween night, and Archer was drunk. When Connor came to the cabin at five, he sized up the situation at a glance: three-quarters empty Maker's Mark bottle on the counter, seven bags of Hershey bars next to it, the usually impeccable kitchen in disarray, and Archer lying on the couch listening to Billie Holiday. She never rested during the day, and Billie came out only when Archer was feeling melancholy. She looked up when Connor came in carrying a big bag of groceries.

"Hey, Arch, looks like I better handle the cooking tonight," he said, putting his bundle on the kitchen counter, slipping off his coat, and hanging it on the back of a chair. "Have a hard day, did we?"

Archer lifted her head, eyes bleary, but she smiled.

"I know, my dear McCall. I'm a wee bit tight tonight. Sounds so much better to say 'I'm tight,' don't you think, than 'I'm shit-faced'"? She sat up and launched into an imitation of characters in *The Sun Also Rises*, complete with British accent. "'I say, Brett, how about a little drink?' 'Oh, Jake, darling, don't mind if I do.' 'I say, Brett, you're a bit tight.' 'Well, Jake, actually, I'm *very* tight, old chap. Do pour me another drink, darling, so that I can stay very tight.'" She held up her glass.

Connor laughed in spite of himself. "When did you start? I can see I've got some catching up to do."

Archer took a long swallow from the tumbler beside her.

"Poor old Jake. He was such a whiner, though. Wasn't he a whiner, McCall? Always going on and on about *his* problems. Jake, you goddamn phony." Archer stood unsteadily, lifting her glass in a toast of scorn.

"Well, you have to admit, Arch, he did have a reason to whine. As I recall, his penis was blown off in the war. The loss of a penis will do that to a man, you know," he said over his shoulder as he unpacked the groceries.

Archer looked doubtful, swayed a bit, then looked up at the rafters, "True, true, Jake, you did have a little problem…a legitimate gripe, I'll grant you that…but *you're* a pretty big mess, McCall, and I don't hear you moaning all the time." She paused for a sip from her glass, then called out, "Hey, Jake. Brett had some problems, too, you know. Ever stop to ask her how *her* day was going? And take McCall here. He's nothing short of a *disaster,* but no one hears him complaining."

Connor shook his head and chuckled. He glanced over as she plunked down onto the couch and slumped forward, elbows resting on her knees, drink dangling precariously in one hand. Connor grabbed the bottle and a glass and sat down on the hearth.

Archer took another swallow of her drink and started up again. "Hey, Jake! Maybe we should go into group therapy together. We do have something in common after all. I myself have had something of a dry spell, too, old man—sexually speaking, that is. 'Dry spell' as in the nature of the Kalahari Desert. Uh-oh, here's an idea. Maybe we could write one of those self-flagellating memoirs—call it *The Unable and the Unwilling? The Frustrated and Dead?* I smell a best-seller, then Oprah, then…who knows? Our own talk show? A book tour? 'Mr. Barnes, how do you *really* feel about your penis—or, rather, the lack thereof? Is it really that much of an impediment to a full life, Mr. Barnes? And, Ms. Loh, have you discovered the real source of your difficulties—aside from the murder of your little girl, that is? Was writing the book cathartic for you in any way?'" At this point, Archer bolted upright, orating to the rafters and tottering. When she started to sit down, she lost her balance and would have fallen had Connor not caught her arm.

"Whoa, there, cowgirl," Connor said, helping her sit back down.

"Jesus, you *are* on a roll, aren't you? Is this what you're like when you're drunk? And what do you have against poor Jake Barnes all of a sudden?"

Archer looked bewildered, then guilty. "You're right, McCall. You're right. Poor Jake. He did have problems." She lifted her glass of whiskey and yelled again in a British accent, "So sorry, Jake, old boy. I'm a bit tight, you see. No offense meant. You do forgive me, don't you, darling? I'm sorry about your penis—I mean, your non-penis, darling." She gulped down the last drop.

"Think we should switch to coffee, Arch?" asked Connor.

She gave him an appraising look, shook her head, flopped back into the couch, and wagged a finger at him. "That's the thing, McCall. That's the thing. You're very sensible. You're a very sensible person." She shook her glass at him for emphasis. "I like that. I myself am a very sensible person. But today I'm not so sensible. Today I'm tight…today I'm drinking. And crying. I cry when I drink, so today I'm drinking and I'm crying." Archer's eyes filled with tears. "Got candy. In case, you know…our special holiday. We always wore the same costume and did this…" Her voice trailed off.

Connor saw it all now. The absurdity of getting candy for the nonexistent possibility of trick-or-treaters knocking on Archer's door was a dead giveaway. She and Annie had always made a special event of Halloween, and now…

Archer held out her empty glass, and Connor poured in the last shot, finishing off the bottle. "Do you ever cry, McCall? *Really* cry? Not like at the movies, but real?" she asked, plump tears rolling down both cheeks.

"Okay, then," said Connor, ignoring her question. "Why don't you just take a little nap here, Archer? Just rest a while. I'll make some coffee."

"No, no. You have to have a drink," she insisted, clutching her glass as if afraid he would try to take it. "If I drink alone, I'm an alcoholic, and I don't want to be an alcoholic. I've been cutting down. Have you noticed, McCall? Have you noticed?" She sounded urgent as she leaned forward.

"Sure, Arch, I noticed." She relaxed again into the couch.

Connor shook his head but got up and opened a new bottle of Maker's Mark. He poured himself a small drink, then sat on the rocker next to the sofa.

"That's good." Archer sat back, sloshing the liquor back and forth in her glass. "So, do you cry, McCall?"

Connor sighed. "Yes, I cry, Archer. But it's like saffron—a little goes a long way. Once every decade, I let go."

"So, when did you last cry, McCall? Tell me."

Connor sat back and thought for a moment. "Well, I guess it's farther back than I thought. It was when I was eighteen. Guess I'm overdue for a real flood."

"When you were *eighteen*? Jesus, McCall, that's, like, decades and decades and decades and decades ago!" wailed Archer, with a theatric roll of her hand at each "decades."

"Just three decades. You did four."

"Oh, whatever," she said, waving her hand in the air. "After three decades, who's counting? You're a goddamn stoic, McCall. You're the goddamn god of stoicism." She refilled her glass. "So what was it? You didn't get into Yale, only Harvard? The prom queen broke your heart? What? *What!*" she demanded, slapping her glass down on the end table.

Connor took a sip of whiskey and said, "It was a horse, if you must know. A horse broke my heart by dying on me. Sabrina. The horse I used to ride when I was a kid at that farm I told you about." He took a swig of his drink, almost exhausting it. "I sat in her stall and cried my eyes out."

Archer stared at him for a few moments, then opened her eyes wide. "Goddamn it! Isn't that the way? Isn't that just the goddamn way? The only time you really cry is because something is really good and you lose it. If it sucks, we don't miss it. Happens every goddamn time." She pounded the trunk in front of the sofa with her fist, grabbed the bourbon bottle, added a little to her glass, then handed it to Connor.

He refilled his glass. "Yup. Happens every goddamn time."

Archer sat, chin in her hands, elbows on her knees again, lost in thought. Suddenly, she sat up. "So what's your secret, McCall? Why are you really up here? The IRS after you? You're in witness protection? What's the real story?"

"No secret, Archer. Just searching like everybody else, and trying to get through the day."

"Connie. May I call you Connie?" she started. Without waiting for an answer, she went on in a whisper as she leaned toward him. "Connie, I have a secret. I only hurt bad people, so good people can sleep again. I think you're a good person."

"What do you mean, Arch, you 'only hurt bad people'?"

Archer didn't answer but picked up her glass again. She looked around the room: polished cedar walls, vaulted ceiling with two beams traversing the room, and a pretty fieldstone fireplace, its hearth neatly stacked with wood. Through the front window, the sun was setting.

She suddenly blurted, "And where is my goddamn knight? My father said I'd have a goddamn knight, who would come for me on a big white horse, only my goddamn knight never came. Or maybe I *left* my goddamn knight. I don't remember exactly now." She rubbed her forehead, confused, then continued. "But he didn't come after me. Somebody should have come after somebody, shouldn't they? A *real* knight would have, wouldn't he?" She looked questioningly at

Connor. She was now sitting cross-legged on the couch, again sloshing the remaining liquor.

"Maybe there's still a knight out there coming for you, Arch."

"No, no, it's too late. It's too goddamn late," she said. "Who said chivalry isn't dead? It's goddamn dead. It's kaput. It's finito. It's fucking D.O.A." She made an umpire's "out" sign. She was quiet for a moment; then she said, "I'm awfully tired. I think I'll take a little nap now. Don't go, McCall. Bad things in the woods tonight. Headless horseman. Can't go out tonight."

"That was in Sleepy Hollow, Arch, down in the Catskills. This is the Berkshires. There's no Ichabod Crane here."

"He *could* be out there. He could have moved. It's not so far," she insisted. "He could be out there looking for a head. You have a good head, McCall. Don't drive. You're too drunk. Friends don't let friends drive drunk."

"I'm not drunk, Arch; *you're* drunk."

"No, I'm tight. That's not as bad as being drunk. You can't leave," she insisted, panic in her voice now.

"Okay, you're not drunk, just tight. And I won't drive. Don't worry. I'll stay here," he soothed as she grabbed his arm.

Appeased, she fell back into the sofa. She pointed at him, then let her hand drop. "You know, I didn't like you at first, McCall. Didn't like you at all. Dislike at first sight, you could say. But then you took care of me…ankle…made me dinner, nice to Hadley…You reminded me of Daddy. Then I liked you."

"Oh, swell," muttered Connor under his breath. "This night just keeps getting better and better."

"And I knew you were a good person, person I could trust. Like my father. Man of honor…" She was lying down on the sofa, eyes closed. She was speaking and slurring more and more softly. Just before passing out, she breathed, "Happy Halloween, McCall. Go see your daughter and stop being such an asshole."

Connor smiled at her. He got up and put a warm alpaca blanket over her, tucking in the edges. He kissed the top of her head and smoothed her hair, then unlaced his Carhartt work boots and set them side by side near the fire, and stretched out in the armchair for the night, feet up on the ottoman.

# CHAPTER
# 17

Several days after the Halloween debacle, Archer sat at the pine table, sipping her morning coffee. Today she would take her run, ride Millie, do her grocery shopping, bake an apple pie.

The phone rang, jarring her out of her thoughts.

"Hello!"

Pause.

"Archer?"

"Yes, this is she. Who is this?"

There was some hesitation.

"Archer, it's Sharon."

Archer spun around at the sound of her sister's voice. She leaned against the counter.

"Sharon? What's wrong?"

"It's Mother, Archer. She's gone."

"Oh, my God. I didn't know she was that sick."

There was silence, then, "Well, how *would* you know? You'd have to call her sometime—maybe even go and see her." The angry tone faded as quickly as it had flared. The voice now sounded weary.

"Uh…anyway, the funeral is Friday, First Congregational in Litch-field, at eleven. I've made the arrangements…not that you'll show up."

"That's not fair, Sharon, and you know it." Archer felt the start of tears.

"Look, I don't want to have this argument again, Archer. I really don't. I'm too damn tired. I called Adam. He can't make it, but I felt he should know. He *was* part of our family for fourteen years. Julie, David, Ted, and I will be there. Come if you want to."

"Sharon, you have no right. You don't know. You have Julie and David. You—"

"Yeah, I know the whole routine, Archer. No one has ever, in the history of the world, suffered as much as you. No one on the face of the earth can understand all you've been through unless exactly the same thing happened to them."

Sharon was quiet for a moment, then continued in an even voice, "Archer, we all tried to be there for you. It was no one's fault, but you acted like it was. You pushed Adam away when all he wanted was to help you get through it. You pushed me away. You have a niece and nephew who don't even remember you. You're a lawyer who does nothing. For God's sake, Archer, do *something*. Yes, Annie's death was tragic, the worst thing that can happen to a parent. But it's ended your life. Now we have two deaths in the family. You make me angry, but mostly you make me so damn sad."

Archer quietly pushed the "End" button on her cell phone and slumped back into a kitchen chair. She put her head in her hands and sat there, with Hadley watching her from across the room, her chin flat on the floor, tail still.

Archer arrived in Litchfield on Friday morning a few minutes before eleven. It had started to rain. The town green was still lush from the mild fall, and the quaint little downtown looked pretty even in the drizzle.

Archer found a parking spot and got out of the Jeep. She smoothed the skirt of her black suit. It was a leftover court suit and the only outfit she had that was anywhere near appropriate to the occasion. *What a loser,* she thought. *Archer Loh, mother of no one, wife of no one, sister of no one, and now daughter of no one as well.*

She approached the church cautiously. She and her sister had once been close. Sharon, her elder by two years, with her curly blond hair, sea green eyes, round face, and pretty smile. Sharon, *my right hand,* their mother would tell people. *Your right and left hand, Zsa Zsa,* Archer would mutter. Even at eleven years old, Sharon could organize the laundry, make out the weekly grocery list, and put together a dinner party for twelve. By the time she was thirteen, she handled the day-to-day cooking for the family, much to their mother's obvious relief.

And what did their mother say about Archer? *Oh, dahlings, Archer prefers to be on da outside of da house, like her father,* she would sniff. True enough—the kitchen was the last place to find her. Or, her mother would say, *nem, Archer prefers da horses to da people.* Also true—more or less. Then there was her mother's classic, *Archer, kerem, if you could stop wit da clomping around with dat horse, a swell fella might take you to da dance, somevon like Shara's boyfriend.* Archer had spun around and retorted that she'd rather go to the prom with Clique than with that idiot Jay Chamberlain, Sharon's then flame, or "flamer," as Archer called him. She had then stalked off, but not before Sharon screamed and threw a high-heeled shoe at her, which Archer immediately threw back, stabbing Sharon's poster of Billy Idol, leaving a heel-size hole in the punk star's forehead, leading to a second shriek from Sharon. *Isten segits! Archer, you are behaving like a vagrant. Vhat am I going to do wit you?* her mother had screeched after her. Ilona Loh had then sighed heavily, shaken her hands as if drying them, and shrugged as if to say, *I can only do so much with that one.*

Ironically, Archer had married almost five years before Sharon. When Annie died, Julie was only six and David was eight. Sharon had continued to live in Litchfield after she and Ted Davini got married. Ted was an internist at Waterbury General Hospital, and Sharon was a pediatric nurse who worked part-time on weekends.

Standing now outside the old church's open oak doors, Archer took a deep breath, lifted her chin, and walked in. Organ music played softly; the church was almost full. She wanted to slip into a back pew and slip out the same way, but others, no doubt with the same idea, had beaten her to it.

In her imagination, Archer envisioned people staring and pointing as she moved down the center aisle. She imagined them saying, *That's Archer, the weird sister. You know, she went crazy when her own daughter died. Never thought* she'd *show up.* But the organ played on, and beyond a few polite nods, the crowd barely noticed her.

Archer walked farther and farther forward, searching for a seat, and then it struck her: she was family. This was her mother, who, with all her faults, was worthy of being mourned and shown respect in this final tribute. Archer moved to the front of the church and slipped into the front pew, next to Sharon.

Sharon was smoothing Julie's hair when Archer moved into the space on the aisle. Sharon turned with a faint smile, which instantly froze.

Sharon's eyes filled with tears. She had not seen her sister for almost three years, since the day Archer told her she was moving away to a cabin in the Berkshires. Sharon had gotten a cell phone number in the mail a few days later, but no address, no e-mail. Since then there had been no photos, no gifts, no birthday cards, no visits.

Archer looked thin and small, but better and stronger than the last time Sharon saw her. Then she'd been a broken woman with dark hollows under her eyes, muddy skin, and a perpetually startled look. Sharon had thought Archer looked like those young horses she used to ride: ready to spook at any loud sound or unfamiliar sight.

Today her dark hair was simple and straight, her light green eyes clear, her skin fresh. Sharon blinked, and a tear rolled down her cheek. Archer's arms reached out; Sharon grasped them.

"I'm sorry, Archer. I didn't mean what I said," Sharon wept.

"Shh, it's okay," Archer whispered as the minister began the service.

Julie and David stared curiously at this woman they did not know.

When the organ swell signaled the service's conclusion, Sharon stood and waved her children, Ted, and Archer toward the West Street Grill on the green for lunch. She greeted mourners as they left, and paused for a few reminiscences about her mother. Ted kissed Archer on the cheek and gave her a hug as he hurried back to the hospital.

Once at the restaurant, Archer and Sharon laughed like old times. They were seated at a big booth, with a solid oak table between them. Rustic chandeliers hung at periodic intervals while blue glasses and white napkins adorned each table. A pretty blond waitress in black pants and a white shirt hurried to wipe off the oak top as Archer and her family slid into the brown leather seats.

Archer and Sharon spoke fondly of their mother, recalling her affinity for all things Hungarian, which went along with her resistance to completely adopting the English language.

"Remember how, no matter where she was, she would find the one Hungarian person in town, and all of a sudden they'd be comparing butcher shops and inviting each other to dinner?" Archer recalled.

"Yeah, a dinner *I* would have to cook. How about the time when she said the steaks were 'laminating' instead of marinating?"

"Oh, God, yeah. Those were some tough steaks. Oh, and then there was the ever popular 'swell fella'—you know, 'He's a swell fella'?" This got them both laughing.

Archer turned and looked at Julie, sitting beside her in the booth. She smiled at her niece, then said to Sharon, "She has the Loh smile— like Annie did."

Sharon eyed her sister, fearing tears but seeing only pleasure in her face. She gazed at Julie and David, noting their enjoyment of the banter and of the attention from their lively, pretty aunt. Then Julie piped up. "Aunt Archer, I thought you lived in a cave with wolves or something and had, like, long fingernails and ate out of cans. *Do* you?"

"Julie!" Sharon yelped. "Don't be silly. You can see that your aunt is perfectly normal."

"But you said Aunt Archer was…" She stopped. Sharon raised a warning eyebrow.

Archer smiled and turned to Julie. "My cabin is small, but it's not a cave. Come and see for yourself sometime, darling." She patted her niece's hand. "Maybe you remember Hadley? Not a wolf, just a chocolate Lab."

And soon it was time for Archer to go. When she and Sharon separated, they hugged again, and Archer promised to stay in touch.

"I'll really try," she said before driving away.

# CHAPTER
# 18

A rcher got back to the cabin in the late afternoon. After changing
into her old jeans, she lay down on the couch, legs up, ankles
crossed. She thought about the day. Connor had wanted to go with
her to the funeral, but she'd felt there was enough in the mix without
adding another wild card. Further, Sharon's comments on the phone
had hit home. She didn't want to be that woman—self-pitying and
ultimately self-centered.

Connor walked in with groceries, Alice on his heels.

"Hey, how are you doing? I didn't know when you'd get back, but I
thought I'd get some supplies," he said, resting two bags on the counter.

"I'm okay actually. It started out rocky. I wasn't sure what I'd find
after that call from Sharon…thought she might physically bar me at
the church door. But it turned out okay. We talked. And I saw my niece
and nephew for the first time in about six years. It was actually better
than okay—it was good."

"That's great. I'm glad. And, now that you've left the mountain,
and the mountain doesn't have to come to Mohammed, maybe we
should try going on an outing."

Archer was up, helping to put groceries away. She looked curiously at Connor over her shoulder as she put a half gallon of milk in the refrigerator. "Just what kind of 'outing' do you have in mind?" she asked.

"Well, I haven't given it too much thought, but maybe like a weekend into Boston," suggested Connor.

Archer put a dozen eggs away. "Boston. Hm-m. I haven't gone out anywhere in over four years." She was quiet a moment, then said, "Hey, do you think I'm self-centered and wallowing in self-pity?"

Connor looked at her, surprised. "Uh, no. Where'd that come from?"

Archer told him about Sharon's attacks.

He stopped putting the rice boxes up on a shelf, caught Archer by the shoulder, and turned her toward him. "Listen, Arch, no one has the right to judge you. Whatever you feel or do is okay. But I will say this. Don't just grieve Annie—honor her. Honor her memory in a way that's as unique and special as she was. You'll know what it is when you find it."

He went back to putting the groceries away.

Connor made reservations at the Four Seasons Hotel on the Boston Green, across the park from Beacon Hill. They planned to go for Thanksgiving weekend, leaving Wednesday night and returning Sunday night.

Without discussing it, Connor reserved two rooms, one overlooking the park, the other across the hall with a view unknown. *Ah, to rent just one...* but that would never be.

He sighed. The moment either had passed or never would come—he wasn't sure which. Since the day in the woods, nothing more had been said about romance or sex. Archer had to be the one to make a move, and she simply never would. He knew it.

He had not been back to Boston since moving to Wyoming seven years ago. It would be fun to eat in a nice restaurant, see a play, maybe even go dancing. Did she even *like* to dance? He didn't know, but he had seen her waltz in fun around the kitchen.

He asked her one night, as they read by the fire after dinner, "So, do you dance?"

"Do I dance? *Do I dance?* Did Martha Graham dance? Did Nureyev dance? Did Baryshnikov dance? Nobody puts Baby in a corner," she declared dramatically, putting her book down.

"Spoken by Johnny, a.k.a. Patrick Swayze, in *Dirty Dancing*, to Baby's a.k.a. Jennifer Grey's, father. So is that a yes?"

"*Yes*, it's a yes!" she proclaimed, and she stood up, took Hadley by the forepaws, and began two-stepping about the living room, with Hadley doing her best to keep up. Alice began barking and chasing Archer around the room, bouncing up and down, as Connor's laughter added to the general uproar.

"Okay, I get it," said Connor. "You dance. Now, does that mean you only dance alone, or just with large dogs?"

"I dance with other people, too—under the right circumstances," Archer said with great dignity.

The plan took shape. Jenny, Archer's dog sitter, would watch both dogs, and Millie was placed with the owner of the feed store, who had an empty barn stall and a small pasture and was happy to have her while they were out of town.

Every few days, Connor called Three Chimneys. Usually, he just got the answering machine and left instructions: call the vet about worming next month; make sure the fields have the fall fertilization; check the barns for leaks before it gets too cold. Sometimes he got one of the men. At other times, his farm manager, Felix, called back. When Archer answered, he stammered.

"Hey, McCall, I think I make him nervous."

"You make *everyone* nervous, Archer. It's your destiny," he chuckled.

One day, after Felix apparently managed to ask if Mac was there, Archer covered the mouthpiece and whispered: "Hey, McCall, are you also known as Mac?"

"Yup, that's my Wyoming moniker."

"Hey, Harvard, no need to show off with big words to impress me," she said with a grin, handing him the phone. Their fingers touched briefly, and Connor tried to ignore the little jolt he felt. "Then I guess this is for you."

Connor talked about tagging the new sheep, outstanding orders to be filled, and business arrangements to move money for funding various projects, payroll needs, and repairs.

"So, Mac," said Felix at the end of the call, "when you coming home?"

"Well, you seem to be running things real smoothly, Felix, my good man," Connor said jovially.

Felix paused and said, "Mac, we need you. I'm doing okay, but the guys aren't afraid of me like they are of you. You know, when you screw up your face and yell at everybody and pound your desk, things are really good for a while."

Connor sighed. "I know. Soon, Felix, soon."

"You're a killer, aren't you?" Connor asked out of nowhere as they sat together on her front porch steps one evening, watching the sky darken.

"What do you mean?"

He turned a cold gaze on her. "Just that. I've seen your gun. And I've seen you shoot, you'll recall. And that's the 'legal work' you sneak off to do, isn't it?"

No answer.

"So, just out of curiosity, tell me, is it freelance or organized?"

Archer sat bolt upright in bed, sweating, her heart racing. She tugged at the neck of her T-shirt, feeling as if she couldn't breathe. Her gaze darted around the room, into corners mottled in dark calico by the moonlight. The snug, comfy room felt mysterious and somehow menacing.

As her eyes adjusted to the dark, she could see Hadley sleeping on the needlepoint rug at the foot of her bed, her breathing steady and regular. Reassured, she felt her own breath slow and her senses relax. *Just a nightmare, silly,* she chided herself. *Connor doesn't even talk like that. If you must dream, at least dream realistically...*But he had sounded so accusing and hostile, even mean—not like himself at all. *What a stupid nightmare.*

Reaching back to pull up her pillow, Archer sank back down in the bed. *A killer?* She had never thought of herself that way. Avenger? Yes. Hit woman? If the shoe fits...But *killer?* No. She folded the white cotton quilt back and got out of bed, padding barefoot into the kitchen for a glass of water.

*Killer.* Such an ugly word.

# CHAPTER
# **19**

Connor and Archer arrived in Boston just before dark, in Connor's F-350 crew cab dually pickup, which, apparently, was something of a novelty at the Four Seasons. The valet, who looked to be about fourteen, was rendered temporarily speechless.

"Yes, please park it," said Connor, "but no joyriding, okay? Though I know the temptation is great." The humor was lost on the valet, who kept staring.

Once the valet recovered, they went into the lobby. For their first evening, Connor had made dinner reservations at the hotel's four-star restaurant: cushioned seats, benches for two, candlelight—the room positively oozed elegant serenity.

After checking in, Archer and Connor went to their rooms. Archer's was big, with a yellow and red chintz sofa under a big window. The cream wallpaper with pink flowers was reminiscent of a Yorkshire bed-and-breakfast she'd seen in one of her design magazines.

She pulled a looped cord hanging along the right edge of the window, and the thick drapes parted to give a view of the Boston Common, all green and yellow in the weak November light. Across the park stood the red brick homes of Beacon Hill, on cobbled streets lit by the faint glow of gaslights. It was peaceful, like a painting of Victorian London.

*I've missed a lot in six years,* she mused.

Entering the white and green marble bathroom, Archer grabbed a thick white towel and ran a hot bubble bath, then undressed slowly, enjoying the pleasure of being in a beautiful place. She lowered herself into the water, gripping the edges of the huge porcelain tub. The little water tank at home allowed for only the smallest, quickest, meanest of baths, making this bath a wild and decadent luxury. She lay back and relaxed, with only her head and toes sticking out of the water. The water sloshed over her, sensuously dipping in and out between her legs and lapping over her shoulders, soothing her.

She wondered about tonight. Connor had planned this trip with her interests in mind. He was so different from Adam, she mused, and yet both were so appealing, so basically *good*. She and Adam had built a history together, while she and Connor had a history to get past. And she didn't know if they could or if she even wanted to. What she did know was that her heart fluttered at the end of every day, when she heard his whistle as he stepped up onto the porch. She thrilled to his huffy whispers at the movies, reliving them for days, and weakened when, after dinner, he handed her a plate to dry and their fingers touched lightly.

Since the day on the mountain when Connor shocked her with his non-declaration declaration, it was as if he'd never said it at all. There was no awkwardness, because it was as if no new element had been injected into the mix. In fact, his behavior was so utterly unchanged that some days Archer wondered if she had imagined the whole thing. Was it just a giddy moment for him, brought on by the high altitude up there on—what did he call it? Mount Loh? Maybe he was embarrassed now and hoped it would never come up again. Then she scolded herself, *Oh, Loh, just enjoy the weekend, for God's sake. Don't analyze everything to death. Snap out of it!*

Archer stepped out of the tub, wrapped herself in a towel, and slowly dried off. Pulling on a clean white T-shirt and cotton bikini underpants, she lay down on the plush bed, imagining she was like any other person in the hotel, on a little getaway, taking a short nap before dinner.

She woke up an hour later, feeling refreshed, and began to dress for dinner. She had brought a black dress—from her past, of course—with sequins and a ruffle along the bottom that had a bit of a Carmen Miranda look. The front was just below knee length, with a back hem several inches longer, falling to just above her ankles. The dress dipped in a swoop to mid back; black stockings and black high heels completed the effect. The only jewelry she wore was a pearl and diamond ring set in platinum, which had been her mother's, and small diamond earrings. She planned to wear her hair down, loose. Closing the drapes, she sat at the vanity mirror to finish getting ready.

Across the hall, Connor felt like a fool. He had rented a tuxedo, and it had just been delivered to his room. This was his chance. His only hope of changing the dynamic between him and Archer was to change the context—to stun her, but in a good way. Now was the time.

He stood in front of the mirror, eyeing himself in the Ralph Lauren black tuxedo and a black cummerbund. It fit his lean, athletic form as if it had been tailored for him alone. His starched white shirt and platinum cufflinks looked graceful, elegant. But what if Archer laughed at him, maybe even secretly pitied him, catching the scent of his desperation? Most women found him handsome, but not all did. Looking appraisingly at himself in the mirror, he decided he looked as good as he ever would.

*This is as good as it gets, at least for me,* he reflected, giving his bow tie a final tug. And he left his room and knocked on Archer's door.

Archer turned from the mirror. She had one earring on and was fumbling with the second one. "Just a minute!" she called out as she finished getting the little diamond stud through her right ear.

She looked at herself, satisfied, and turning away from the mirror, she walked to the door and opened it. And stared.

Was that Connor? It looked like him, but it didn't. She had seen him only in jeans and a rough jacket, and thought he couldn't possibly look better in anything else—they suited him. But in this tuxedo, with crisp shirt and hair freshly washed and combed, he looked amazing. Yes, "amazing" was the word. Amazingly good-looking. She swallowed hard and then smiled.

For his part, Connor was frozen. When he saw her, sparkling there in a black-sequined dress, eyes expectant and smiling, and dressed up for no other reason than that he had asked her to dinner—well, she could have worn anything. But she had chosen to adorn herself in such finery, knowing that she would be with him alone. Clearly, she had made an effort to look good. But she had overshot the mark—she was breathtaking.

"Okay!" she said nervously, turning back to get her room key and then quickly drawing open the drapes to let in the lovely scene of Boston Common. "Let's go!"

Closing the door behind her, she checked the handle to be sure it had latched, and then turned to Connor, who was waiting patiently for her, leaning casually against the corridor wall.

"Hey, cowboy, stand up straight," she said. "We're not in the hills anymore."

"Thank you for doing this, Ellen." he said awkwardly, unsure how to break the ice with this goddess standing before him.

"McCall, that's way too easy!" she hooted. "Don't patronize me! *Dave*, in the White House, just before Dave, a.k.a. Kevin Kline, and

Ellen, a.k.a. Sigourney Weaver, are going to appear on the balcony."

"Well done. Gold star," said Connor, taking her elbow and guiding her down the hall to the elevator.

Arriving at the restaurant entrance, Connor stepped up to the maitre d'hotel.

"McCall, two for eight, please."

"Very good, sir," said the host, leading them to a table for two in a corner. There was a fresh pink carnation in a cut-glass vase, and a candle with a beaded shade.

The whole room was golden, with a sky blue ceiling and patches of red light thrown by the red-beaded lampshades on the tables. The chandeliers had a soft peach glow.

Arriving at the table, the host seated them, and Archer laid her black beaded purse on a corner of the table, smiled, and looked around. The host handed each of them a menu, thanked them, and backed away.

"So, have you ever been here before?" Archer asked as she opened her menu. "I mean, being brought up in Boston and all."

"Not exactly. Where I grew up in South Boston, we were lucky to afford a dinner at the local pub once in a while. Forget this part of town—it may as well have been on the moon. And then at Harvard, I was on pretty much a full scholarship. My part-time job was as a waiter at the Crimson Joe's, a little Irish pub, behind Harvard Square—that was for spending money. No Four Seasons for me... Ever been to South Boston?"

"No," she said, shaking her head, "I don't think so."

"You'd remember if you had. I laugh like crazy when I read about it now. It's become gentrified and desirable. When I was growing up, it was mostly welfare cases, with real divisions between black and white, and serious crime and drug problems. My parents held their own and were proud that they owned their home, but they were the exception."

"Lots of changes in twenty years."

The waiter came, and Connor ordered a nice bottle of pinot grigio.

"You know," he continued, "most of their friends had at least six children; some had eight or nine. They would always say to my mother, 'Colleen, why just one?' But Mom was this pretty, fragile daydreamer who got pregnant only once—at least that I know of. And that was that.

"When she was growing up there, the least desirable area was the waterfront—overrun with rats and trash and the homeless. She would never believe the million-dollar condos there now. She'd just say, 'Now, Connor, don't toy with me,' and shake her head, smiling coyly. She was something, that woman."

"Really?" said Archer. "You don't talk too much about your parents. What were they like?"

"Well, I spent a lot of years resenting them. My father really didn't seem to like me much, and my mother seemed like she had no life, so she stayed too interested in mine. At least that's how I felt while I was growing up. Now I feel like they just didn't know how to be any different, and they gave all they had to give. My mother died of cancer about ten years ago now, and my dad died at a Red Sox game about eight years ago. Heart attack. Life just throws a lot of stuff at us that we don't expect," he added, sighing. "You know, when I left Harvard Business School, I thought I knew exactly how my life would go. It was mapped out, blueprinted. And for a while it went according to my plan. And then it didn't."

"Yeah, I know. I wish so hard sometimes for a redo. You know, like in *Back to the Future.* You can go back and change the things that went wrong, put the pieces in the right order, then go on from there.

"We all want a redo, Archer. We just don't get it. We have to take what we get and work with that." He fell silent for a moment, then said, "So tell me, how'd you happen to be named Archer?"

"Oh, that. My father's mother's maiden name. I think he always regretted giving me that name, because I was teased pretty relentlessly about it in school. Litchfield was full of Debbies, Lisas, and Amys. I was Bow-and-Arrow girl, Orca the Whale, Archer Smarcher, et cetera, et cetera. You get the picture. I think Daddy would have just called me Mary, had he known. But I never gave it a second thought. I liked my name. I guess I was a weird kid—I always wondered what was wrong with them, not what was wrong with me." She laughed at the memory. "How about you? Connor wasn't all that common a name when you were born, was it?"

"No, not really. My mother, with her romantic notions, thought Connor McCall—you know, all those 'C' sounds—sounded like some hero in a romance novel. For years I wished my name were Joe or Tom. But then, we each have our cross to bear. She could have gone with Rhett McCall, and then I would have had to move to Europe."

Archer laughed.

The waiter came and poured the wine, then took their order. Archer ordered the Dover sole, and Conner the trout almondine.

Just then a flash of light made them both look up. A photographer had just taken a picture of the couple at the next table. They appeared to be in their eighties and sat at a table for eight with two younger couples—probably their children—and a ten-year-old boy, and a girl of perhaps twelve. All were elegantly dressed and glowing.

The photographer lowered the camera, looked around, and saw Connor and Archer eyeing him curiously. He smiled broadly and took a step toward them.

"Sorry to interrupt your dinner, folks. Sixtieth wedding anniversary dinner. Wanted a few photos with the family." He stopped, cocked his head, and said, "How about one of you two? All dressed up and looking good. Show it to the kids at home?"

And before either of them had a chance to respond, he stepped away from them, twisted the lens once, focused, and shot three photos in rapid succession. He then picked up a second camera and shot two more.

"Write your name and address down for me, and I'll send you a few copies," he said, shoving a little white memo pad at Connor.

Connor, startled but game, wrote down his P.O. box in Lenox and handed the pad back. Smiling, the man packed his equipment away, said his good-byes to the anniversary couple and their family, and left.

"Happy anniversary," Archer called gaily to the elderly couple.

In response, they held up their two champagne glasses to Connor and Archer and clinked them together.

"Thank you, dear. Hope you two make it to sixty years, too," the wife said, beaming with pride and contentment, surrounded by her loved ones.

Archer returned the warm smile. "Thank you very much." Then, turning back to Connor and smiling, she said, "You'll never see any pictures. You do know that, don't you, McCall?"

"Oh, ye of little faith," he scolded. "But, yeah, I do know I'll never see any photos. No one ever does what they say they will these days. It's epidemic. It'd be cool if they showed up someday, though, wouldn't it? It would help restore my faith in mankind."

"I know... So what do you have planned for us tomorrow?"

"Well, I thought I'd take you to the old neighborhood in the morning and take a walk by the river. Not much open on Thanksgiving Day, but I found a restaurant in the North End—Italian—that's supposed to put out a hell of a Thanksgiving spread. So we have a reservation there. Then maybe a movie. For Friday I got tickets to this show called *Mama Mia*—music from your youth: ABBA. Anything in particular *you'd* like to do?"

"Well, I thought we could have dinner with Gavin on Saturday night. Other than that, nothing in particular. And I *do* like ABBA, by the way. It's happy music; don't knock it!"

He smiled.

Dinner was sublime. Afterward, over cognacs and then coffee, the talk ranged from international terrorism to the wool market, to what book they would read now that they had finished *The Good Earth*. They agreed on *Seabiscuit*.

Archer spoke animatedly, gesturing to emphasize her points, and

Connor tried his best to listen, though it wasn't easy. She looked as if she were twenty-one and in the city for a big weekend—so full of life and beginnings. As she spoke, she sometimes twisted her pearl ring absentmindedly, and her hair would fall over her right eye.

Archer talked rapidly, noting that Connor's eyes were a deep, almost royal blue with flecks of yellow and green, and that the corners turned up when he smiled. She had never noticed the flecks before.

Archer was playing one of their games: a quick series of associations, often trivial, the objective being to answer with the first word that sprang to mind.

"Flower?" Archer asked.

"Rose."

"Dog?"

"Bouvier."

"Elton John song?"

"'All the Young Girls Love Alice.'"

"Whoa, now! Where did that come from?" interjected Archer.

"Wouldn't *you* like to know? Just kidding. I wanted to see if you were really listening. Okay, uh, 'Tiny Dancer.'"

"Book?"

"*Youngblood Hawke.*"

"Movie?"

"Oh, no fair. Too many possibilities. Depends on the day, the genre."

"Okay, okay. Blue."

"Sky."

"Forever."

"Archer." He looked down, embarrassed.

Archer stopped smiling and examined her snifter of cognac. She lifted it to her mouth, her hand shaking.

"Archer, I'm sorry. I guess the candles, the wine...you...I got carried away. I thought I was over my grand pronouncements after the last one."

Archer lifted her eyes to his, and he saw that they were misty. Her left hand, the one with the pearl ring, was still resting on the table, his right hand almost touching it. She moved her fingers forward to cover his. He looked up. She smiled, and he raised her hand and clasped it in his.

It was nine thirty, and the six-piece orchestra and female vocalist had just begun to play. The music was eclectic. She started out with a rendition of the Sinatra classic "That's Why the Lady Is a Tramp," then Faith Hill's "Breathe," followed by Martina McBride's "Valentine." Connor and Archer sipped their coffees with a second cognac, and the piano began a single strand of the theme.

"Shall we?" asked Connor.

Archer smiled and rose gracefully, taking her offered arm. Connor put his arm gently around her, but as the song went on, he pulled her closer. She was light and responsive, moving easily. Even in heels, she barely came to his shoulder. They turned and turned, slowly, lost in the moment and each other. When the song ended, they stayed on the dance floor a few moments, as if unwilling to separate, then went back to the table. Connor motioned for the bill and paid with cash.

They walked to the elevator holding hands shyly, laughing, leaning into each other. They got on and pushed "7," and as the doors closed, Connor immediately turned to Archer and pressed her against the mirrored wall of the elevator. They fell together, kissing passionately until the car finally stopped at their floor. Archer thrilled at the feel of Connor's hard body against hers, and pressed back breathlessly into him. When the elevator doors opened, they stepped out, disheveled and excited.

"I've dreamed of this for so long," he said, turning to her. "But I thought I was a fool to think it was possible."

"Me, too," said Archer. "And you wasted good money on two rooms, McCall. I choose you." And opening the door to her room, she pulled him in.

# CHAPTER
# 20

They woke up to the sun pouring in the window. Archer stretched and then collapsed over onto Connor, snuggling close. He put his arm around her shoulders and pulled her to him.

"Hey, I would have seduced you sooner had I known," laughed Archer.

"Yeah, right." He kissed the top of her head.

"Good you practice safe sex, McCall, because *I* sure as hell wasn't planning a tryst. How long has that condom been in your wallet?"

"Wouldn't you like to know? Probably so long it's worthless." He stroked her hair.

"And hidden behind Lauren's baby picture, no less. Tsk, tsk," she quipped. "Poetic irony, McCall, although a bit sacrilegious, you must admit."

Connor laughed. "It's actually quite appropriate, if you think about it."

Now Archer laughed and snuggled tighter. She felt him growing hard, and it excited her, reminding her of last night.

"You're unbelievably beautiful," he said, reaching to push her hair back from her face. "You make that picket fence look awfully good to me."

She leaned forward to kiss him. "And you make me want to be standing at the gate."

Eventually, they got into the shower together, reluctant to be apart. They soaped each other up, rinsed, and hopped out, aglow and steaming.

The day was lovely, sunny and crisp—perfect Thanksgiving football weather. They took a cab to South Boston, and Connor showed her his old house. Like many other homes in the newly gentrified neighborhood, it had been transformed by an addition as large as the original house. He showed her where he had gone to school and church, and where he had caught the bus to go to Rose's farm in the summers.

"I never had to work going through college," Archer reflected. "Guess I was lucky. Daddy said my job was to study, and if I held up my end there, that was all he could ask for. I had Clique at school, too, so between classes and riding, I loved my life. I thought life would always be that exhilarating, and that everything I did would be topped by the next thing in some endlessly growing crescendo. Naive, huh?"

"No, just youth—and that's how it *should* be. I love seeing kids fighting for some stupid cause, working to save the seals, or backpacking through Europe and feeling like they're the first kid who ever took to the hills and highways. There's plenty of time to feel jaded and cynical later, after life beats you up a bit—no need to rain on their parade too soon."

Archer and Connor had dinner at Antonio's—turkey surrounded by stuffing, with a side of polenta.

"Good we're not on Atkins," Archer whispered.

They laughed with Antonio when he came out to greet his

patrons, to offer another bottle of valpolicella, and hear them rave about his latest creation. The spectacle was complete when his staff dimmed the lights and paraded out in formation, bearing aloft flaming baked Alaskas. The diners applauded and cheered.

On Friday, they went to Faneuil Hall to browse, then to a place called the Dog House for lunch, where they sat on tall red leather-padded stools and ate hamburgers with mushrooms and grilled onions.

"Boy, they must think everyone's over six two," grumbled Archer, trying to get comfortable, shifting right and then left on the slippery stool. She tried both feet on the highest rung but felt like a jockey, knees almost under her chin. But the next rung was too far down, and hanging naturally, her feet cleared the floor by four inches. Connor sat comfortably with one foot on a middle rung and the other on the floor.

He watched with an amused gleam in his eye. "Well, the midget people are dying out—inferior genes, you see—and this place is on the cutting edge of evolution. Yeah, the Dog House is known for that. They say when the little people get angry, they begin to push and shove and make a terrible ruckus, sometimes biting the ankles of the big people."

Archer pushed him almost off his stool.

He grabbed the edge of the counter. "Oh, see? *See?* Here's one of the little people now, in one of those frenzies they talk about. I better cover my ankles."

Archer waved off his comments as if they were unworthy of response, but she giggled. "Hey, McCall," she began, gesturing with her burger at the throng milling around them. "See all these people walking around, living their lives, doing Christmas shopping, seeming like ordinary people? But each one of them—*every single one* of them, including that bag lady out there on the corner—has one unique fabulous moment tucked inside them that they can pull out on a rainy day. I sometimes try to guess what it is for each one. Do you ever do that?"

Connor turned and looked at her.

"What *are* you talking about, Archer? Maybe the little people also have some weird world vision, too?"

"Well, don't you have one moment that you…you know, *savor*, that you replay again and again in your head, and that when you're down, it absolutely, one hundred percent, works every time without exception to pull you up?"

Connor thought about it for a few seconds, then shook his head. "Nope, I don't."

Now it was Archer who stared. *"None?"*

"Maybe I don't get it, but there just is no one occasion I can think of that ever did that for me. If it's important to you, though, I'll get one." He leaned over and kissed Archer's neck. "So, what's yours?"

She tilted her head and looked up at him. "McCall, my moment is so spectacular, I'll need a whole dinner to describe it to you. So spectacular, in fact, I may need a dinner *and* dessert. It's saved my life on more than a few occasions, and someday, when I have enough serenity and time to do it justice, I'll tell you."

Connor looked into her bright, spirited eyes. He reached over, pushed her hair back, and tucked a loose strand behind her ear. "Well, if that's the case," he said softly, "I've got a lot to be grateful to your moment for. I can't wait to hear about it."

They finished their burgers, poked around in some of the boutiques, and walked around Beacon Hill, admiring the cobblestone streets, ornate wrought-iron gates, and elegant brick townhouses. They went to *Mama Mia* on Friday night and laughed uproariously when the cool Australian fell for the pudgy but aggressive friend of the main star, and they danced along with the rest of the audience in the encore.

On Saturday night, Gavin was to have dinner with Archer at the Impudent Oyster. He had mixed feelings about it. Archer had called him a week ago to say she would be in Boston with a friend—a man. He knew from the way she talked about him—Connor, his name was—that she was in love with him. Hearing her talk about him wounded Gavin in a way he had thought he was beyond. Even hearing her say his name, as though it were special, made him wince inside. He had always felt that someday he and Archer would end up together. She understood him—his pain, his heritage, his legacy. He had never wanted to rush her. But now she was bringing someone, a man, here. What could he say?

If Gavin had any doubts that this was something more than a friendship, those doubts vanished when he spotted them walking in. They had the look of new lovers: flushed, buoyant, touching, thoroughly smitten. As Connor helped Archer off with her coat, he stroked her cheek gently and actually seemed to savor the slip of its weight from her shoulders. They were still in that bubble, insulated from the rest of the world. Nothing could pierce it—at least for a while.

Gavin saw more. Soon Archer would leave them. She would reenter the world, start over. He saw it as surely as he saw that his chance was gone, and it made him inconsolably sad. But because he had loved her for more years than he cared to think about, he was happy for her. She had a chance at a redo. He had hoped it would be with him, but at least she was doing it with *someone. Way to go, Archer,* he said to himself. *Way to go, baby.*

As Archer and Connor approached the table, Gavin stood up and leaned forward to shake hands with Connor. "Well, hello. Gavin Kennelly."

"Connor McCall. Nice to meet you. Archer has told me so much about you—all of it good, of course!"

They shook hands, one watching his clear picture of the future now blurring and fading away, the other seeing a vague image of the future taking shape and sharpening. Archer looked at the two men—so different, each distinguished and determined in his own way, both in love with her. She felt not so much flattered as honored. They were two good men, true and honest, gentlemen in the best sense of the word.

The two men got along well, both self-effacing, each setting the stage for the other to shine, and, in the act, both shining. Archer felt something she had not felt in a long time: a sense of satisfaction at seeing two people who were dear to her joust, laugh, exchange stories, and tease her about her great taste in friends. The evening was a joy, a grand part of a weekend that came as close to perfection as this life allowed. Archer felt shamelessly greedy for more—more laughter, more love.

# CHAPTER
# 21

When Connor and Archer returned from Boston, Connor moved most of what he had to Archer's cabin—starting with Millie. Archer glowed when she saw him emerge from the woods, leading the black mare by her halter. Flinging open the back door, she ran to greet them, laughing, carrot in hand for Millie. Connor had left his tent up, but his base of operations had changed.

Meanwhile, Felix's awkward but persistent entreaties to Connor to return to Three Chimneys had become more pointed since their return from Boston, though Connor responded by delegating more and more responsibility to his foreman. It was clear to all that he would not be getting back to the ranch before Christmas.

Calling to check in, Connor said, "Hey, Felix, you can arrange for the vetting in March, okay? And get Joe Ross in to fix the waterers. How are the lambs out in Jacob's Field doing?"

"They're doing okay, Mac. But I already called Joe and he wants to hear from you. And I'm not sure we fertilized the west hundred enough—may have to do more this spring. You'll need to check it out, Mac."

"Fine. We could do without that pasture this season if we had to. Let it rest, then hit it in the fall."

Pause. "Mac?"

"Yeah, Felix?"

Pause. "Nothing."

"Okay, Felix. I'll ring you in a few days."

For Archer and Connor, virtually no changes were necessary; they were compatible by natural inclination. Both were flushed with the incredulity that in the middle of nowhere, completely unexpectedly, they had somehow found each other. Archer seemed happy, but she seemed to give little thought to the future. Connor was happy, too, but he worried enough for both of them. He had to get back to Three Chimneys, and he was unsure if Archer would come. The matter needed more thought, but, like Scarlett O'Hara, he would think about it tomorrow.

And yet he couldn't turn it off. He wanted—no, he craved—connection. He wanted someone to mourn his absence, to rejoice in his return. He wanted Lauren to know he cared for her more than his monthly check suggested.

Christmas was just two weeks away. For the first time in six years, Archer felt like celebrating, maybe putting up stockings on the hearth—and shopping. Driving to the Farmington Mall, she remembered the fun of finding just the right present, the anticipation, the look of surprise, then glee. She pulled into one the few remaining parking spaces, slipped her shoulder bag strap over her head, and entered Lord & Taylor. The whiff of clove and evergreen hit her, and she smiled.

At the top of the escalator, she found a directory and traced a route to Abercrombie's, the place Sharon had suggested for Julie's gift. The interior was dim but lively, with crowds of preteens hovering over tables filled with shirts and jeans. Loud rock music she didn't recognize blared from unseen speakers as she browsed through racks jammed with sweaters, shirts, and pants, darting occasional glances at what the other girls were buying.

The clothes were tiny. Some had tears in them. Was this what girls were wearing these days? Torn, grubby-looking jeans? Tops that looked as though they wouldn't fit a toddler? Archer looked at the mannequins, and sure enough, wrinkled shirttails were hanging out over small dirty-looking denim skirts, all topped by a tiny sweater that covered precious little. *Hm-m.* She nodded to herself. *So that really is the look...*

Archer selected a pretty blue sweater with "STAR" in sparkles on the front, and a black denim skirt that several girls around her had also selected.

From there, she went down an arm of the mall to Williams-Sonoma, for a copper soup pot for Sharon, and on to Brooks Brothers for a sweater for Ted.

Finally, she found Sam Goody's on the directory and hurried there to get the CDs Sharon had suggested for David. She quickly found the three on Sharon's list, then sauntered up to the checkout counter, pleased with her purchases.

As she stood waiting for assistance, the speakers started punching out the old Temptations song "Ain't Too Proud to Beg." Archer looked at the cashier. She had piercings in each eyebrow, and hair that bordered on neon blue. The girl was singing along and doing a dance step behind the counter. It made Archer laugh to herself. Annie, too, had loved Motown—no surprise, since Archer and Adam had played it endlessly when she was young. It was from before their time, but it didn't matter—they were addicted. "Berry Gordy is, and always will be, the king in this house," Adam would declare as he cranked up the record player to throbbing levels and pulled her to her feet for a dance around the kitchen.

Annie and her best friend, Sophie, would giggle, then lip-synch the parts, making Archer and Adam weak with laughter. The girls would strut, bend, arch, and howl the high falsetto notes, sometimes enlisting Archer to be the third in a Supremes number. Archer would groan but still got up holding a cucumber or Coke bottle as a makeshift microphone, swooning like Diana Ross or Mary Wilson, and Adam was sometimes persuaded to be their fourth in the Four Tops numbers. The girls had their favorite, the Isley Brothers' "This Old Heart of Mine," down pat.

Archer smiled at the memory. The song ended, and she pushed her credit card toward the girl at the counter.

"Great song," the girl chirped with a shake of blue dreadlocks.

"Yes, it is. Somewhat before your time, though, wasn't it?" asked Archer, signing the credit slip.

"Yeah, but the really great ones are timeless, you know. That one was a *really* great one. Classic, you know," she advised with a nod.

"True enough," Archer said, smiling and collecting her bag. "Thanks." And she headed back out into the mall.

What to get for Connor? She paused. He hardly ever bought anything for himself and was always in blue jeans. He wore no jewelry. A book? A new winter jacket? She had to get him something unforgettable, something that would make him swoon.

# CHAPTER
## 22

It started to snow lightly on Christmas Eve morning. Archer got up first, started the coffee, and opened the back door to let Hadley and Alice out for their morning run. She peered out the kitchen window, then began to assemble the ingredients to make three kinds of Christmas cookies.

"Hey, Sleeping Beauty, I need butter if we're going to have more than four cookies. And judging by the snow, you might want to get out now while you still can," Archer called over her shoulder toward the bedroom.

Connor emerged pulling a faded green sweatshirt over his head, rubbing his eyes. Coming up behind Archer, who was leaning over the sink, he put his arms around her and nuzzled her shoulder. She turned to him, laughing, and threw her arms around his neck. In her bare feet, she was tiny next to him.

"Hmmm, maybe we don't need butter all that badly," she purred, feeling light-headed in his warm embrace.

"Ha, too late! I'm holding you to that offer later, though—hey, look at old Millie out there, rolling in the snow!" He chuckled, pointing outside.

The mare had all four legs in the air, rolling to one side, then the other, not quite managing to get all the way over. After several rolls, she righted herself, shook off, and ran to the front of the house, bucking and crow-hopping.

"We should just put some lights on Millie, and she'll be our holiday decoration," Connor said. "I'll just give her some hay, hop in the shower, and get that butter."

"That didn't even make sense, McCall!" Archer laughed, opening the back door to let the dogs back in.

"Well, look at you, Haddie," she said to the snow-covered Lab who waddled in. Alice followed right behind, looking like a giant, frosted Rastafarian Scottie.

Connor got back from the store two hours later with butter and some big bayberry candles.

"Have to put one of these in an east window tonight, for good fortune in the New Year," he said.

"I never heard that one, but I'll try anything once. That reminds me, did you ever see that bumper sticker—you know, the one that says, 'I'll try anything once except anal sex and square dancing'?"

"No, Archer," he laughed, "it seems I've led a sheltered life—but the sentiment is well expressed."

"How were the roads?" Archer asked.

"Not bad," he said, "if you're used to Wyoming weather. A couple of spinouts on the side roads, but no real trouble."

Archer began the cookies, and by lunchtime she had made pinwheels, linzer tortes, and her specialty, Hungarian nut rolls. The recipe for the nut rolls was a closely kept family secret from her grandmother, the two secret ingredients being a little grated orange peel mixed into the walnuts, and sour cream whipped into the crust mixture. Sharon had the only other copy.

Helping himself to one of the pinwheels, Connor observed, "Yum, these are great, Arch. Oh, I filled the car with gas, so we're all set for tomorrow."

They took a long walk in the afternoon, dragging an ax along. When they found a tight stand of spruces on the edge of Archer's land, they chopped down a nice round one and hauled it home to set up in the main room.

Back at the cabin, Connor got a saw and evened up the fresh-cut tree trunk, then trimmed off a few drooping lower limbs. Archer peeled off her coat, hat, and gloves, and piled them on one end of the sofa before grabbing a small flashlight and heading down the steep basement steps for the Christmas ornaments and trimmings stashed there. She hadn't put up a Christmas tree in six years, but when she and Adam divorced, she had insisted on keeping her family's simple glass ornaments.

Archer flashed the narrow beam of light around the small dirt floor: a few lawn chairs in one corner, some laundry supplies along the wall, a pile of six large boxes in another corner. Going straight to the boxes, she opened the top one: Lenox china. Ha, fat chance of using that again! The last time was Easter Sunday the year Annie died. After an Easter egg hunt at which Hadley discovered at least as many eggs as Annie, Archer had made a big honey-mustard ham and served it on the pretty gilt-edged china. Archer shook her head. It seemed as if all that had happened to someone else.

Archer closed up the box reverently, moved it to the side, and opened the next box: Clique's bridle, saddle pad, and blanket monogrammed "AEL"—Archer Elizabeth Loh. Maybe someday…She closed the flaps of the box and set it to the side.

Third one. Unmarked manuals from her training for the Group. God, she remembered that year. The first six months were mandatory and held at one of the temporary training facilities. The second six months could be spent "off base," at the trainee's option. Trainees could quit anytime they wanted, but if they were to be part of the program, the requirements were inflexible.

During the initial six months, the trainees' talents and deficits were clinically assessed, without any shred of sentimentality or compassion. There was no place for a Charles Bronson character with visions of reckless vigilante revenge. This was about careful, businesslike justice, albeit outside the lines. It was about intensive training, objective evaluation, and meticulous planning.

After the preliminary interview, psychological testing, and skills review, a five-member panel determined whether the trainee's talents were best suited in public relations, financial recruitment, administration, or "in the field"—another word for sharpshooting.

It was quickly apparent that Archer fell into the last category, given her previous training and natural talent. This was a useful development for the Group, since it was generally agreed that women snipers roused fewer suspicions: it went against type, so the myth went. *That's a good one,* Archer had thought wryly. *Peter will love this when I tell him.*

For the first six months, you were paired with a mentor, who became your alter ego. Archer had been partnered with Katharine Barnett. Katharine had been a Group member for over ten years. She dealt primarily with fund-raising but was also on the committee that made the determinations regarding assignments. For every hit the Group did, there were at least thirty it didn't take on. The egregiousness of the crime, the lack of other remedies, and the accused's certain guilt all played into the decision to accept, defer, or decline a request.

For a year, Archer had spent sixteen hours a day in training. Marksmanship was her exclusive focus, including ballistics, advanced ballistics, matching weapon to job and conditions, steep-angle shots, the impact of altitude, wind, and temperature variations, low-light and night shooting, urban and rooftop environments, night vision theory and technique, mental preparation, shot placement, weapon maintenance, and long-range shooting. The fact that she already had training, even though rusty, was a windfall.

Everyone in her class eventually developed a specialty. Archer's niche was urban environments with long-range targets, with an emphasis on night and low-light settings. Gavin's specialty was rooftop and steep-angle shots. One of Archer's other close friends from training was a dead shot in windy conditions. Above all, the motto of the Group was "one shot, one kill." The target had to be dispatched with certainty in one—or at most two— shots. No mistakes were excused.

As Archer put the top manual back in the box, a square Polaroid photo fell out. It showed Katharine and Archer smiling, holding trays in the cafeteria line. Archer had no memory of who took the picture, or the circumstances beyond the obvious. Katharine was one of a handful of true friends Archer had ever had. She was smart, funny, and lovely. With her curly black hair and violet eyes, she looked like a young Elizabeth Taylor. She had been an accountant with Arthur Anderson when her husband and son were killed during a mugging on their way to meet her for dinner in downtown Chicago. Her husband had taught ancient Near Eastern history at the University of Chicago, and her fourteen-year-old son was a high school student and a star swimmer in the Chicago suburb where they lived. Her husband's hand had been chopped off for a Rolex watch whose elastic band would have slipped off easily, and her son's head was beaten in with a bat. And yet it was Katharine who had helped Archer get up each day—no mean accomplishment at the time.

Archer sighed. Katharine had killed herself with a revolver about two years ago. Despite all her own training, she had never gotten over the complete obliteration of her family, and she finally could not face another night. She had once told Archer that the nights were the worst. During the day, she could push it all into a compartment and keep it closed, but at night...oh, at night, out it all came. The night was so ruthless and unforgiving.

Archer closed the box tightly and pushed it back into place, then opened the fourth box. Eureka! This was the one: Christmas ornaments. She lugged it up the stairs, pulled everything out, spread the contents on the floor, and began testing the strands of lights by plugging them in. Connor was busy attempting to set up the tree in the corner of the room, holding it with one gloved hand and crouching under it, trying to position it without too much lean.

"Hey, we got a crooked tree!" he called out through the branches.

"No, we didn't; you just put it in crooked!"

"Hm-m. Hey, Arch, can you just hold it for me while I tighten up the stand?"

"Sure. No problem," Archer said, coming over and grabbing the tree with a potholder still on her hand.

Connor was bending down on the floor, tightening the bolts while Archer held the little spruce upright.

"I think I've got it!" he said finally.

"*My Fair Lady*, Eliza Doolittle, a.k.a. Audrey Hepburn in the movie, or Julie Andrews on Broadway, in Professor Higgins's living room after she nailed the accent!" crowed Archer. "Ten points for me. I see a week of kitchen chores in your future, McCall."

"I wasn't doing the game," Connor protested, slowly unfolding his frame from under the tree. "I was just saying it myself."

"We're never not playing the game," retorted Archer, beaming. "But in the Christmas spirit, I won't insist on getting credit for my answer."

"Oh, thanks ever so much," Connor grumbled.

"Hey, Christmas Eve is a big deal, don't you think? When you were a kid, did you celebrate on Christmas Eve or Christmas day?"

"Christmas day was the thing in my house. All presents opened then, big dinner around two. Visits to the neighbors in late afternoon to see their loot."

"We were a Christmas Eve family. Big dinner, lots of carols, a few gifts in the evening, the rest in the morning. I'll tell you, there's a big,

big difference between Christmas Eve families and Christmas day families. Christmas Eve families, I think, want two celebrations—kind of greedy don't you think?" She looked pensive for a moment. "Hey, McCall, were you an all-white-lights family or multicolored?" Archer asked as she began stringing lights on the tree.

"Multi, unquestionably," he replied.

"Absolutely. That's the right way. White is good for businesses but not for home. Multi, that's the ticket." she affirmed, nodding as if approving of her quick pupil's correct answer.

"You're wound up today, aren't you? The two-shot deal of those Christmas Eve families does sound pretty good to me, but I think we should make our own traditions, beginning this year." Connor got up, grabbed Archer, and swung her around.

She held on and savored the sound: *our own traditions*. Just then, on the radio playing softly in the background, they heard the Motown tune "You Better Shop Around."

"Hey, that's not Christmas music. But I do love the Miracles," exclaimed Archer as Connor grabbed her around the waist and pulled her into a fast Lindy hop. Dancing by firelight, she laughed, bending forward, limp in the middle from watching Connor do his fancy turns, as Alice began to jump alongside him in a frenzy, and Hadley, not to be outdone, began to run around and howl.

# CHAPTER
# 23

On Christmas morning, Connor and Archer both woke early. It had snowed several inches during the night. Outside the kitchen window, the woods looked fresh. Archer started the coffee.

After the essential first cup, they walked with the dogs through the woods, making the first tracks in the new snow. Hadley sniffed about, jumping and rolling. Alice was more cautious but seemed to love the fluffy white coolness, every few minutes stopping to bite the little snowballs that gathered on the hair of her paws.

Back in the house, Connor built a fire while Archer made two cups of hot chocolate and set them on the coffee table. She flopped down on the floor cross-legged and reached for her cup.

Connor went into the bedroom and came out with a little cubical baby blue box. Tiffany's. He handed it to Archer.

"Merry Christmas, Arch. In memory of Holly Golightly."

"Oh, Connor, *thank* you."

"Hey, don't thank me yet. You haven't opened it—you may hate it."

"I doubt that," she said as she pulled the fat red bow.

Gently, Archer opened the box and lifted the cotton covering. She gazed at it: a slim silver oval locket, shiny and chaste, on a silver chain. It was honest and simple, designed to hold memories, but not just any memories—the best of all edited memories. Lifting it from the box, she opened the delicate clasp. It would shelter two photos. She held its smooth coolness in her hands and turned it over to read the engraved back: "To Archer. Forever, Connor."

Archer looked up at him, her eyes moist. "It's the best present I could ever imagine. Thank you, Connor. Now I feel funny about mine to you. I'm not sure, but…it's what I have for you."

Archer got up and opened the middle drawer of her desk, and handed him a slim saffron-colored envelope. He took it with apprehension—Archer's nervousness seemed to be catching.

Turning the envelope over, he pushed the prongs of the fastener together, lifted the flap, and slid out two pieces of paper and three photocopied pictures. He set the pictures aside and began to read from the first sheet of paper:

*Dear Ms. Loh:*

*In accordance with your request, we have gathered as much information as we could in the past three weeks regarding the status of one Lauren Jane Giordano. As per your request, we have used only public records and have not undertaken personal surveillance beyond the superficial. Given the limitations you circumscribed and the short time frame, we determined the following:*
*Miss Giordano is nine years old, having been born on October 1, 1992, in Chicago. She is in the fourth grade at Greenwich Country School, a private school, in Evanston, Illinois, where she excels in her daily studies. Last year and this year, Miss Giordano played the flute in the school orchestra and participated in intramural soccer, where she generally plays center halfback. Her*

*most involving extracurricular activity is horseback riding. Miss Giordano takes two lessons a week at a stable called Hawthorne Farms in Granby, Illinois, and has ridden in competitions for the past two years, based on the local newspaper clippings of horse show results. Ms. Giordano's report card consists of mostly A's, with a B+ in applied science and a B in art. Her class behavior and citizenship are superior.*

*Miss Giordano lives in a two-story saltbox-style colonial in a neighborhood of similar homes. The home is tidy and well maintained. The family appears to consist of two adults and two children, Lauren Giordano and a younger brother of about four years. Neither Mr. nor Mrs. Giordano has a criminal record. The family has two vehicles: a 2000 Saab and a 1999 Plymouth Minivan.*

*Miss Giordano is popular with her classmates. She is on the elementary school student council and won an award for a poetry contest in the third grade.*

*We hope the above is satisfactory. With additional time and the removal of constraints, I assure you that more data can be compiled. Please feel free to call on us again. We enclose three photos that we were able to acquire.*

*Respectfully yours,*
*James Mason Brock,*
*Personal Investigations*

Connor was absorbed in reading. He completed the second page and then looked at the three photos, each with a handwritten explanation attached on a yellow sticky note. The first was a picture of Lauren from St. Margaret's Catholic School Sunday picnic with two other five-year-olds, sitting on a blanket near a lake. It was in color, the delicate blond girl between the two boys, squinting at the camera and smiling sweetly, holding up a bagel as if offering it to the photographer. Connor smiled and turned to the next photo.

It showed a grinning six- or seven-year-old little girl on Santa's lap. She wore a red snowsuit, but there was no mistaking that coquettish tilt of her head as she posed with Santa—pure Colleen McCall.

He then turned to the third picture. A clipping from a local paper, dated this past summer, it showed Lauren on a pony named Nikki, posing with the blue ribbon for short-stirrup hunter. She had her riding helmet on. Was it his imagination, or did she have almond-shaped eyes that mimicked his own?

"I hope I haven't intruded," Archer began.

"No—oh, no, Archer, it's a fabulous…a *wonderful* gift. You have no idea how wonderful," Connor said, opening his arms for her and hugging her close. He felt he had no right to know about Lauren, no right to *think* he had any right, but he did want to know, and he had read the two thin pages greedily, hungry for more.

At noon, Archer and Connor got in the Jeep and headed for Litchfield, about an hour away. Archer was in a long black wool skirt with her black and white tweed sweater and low boots. Connor was in dark blue jeans, a dark green turtleneck, and green and cream tweed sweater, with brown cowboy boots. He wore his shearling coat and Stetson.

The traffic on the back roads was light. New snow lightly covered the tree branches. Hadley and Alice were in the back, Hadley lying down and Alice pacing back and forth, finally relaxing twenty minutes into the trip.

"So, what am I walking into?" asked Connor.

"Oh, it'll be fine. Ted's a doctor, internal medicine with specialization in emergency room medicine. Sharon's a nurse part-time. And the kids are…well, kids. They're great. You'll like them."

"What have you told them about me?"

"Well, um, not much." Archer replied, looking down.

"How much?" he asked, sounding a little alarmed.

"Well, actually nothing."

There was a long moment of silence. Connor then said slowly, "Archer, don't you think this will be a bit of a surprise? I mean, to them you've been a recluse for years; Adam is gone, and now you bring me."

"Well, I thought rather than tell them about you, they could, you know, just see you and it would sort of take care of itself," Archer replied uncertainly.

"Oh, now, did you?" He paused, then gave a resigned sigh. "Well, I guess I'll have to be particularly charming today to pull this off."

They pulled up twenty minutes later at a lovely old colonial, set back from the road. It had a center chimney, two big trees framing the front, and a stone path leading to the door. The house was white with black shutters. Through the left front window, Archer could see the lights of a big Christmas tree.

They pulled into the driveway, and Connor let the dogs out. They ran around the car, chased each other, and finally fell into line behind Archer. She was laughing and carrying a stack of neatly wrapped gifts. Connor slammed the Jeep's rear door shut and hefted the bigger group of presents.

Archer lifted the heavy brass knocker and rapped twice. She could hear laughter and someone running to the door. A breathless Julie flung the door open. She had on a bright red sweater, and her blond hair was in a ponytail with a red velvet ribbon.

"Aunt Archer! Hi! Merry Christmas! Hi, Hadley. And who are you?" Julie asked the fluffy black dog following Hadley.

"Julie, Merry Christmas, darling," said Archer. "That's Alice. And that, coming up the path, is the human attached to Alice—his name's

Connor." She pointed to Connor, who was slipping up the path with his pile of presents.

Connor entered with a gust of cold air. Archer thought, if Wyoming were a person, this was what it would look like: crisp and clean and a little wild.

"Hi," he said, walking into the spacious front hall with its yellow floral print wallpaper. "You must be Julie. I'm Connor. Merry Christmas!"

Sharon speeded from the kitchen to greet Archer. She had a white and red checked apron over black corduroy pants and a bright yellow turtleneck sweater.

"Hi! Hey, Arch, how were the roads? Merry Christmas, baby sister." She spied Connor. "Oh, hi, I'm Sharon."

"Hi! Connor McCall, a friend of Archer's."

Sharon and Connor shook hands and smiled. Sharon looked at Archer, her eyes curious, and then said, "Can I get you a drink, Connor?"

"Oh, just some soda would be fine, thanks," he replied, hunkering down in the living room to put the presents under the tree. The fireplace was crackling merrily, and the room looked festive. After placing the gifts in piles, he moved to the back of the house, where voices were chattering gaily.

"Arch, who *is* that?" Sharon whispered once they were in the family room away from the men. "You never mentioned anyone. What gives?"

"He's cute. He looks like a cowboy," said Julie, giggling conspiratorially.

"He *is* kind of a cowboy, actually. He owns the three hundred acres next to me, and we met last fall when he came here from Wyoming to check it out. We've become good friends over the months, and he has no family, so I thought he'd have some fun here."

"Is this like a romance or something?" said Sharon, obviously excited.

Archer squirmed. "Shar, don't get carried away. We met. We get along well and have become good friends. If there are further developments, you'll be the first to know."

"Hey, Shar, help!" yelled Ted from the kitchen. "Should I put the meat in now or wait another fifteen minutes?"

Sharon rolled her eyes. "He can manage forty patients in the ER, but a simple meal overwhelms him."

Sharon, Julie, and Archer all moved into the kitchen. Connor and Ted were chatting about Ted's recent effort to form a consortium with other doctors for a complete interactive referral system. Connor already had sketched Ted a business plan, marketing options, and sales projections on a long white pad.

"Hey, Archer, this guy is more than a cowboy—he knows a lot of business stuff," said Ted, leaning on the granite countertop, sipping eggnog, fascinated with the diagram Connor had made.

"Yeah, well, that's what Harvard Business School does to you," said Archer. You can never shake that stuff even when you try to bury it in sheepskins."

Ted and Sharon looked puzzled, but they smiled. Connor, seeing their bewilderment, quickly explained the sheep reference. Julie and David thought it was simply too cool for words.

From there, the late afternoon and evening swung along. The roast beef, Yorkshire pudding, and salad were delicious. Archer was sparkling and talkative.

"So, what I want to know, Sharon, said Connor, over coffee and apple pie, "is if anyone ever called Archer 'Archie.'"

"Ha! No one who lived to tell the tale!" Archer broke in.

"Actually, no one ever did," Sharon said. "She was always just Archer, or Arch. Daddy sometimes called her Scout—you know, after the little girl in *To Kill a Mockingbird*—but that's about it. She was scary even as a kid. No one messed with her."

"I believe that."

As evening grew late, Connor and Archer got up to say their good-byes, and Sharon packed some dessert for them. Archer gave Julie and David a hug, and both kids hugged the two dogs.

"I love Alice and Hadley," declared Julie. "Mom, can we get a dog?"

"Honey, you know we're out sometimes for twelve hours, and it's not fair to the dog. Archer, honey, you be careful going home. Call me over the weekend. Connor, I am so glad to meet you! Please come back."

Archer turned to her niece and nephew and said, "Now, you guys come and see us soon. We'll take a walk in the woods and watch movies with the girls. I love you guys," she said, waving good-bye.

Connor shook hands with Ted, gave Sharon a kiss on the cheek, and hugged each of the kids. He took Archer's arm in a proprietary gesture and guided her down the snowy path to the car. Connor opened the door for Archer, opened the back of the Jeep for the dogs, and then got into the driver's seat. He looked over at Archer. She was smiling at him.

"See, it went fine," she said, a smug grin on her face.

"Okay, smarty-pants, I liked your family," replied Connor. "Hey, what can I say? It worked."

# CHAPTER
# 24

January was cold but mostly sunny. There was little snow, and Connor and Archer could run or hike most days. Connor spent most afternoons during the week working on an article about Rambouillet sheep for *Agricultural Digest*. He had outlined most of it but needed a library to check a few facts and beef up—or rather "sheep up," as Archer suggested—some of his references. They planned a trip to a college library, then lunch.

One afternoon at the end of January, while Connor was in town picking up the mail, Archer sat by the fire reading. She turned the book over on her lap and leaned her head on the high-backed chair. Until a few months ago, she had only enough energy to get through the day—no more, no less. Now she had more. At times she felt almost restless. She rarely drank to get to sleep anymore, and she awoke clear-headed and almost, well...*cheerful.* "Honor Annie; don't just grieve her," Connor had said.

What would Annie be like now? she wondered. She would be eighteen this coming May. Daydreaming was a luxury Archer rarely allowed herself—too much potential for taking that path back downward to serious depression. Still, she wondered. Would they have had one those tense mother-daughter relationships, like the one she and her mother had had, with doors slamming, recriminations flying, miscommunication at best, no communication at worst? Somehow, she doubted it.

With Annie, the tight connection had been there early, although not, as some mothers claimed, the moment she laid eyes on her bawling baby girl. Archer's first sight of Annie came after twenty-two hours of labor. Beyond being utterly wrung out, she had been woozily pleased, but that was about all.

It was what came afterward that cemented the bond: Annie's squeals and upraised arms when her mother came through the door at night; those stubby legs sticking out as she sat, enraptured, high up on the aging Clique, the horse trotting gently, keeping safe the little girl entrusted to him; Annie beaming out at her and Adam, stumbling over the word "incense" in the church pageant, her hair plaited in uneven, almost horizontal braids she had insisted on making herself. It was all those little vignettes, each one barely a blip at the time, that had grown into a ferocious, roaring love unlike anything Archer had ever known before or ever would again.

Archer got up and went over to the kitchen counter. She opened a drawer and grabbed her PDA. Tapping her way to her subfolder on lawyers, she moved to the "C's" and found it: *Rachel Cohen, 555-278-3303.*

She dialed the number, her fingers drumming on the counter. It was Thursday, and most family lawyers, unless they had a trial, were in their offices.

"Good afternoon, Center for Child Advocacy."

"Attorney Cohen, please."

"Attorney Cohen is on the other line—oh…she just hung up. May I say who's calling?"

"Uh, yes—Archer Loh."

On hold, Archer waited. Rachel was one of the best people she knew. A fine lawyer who, by choice, remained with the Center for Child Advocacy, she was underpaid and underappreciated. She worked diligently, head down, to improve the lot of children whose parents were in the midst of divorce. Rachel was fifty years old, with long, curly gray hair that she usually wore in a wiry halo around her head or, when she went to court, wrapped in a tight, tidy bun. Undeterred by the judges who had no understanding of her mission, and buoyed by those who did, Rachel approached life with spirit, a sense of humor, and an unsentimental love of kids. She and Archer had started at Legal Aid together, but Rachel had stayed in the nonprofit sector long after Archer switched to the big-income cases of private practice.

A voice broke into her thoughts. "Archer? Is it really you?" Rachel asked in a whisper.

"Yes, Rae, it's me. How are you?"

There was a long silence. Rachel, in truth, had thought it likely that Archer was dead. There had been rumors about self-cutting as well as about her divorce, and no one had heard from her for years. After a while, even her best friends and closest colleagues had given up hope. They took it as an object lesson. Archer was the most solid, least mercurial person any of them knew. If this tragedy could befall *her,* what chance did any of them have? There but for the grace of God…

Rachel burst out: "Archer! My God, darling, where *are* you? *How* are you? What have you been doing? Are you in town?"

"No, Rae, I'm at my cabin."

"Cabin?"

"I live in the Berkshires. I'm calling, Rae, because I need to work."

"Work? How can I help, Archer?"

"Well, I want to work with kids, help them. The only skill I have that could help kids is the law. I've kept up my occupational tax in Connecticut and I'm still licensed. I thought maybe I could work for the center part-time—that is, if you need anyone," Archer said, hurrying on.

"If we *need* anyone? Surly you jest, Arch. We'd love to have you—

I mean, what a boon! But our budget is pretty limited. Given your experience, though, I could go to the board and see—"

"No, no money, Rae. I need to work now. No pay. I just want to work. Do you have enough work for another lawyer?"

"God, Archer, we have enough work for *five* more lawyers! You know how it is here. Everyone says kids are the most important people in the case, until it comes time to represent them. Wow, I feel like I just got a brand-new Mercedes, free! So how about starting...oh, say, today? I have files sitting right here waiting to be worked."

"The, uh, Mercedes is a bit used, but how about Monday, then?" Archer said, laughing at Rachel's glee. "If that's okay."

"Perfect. Our facilities will seem primitive after what you're used to, Archer, but I'll set up a corner in the library for you, and we'll go from there."

"Great. I know it will be fine," said Archer. She paused a moment, then added, "And thanks, Rae. This means a lot to me."

"It's me who should be thanking you, Arch."

After catching up on Rachel's children, Archer clicked the off button. She stood at the sink, phone resting against her chin, and smiled. *I can still be useful,* she thought.

On Friday, Connor and Archer drove to Northampton, home of her alma mater, Smith College. They took the Massachusetts Turnpike through pretty wooded hills.

About twenty miles before Springfield, they got off onto back roads, and farms, fields, and woods gave way to town greens and white church steeples.

Archer pulled the Jeep onto the main street in Northampton. It was wide, with a brownstone Congregational church dominating the lower end. She thought the town had a Norman Rockwell quality but for the many gay couples strolling arm in arm along Main Street.

Smith, one of the few remaining all-women's schools, had given her something invaluable: the knowledge that being a woman was not a disability.

Connor was impressed and said so.

"Everything is so pretty here," said Connor. "And everyone looks so healthy and smart—and athletic," he added, looking around at young women cycling and roller blading on the bike lane and rowing on the lake.

Connor and Archer went to the library, which was in the center of campus, its entrance sheltered by two spreading elm trees. Even without leaves, the trees were stately, lending gravity to the building.

After seeing Connor off at the library entrance, Archer walked over to Green Street, with its cafés, bookstores, and specialty shops. After stopping for a latte at a cute little coffee bar, she wandered to the Smith Art Museum with its world-class collection, then strolled by the botanical greenhouse, out to the quadrangle, and by her old dormitory, reliving in the process the excitement and promise she had felt at eighteen.

Finally, saving the best for last, she headed down to the stables, a good twenty-minute walk across the athletic fields. As she approached the barn complex, Archer noted the new arena, the spotless white fencing, and the four modern ten-horse trailers lined up next to the barn, ready to hitch. She ambled over to the new main barn to watch two women schooling their horses over the jumps. Between jumps, the two chatted, each critiquing the other's performance.

Archer then walked into the older barn that had been her daily refuge twenty-five years ago. She looked up at the rafters, where barn swallows played, and remembered arriving with Clique all those years ago. While other girls had been setting up stereos and popping into town to buy curtains, Archer and her father had walked the high-strung thoroughbred in shifts in a vain effort to calm him down enough to settle into his new stall. They had led Clique, snorting and pawing, up and down the aisles of the barn, and when that got too tedious, they'd moved outside, traipsing him around and around the outdoor arena, holding tight to the lead rope as he spooked and bolted, trying to pull away. Finally, after six hours, he had tired, and Archer had led him like a lamb into his new quarters. That was what it had taken to get him into his stall without him kicking it down.

Archer smiled at the memory. Her father was a real trooper who never let her down. *God, how did Daddy put up with me?* she wondered. Other fathers either would have insisted on selling the horse or would have left her to work out the logistics on her own. But she knew why he had put up with her. Simple: love. Love was what made the difficult manageable, the impossible merely challenging, the unfathomable comprehensible.

Archer peered into Clique's old stall, now occupied by a steel-gray gelding, peacefully munching his hay. She watched him with interest for a few moments, then put on her gloves, preparing to head back to the main campus. Just then the gray lifted his well-formed head and gazed at Archer with soft brown eyes, ears twitching lazily. She smiled at him and put both her gloved hands on the stall edge. He pressed his nose through the bars, and Archer reached out to him.

"Give your girl a great ride, fella. Give her something to hold on to," she whispered. She touched his muzzle, now close, then stroked it gently. "Give her something she can keep forever."

And with that, she turned and walked briskly back across the fields to the library.

At a table on the second floor, Connor looked up as she approached. "Hey, what's up?"

"Not too much. How's your stuff going?"

"About done," he said, closing up a Web site and making a stack of the agricultural books. "Just have to finish printing a few Web addresses."

As they walked out arm in arm, Connor said, "You know, I can see you here, Arch, running from class to class, bossing everyone around. Yeah, I can see it."

"Hm-m-m. Hey, what do you think about my job, McCall? You haven't said much."

"You know what I think—I think it's great. Lucky them, but even better for you. You're just gathering dust up on the mountain. Don't get me wrong—I love having you cater to my every need, but sacrifices are necessary for the general good," he said, striking a noble pose.

"You goon!" Archer said, poking him in the ribs.

When they arrived home, Connor called Three Chimneys on his cell phone while Archer busied herself in the kitchen.

"Hello, Felix?…Great, I'm great. How are things there?…Is the barn staying dry enough?" Connor paused, listening. "Okay, that sounds okay. We may have to buy a few more ewes, though, if that's the case. How's the fencing holding up?…Were you able to hire any more help for shearing?…How about a few of Bill Randall's men? He won't need them until later in the spring, and some like to make extra money on the weekends… Right. Well, you might check it out. Some of the kids from Bozeman might be willing to come down in March, too… Yeah, I know—we can do it first thing in the spring. Speaking of which, how's the weather?…Yeah, well, stay warm, Felix… I know, I know. I'm working on it. It's always on my mind… Right. Well, I'll talk to you in a few days. Say hi to the guys for me." Connor hung up and stared at the phone for a moment.

"So, how are things on the ranch, cowboy?" Archer asked, putting water on for tea.

"Not bad, but the natives are restless. Felix is doing a great job, but he's only twenty-four and not seasoned enough. I'll have to go back for shearing and lambing, starting in late winter, early spring.

Felix has only been through one lambing season, and he just can't run the show. A little psychological muscle from a crotchety old man sometimes helps to get my less-than-reliable ranch hands to show up and perform." He sighed.

Archer turned away and said nothing.

Unspoken was the fact that Connor had another life in Wyoming, and at some point he had to get back to it or shut it down. Silently they agreed to think about it…tomorrow. Fiddle-de-dee.

Archer's work at the Children's Center was a roaring success. She drove into Hartford and did most of her interviewing on Tuesdays, then wrote on Thursdays. The first time she had to go to court, she had been as nervous as she was nineteen years ago. Her old colleagues greeted her with surprise and warmth, treating her absence as if it had been merely an extended sabbatical.

The best part was the kids. The little ones were proud that they had their own lawyer. The teenagers were angry but very clear about their wishes and needs. And the parents, well, they were mostly good people who could not separate their own desires from their children's needs. Archer saw her role as liaison, educator, advocate, and mediator.

She sat at her Irish pine table in the cabin, reading through the file she had brought home. She looked up as Connor came in with a load of split wood.

"Hey."

"Hey, yourself," he said with a grin, carrying the wood to the hearth, where he began stacking it.

"Hey, would you be upset if I were an exotic dancer?" she asked out of the blue.

Connor looked at her over his shoulder, amused.

"Oh, contemplating a career change, are we?"

"Yeah, right after my implant surgery," laughed Archer. "No, I have this custody case. The mother is a topless dancer, and the child's father thinks she's a bad role model. It got me thinking about it. Do you think an exotic dancer is by definition a bad role model as a mother?"

"Oh, boy, how'd I get in the middle of this?" Connor moaned as he stacked the last split of wood. He stood up, brushed off his hands, and sighed. "Okay, well, I'd say it's a living for someone who may have had few other opportunities. It's not illegal—at least that I know of—and she's supporting herself and her daughter, I presume.

"On the other hand, who wants their daughter to grow up to be a topless dancer? For that matter, who wants their *mother* to be a topless dancer? Actually, that's a *really* repulsive thought, now that I ponder it. Anyway, it's not exactly a high aspiration for yourself, or one brimming with bragging rights for either side, so from that point of view, I'd have to say I'd be lukewarm about the lady's judgment."

Archer looked at him curiously. "I like that you answer questions and don't duck and weave. My father was like that. He was a very low-key, courteous man who tried not to offend or hurt anyone, but he always answered directly. You remind me of him sometimes."

"So you said in your drunken Halloween stupor. I wasn't too thrilled about it at the time, though, I can assure you. No man wants to hear that his dream girl sees him as Dad instead of George Clooney."

Archer laughed. "Oh, God. Was I *really* that bad? I have no recollection at all of that night, other than of feeling ghastly in the morning and being eternally grateful that the coffee was all set out in a carafe when I stumbled into the kitchen. A real lifesaver."

"Nah, you weren't that bad. Plus, you are extremely talkative when intoxicated, not to mention hilarious. I gained a fair amount of classified info about your sex life that night, which I plan to put to good use." Connor leered at her.

"I have plenty of classified tricks left, old chap, so stay tuned," she laughed, returning to her file.

Connor sat at the pine table, putting the finishing touches on the article for Agricultural Digest. Archer was out getting the mail. Despite a deadline to complete the piece, he couldn't keep his mind from wandering. He shook his head, stretched, and leaned back in his chair.

Archer Loh, his "dream girl," was in many ways still a mystery to him. He knew she had a secret life involving some clandestine work of a violent nature. Her familiarity with guns, along with her sharp-shooter's aim, her impromptu three-day trips, her vague descriptions of the work done on these "business" trips—it all added up to something most troubling, although he said nothing. While she was away, he feared for her, and whenever the phone rang in her absence, a chill ran through him. Still, he feared even more a change of heart in her, an epiphany that this—that he—was a big mistake. He knew with absolute certainty that whatever Archer did was essential to her sanity and survival in some way, that it allowed her some control in a world in which she had lost so much control. He also knew something else: that whatever she did, whatever she was, didn't matter to him. What he felt for her was sacred and undamaged, because he knew, that when she was with him, she was the girl before it happened, the one who rode in Madison Square Garden on a magical horse with wings for feet—the girl and the horse who could jump higher than all the others.

# CHAPTER
# 25

Connor drove slowly down the back road, glancing occasionally at his map. He'd been on the road for about an hour and a half and suspected that he was near his destination. He pulled over to the side of the road to read the address on the letterhead of the billing and then studied his map again. He was close. He pulled out onto the road, and, in less than a mile, saw the sign for Mad River Farm. He turned into a dirt driveway, drove up to the main barn, and got out of the truck. *Pretty farm,* he thought.

A large indoor arena was attached to the main barn. The arena doors were rolled aside, and he could see two women working their horses over the low jumps. Though the January air had a bite, the day was sunny and still. The natural daylight was probably welcome, he supposed.

He went in the door to the main barn. He had walked only a few stall lengths when he was greeted by a middle-aged woman in riding clothes. She had her faded blond hair pulled back in a ponytail, and a green John Deere ball cap on her head. She stepped up to Connor and stuck out her hand. "Hi. I'm Jane Russo. You must be Connor."

"Yes, I am." He shook her hand. "Thanks for seeing me."

"Not at all. I was actually delighted to hear from you. Everyone here really liked Archer, and we loved Annie. We were all a little nervous when they first came, you know, given Archer's background as one of the top riders in the country. Some of the instructors were afraid she'd be a real pain in the neck—real critical, you know—but she never was. And Annie—she was the kind of kid everyone hopes for." Jane's voice trailed off. She looked away, then said, "It was all so utterly tragic." Her face dropped when she got to this part, and she looked up at Connor. "How is Archer doing?"

"She's okay," Connor replied. "Mostly she's coping. She got a volunteer job working for legal aid in Hartford. She's there this morning. But the reason I came down is, I understand that Annie's horse—Allegra, is it?—is still here. Is that right?"

"Sure is. Archer never showed up again after Annie died, but she always pays Allegra's board on time. I thought for sure she'd eventually come down, start riding her, or lease her out, but no. The horse is stagnating, and it makes all of us really sad. Annie loved that mare the way only a twelve-year-old girl can. You know, like it's all that matters in the world. Those two were best friends. Annie would talk to Allegra from the moment she got here until she left again, and Allegra seemed to understand it all. That horse had a lot of potential to handle high-performance jumping courses." Jane shoved her hands into her jacket pockets and looked down for a moment, then back up at Connor.

"I see," he said. He paused. "May I see the horse?"

"Sure. Come on along." Jane led him down the aisle, turned a corner, and stopped at the second stall on the left. She slid the door open, and a dark bay horse turned around, a white heart on her forehead. "This is Allegra."

Connor entered the stall and held out his hand, and Allegra sniffed it and moved toward him. Patting her neck, he fed her a peppermint. She crunched on it, then stretched out her neck for another. "She's a beauty," Connor said, never turning from the horse.

"Yeah, she is—and a real sweetheart. No quirks. Real quiet. I hate to see her just languish on the vine. She can't go backward, but she can't go forward, either. It just breaks your heart to see her like this."

Connor stroked Allegra's neck. She stood quietly, nuzzling the collar of his parka. "Yeah, I know what you mean."

That night, as they were cleaning up after dinner, Connor said, "I saw her."

Archer turned from the sink, eyebrow raised. "Saw who?"

"Allegra. You know, your horse?"

Archer's face hardened, and she turned back to the sink.

"And how, pray tell, do you know about her?" she asked.

"I saw a bill for her board sitting on your kitchen counter last week."

Without turning, Archer said flatly, "So instead of asking me about it, you took it upon yourself to snoop." Feeling herself flush, she kept her back to Connor, knowing she had done far worse when she invaded his notebook.

"I wasn't snooping. It was there and I was curious. I mean, you said Annie had a horse, and I didn't think it was some big secret. I just didn't know you still owned her. I thought maybe we could bring her here—you know, we could both ride."

Archer put down the plate she was drying and half turned toward him, twisting the dish towel in her hands. "Hey," she said, "if you don't want me riding Millie anymore, no problem. Just say so."

"That's not it at all, and you know it. I love that you ride Millie. I just think that if Annie cared about that horse, maybe it makes sense to bring—"

Without warning, Archer whirled around with the plate and hurled it to the floor, where it exploded into hundreds of slivers. She grabbed another plate from the drying rack and smashed it, then a third. More fragments flew.

"No!" she shouted, slamming her hand on the counter. "No, no, no, no!" She steadied herself against the counter, breathing hard, trying to regain control.

Connor looked stunned. But he stood his ground and said, "Archer, life goes on whether you want it to or not. You think doing whatever it is you do…on your outings…is going to make you forget. It won't, and it's killing you. I see it."

Archer took a step closer to him, fists clenched. She then stepped back and roared, "Oh, really! You see? You *see nothing*. You *know* nothing." She turned back to the sink, but Connor caught her arm.

"I know, Archer. I know." He hesitated. "Well, I think I know. You do something that you think is justice. But it's not, you know. It's revenge, for sure. It's even fair, maybe, but it's not justice. Justice is the system that keeps it all in a box, the box that keeps us all from reverting to *Lord of the Flies*."

Archer jerked her arm away. She brushed back a disheveled lock of hair and glared at him. "Oh, this pearl of wisdom from the man who's never seen his own daughter. Come and talk to me when someone *you* love so much that you can't breathe without them is ripped from *you*." She looked away, then spat out, "Oh, I forgot. You've never in your life loved anyone that way." She gulped a breath. "So spare me your armchair psychology, would you?"

She stopped and leaned against the counter. Then she said in a level voice, "You don't know anything about me or what I do. You presume some easy fix. You think maybe I see the horse and it's some instant healing thing. *Bullshit*, McCall! I am so damaged, they need a new word for it." Her face was blazing now, and she looked as if she wanted to run out of the room but couldn't. Now she shot out each word distinctly. "You just don't get it, do you, McCall? The day I see that horse is the day I choose to die, because it would kill me. It would kill what's left of me to see that horse. Whatever soul is left of my daughter is with that horse, and I can't bear to contaminate that, too."

She was still propped against the counter to keep from slumping onto the floor. After a minute, she quieted and said in almost a whisper, "*You* find Lauren in a dirty little alley, jeans down to her knees, torn underpants, claw marks on her face, and *then* we'll talk about justice. You know *nothing...nothing*. You're an amateur, McCall, who's stepped unwittingly into the show ring with the heavyweight champ of the world. *Get out of the ring, newbie, before you get hurt!*" Each word rang menacingly.

Connor recoiled as if she had struck him. Then he straightened, as if with newfound resolve. "I still say you become what you do. It's going to kill you, Archer. It's going to change you, and there'll be no coming back."

"Coming back to *what?* You tell me that, McCall. Coming back to what!" Archer spoke in almost a whisper as she leaned over the sink, sobbing now. Then she raised her head. "Leave me alone, McCall. I can't do this."

"Can't do what?"

"Oh, forget it."

"No—say it."

She pushed back from the sink and stood facing the kitchen window, still holding the edge of the counter, just staring. She said nothing.

"*Say it.* I want to hear you say it." Connor enunciated each word and stared at her back.

She spun around to face him, tears running down her face, and bellowed, "Have *you* and *her!* I can't have you and her. And I chose *her.*"

Connor started toward her, then hesitated. He stepped back, crossed his arms across his chest, and shook his head, and after letting a few moments pass, he said quietly, "That's just not true, Archer. I may not know anything about you and this horse or about you and Annie. But I do know some things about just plain old you. You can't bring her back, no matter what you do. Her death wasn't your fault, but somehow you think it was. It just happened because some sick pervert was loose, not because you failed her in some way. I know that. And you do, too, if you'll let yourself. And your love isn't limited. If you give love to me, it doesn't mean there's less for her. I know that I love you, and I can't stand to watch you destroy yourself."

"Then don't." She straightened and moved stiffly to a kitchen chair, where she just drooped, head in her hands. Slowly she looked up. Connor was still standing, looking anxious, unsure, hands in his jeans pockets. After a minute, she said softly, eyes dry now, and voice drained of emotion, "McCall, I love you, too, but don't ever mention that horse again... I can't take it."

# CHAPTER
# 26

The last week of February, the mood at Three Chimneys felt expectant. Connor's calls had grown more frequent, until he was calling almost every day. Felix had all the shears, vehicles, and lamb incubators serviced in anticipation of shearing and the lambing that would follow, and he had arranged for roof repairs on the larger of the two barns and hired additional seasonal help. And although Felix was coordinating all the preparations, he sought approval and reassurance from Connor for anything bigger than a hundred-dollar plumbing job. Connor didn't mind; he expected it as a necessary part of running a good-size operation from long distance.

On the mountain, Connor was restless. He felt like a politician about to throw his hat into the ring. While a win was no certainty, not by a long shot, the mere fact that he was jumping into the fray…well, it was enough to make you wake up tingling.

Connor's excitement was tempered by fear. Archer never talked about tomorrow—only about today and, more rarely, yesterday. After the blowup over Allegra, Connor had tiptoed around the edges of Archer's heavily fortified boundaries. It troubled him, but he felt certain they could talk things through, given enough time and trust.

Connor's original plan had been to take Archer to dinner somewhere intimate and romantic and ask her to return to Wyoming with him. However, though he was a master at speaking to a boardroom full of executives or a crew of ranch hands, the thought of facing Archer and pleading his personal case was unnerving.

Connor wanted to say everything at once, so that Archer would have the full scope of his intentions before she gave her answer. He feared that he couldn't talk fast enough to get his plea out before she raised an objection or reservation—she was awfully good at that. Then he would lose the advantage of the cumulative effect of his argument, perhaps never to recover.

His backup plan was to put his thoughts in writing so that Archer would have to read them through in their entirety and consider them in her deliberate way. She wasn't good at being rushed or pressured, so this became his working plan.

It was a cold and dreary February afternoon, and Archer was out with Hadley getting the mail. Connor went into the kitchen and, opening the top drawer of Archer's little desk table, took out two sheets of crisp white paper and a blue fine-point pen. Taking these over to the sofa, he sat down, leaning forward to rest the paper on the pile of books on the coffee table.

He sat with his elbows resting on his knees, thinking about what he wanted to say. After a moment, he knew what to say, but not how to say it in a way that gave it the proper texture. He needed three dimensions to explain himself, but his talents only enabled him to work in a straight line. His prose seemed flat to him, incapable of conveying the depth and nuance he felt. He was disappointing himself.

After laboring at it for an hour, Connor reviewed his note. It was unsatisfactory, but he could think of no way to improve it. He reread it once more:

*Dear Archer,*

*I was at a low ebb when I came here. You screeching at me from behind your closed door was just about par for the course. I wish I had the skills of your hero, Mr. Hemingway—then, in a few sentences, I could make you feel what you've done to me. But I'm more Excel than PowerPoint, so I'll just say what I need to say.*

*You blindsided me completely. I expected nothing when I came out here—nothing. I wasn't unhappy, but I wasn't happy. After meeting you, though, everything changed. For the first time in my life, I wanted to share my life. Until now, I never wanted to have responsibility for or to anyone else. This is a long way of saying I want you to come back with me to Three Chimneys. Share life with me. If you don't like Wyoming, we can go anywhere.*

*I know what you do, Archer. Or at least I have some idea. Mrs. McCall's boy didn't get out of Harvard without being able to add two and two. I'm afraid for you, and I see what it's doing to you. It's keeping the pain fresh, Archer—always alive, always close at hand. With this thing that you do, Annie's death is the entirety of your life. Grieve her, yes, but also honor her, but not by killing. That's no legacy to leave her. Just because something is fair doesn't make it right. What you do is fair but not right. Believe me, I don't judge you. I just love you and want you safe and at peace.*

*Whatever happens, I plan to see my daughter on the way back to Wyoming. I've thrown away without a second thought what you tragically lost. You were right on that point (even though you could have said it a little nicer!). Shame on me. It's too cowardly on my part to countenance. It's too late for me to be a father to Lauren, but maybe not too late to be her friend.*

*Archer, the thought of living without you is so painful to me that I'll only ask you once to come with me. If you say no, I respect you way too much not to believe that you mean what you say, and I will view our six months as just that: the finest, most wonderful six months I'll ever live. If your answer is yes, meet me at three tomorrow at the Cloisters. If you're not there, I'll know your answer. I'll stay at the camp tonight so you can think.*

*Whether you come with me or not, Archer, you are the love of my life. Know that.*

*Connor*

After folding the letter in thirds, Connor tucked it in a white envelope and wrote Archer's name on the front in his bold, blocky print, all in capital letters. He licked the envelope flap, closed it, and left it on the kitchen counter for her to find when she returned.

Archer found the note on the kitchen counter when she arrived home from shopping. She read it twice, tucked it into her jeans pocket, pulled it out, and read it again. Then she put it down and went over to light the fire. Once it was going, she pulled her chair close and, sitting with her legs tucked under her, read it yet a fourth time.

After the fourth reading, Archer let the letter fall into her lap. She leaned her head back against the chair and shut her eyes tight to hold back the tears. She loved Connor; that wasn't the issue at all. If she went to Wyoming, she would be moving on, forsaking Annie. This was her penance. Bottom line: she knew she didn't deserve to be happy. Her suffering was limitless; she'd earned it, and there would be no reprieve. The memories of her life with Annie and Adam were her torment. She couldn't give to Connor what was left of her ability to love, lessening what was there for Annie. She couldn't give him the allegiance she gave the Group. She was going to lose him, she knew. This was her karma, her fate, her legacy—more losses on the growing heap. But this she knew. She could do this until her time was up.

After carefully writing her answer, she jogged up to the Cloisters and left it there on the big rock, in a white envelope secured by a stone. Connor would see it. It was where they always sat and viewed the glory of the mountain during their jogging break.

She walked home quietly, taking her time, wending her way through the leafless trees. When she got back, she sat in her chair by the fire and wept. This time her tears were for herself and for what might have been.

Connor walked up to the Cloisters with a light step. He had a bottle of champagne under one arm, and a small bunch of flowers he had carefully selected at Stop and Shop that morning. They had wilted a bit in the crisp air but were still pretty and merry. Alice pranced by his side, not sure why the day was special, but appearing to know that it was. It was a beautiful February afternoon, sunny, about fifty-five degrees. The days were getting longer, and the sun felt cheering and somehow auspicious.

Maybe they would get a redo, Connor thought. Maybe everyone deserved a redo. He paced along the ledge, anxious for Archer to arrive. She loved him. She would come; he knew it.

At three, Connor began to pace in a wide circle, hands in his jacket pockets. She would be coming now. Soon Hadley would come bounding through the clearing a few steps ahead of her. He would hear them soon. She would smile and throw her arms around his neck. He stood impatiently at the edge of the cliff. He could see almost to Mt. Tom from here.

At 3:15, Connor began to worry for the first time. Maybe she wouldn't come. Maybe she hadn't seen his note on the kitchen counter. He turned away from the logging path to sit on their rock, and then he saw it, small and very white: an envelope. In her direct, angular script, she had written his name on it. It lay under a stone.

Connor moved the stone, picked up the envelope, and sat down on the granite boulder. Slipping his thumb under the glued flap, he opened the envelope and pulled out the short note, feeling a landslide in the pit of his stomach. He read:

*Dear Connor:*

*This is the coward's way out. Please forgive me. I could not face you. Hemingway and I both agree that less is more, so here it is.*

    *I can't go with you. To leave here and all that keeps Annie alive to me is too terrifying. Also, I lied when I said I didn't feel guilty about Annie's death. I am plenty guilty. I know as sure as I know the sun will rise tomorrow that if I had agreed to be a chaperone on that trip as I should have, Annie would be alive. If I'd been there, I would have looked for her and made sure she was on the right bus. If I'd been there, she never for a minute would have been alone or confused. I should have been there. Living with that knowledge is my burden, and I must pay forever. There's no room for anything else.*

    *You have given me a clean space in my life, however briefly, that I never thought I would have again—just a whiff of what could be but can't. To laugh again, to dance again, to smile just because there's a beautiful sunset to see—well, I haven't had that for six years. You did this for me and it was real. It was real. But I knew it couldn't last, because I'm unworthy of happiness. I wish to the very core of my being that it were different. Don't pity me. It is both fair and right. As for "this thing I do," I do what I do so I can still breathe. It's that simple.*

*And we'll always have Boston (please smile a little here).*

*I love you, McCall, and I will for as long as I live, and then some.*

Archer

Connor finished reading and had to will himself to breathe. The once jaunty bouquet bent sadly between his fingers, then slipped from his hand and tumbled to the ground. The green champagne bottle sat untouched, still chilling in the snow, the glasses upright and still tipped toward each other. A celebration stillborn.

Connor leaned against a tree for support. His body crumpled forward, and he slumped to his knees, lacking the strength to remain upright. An owl in a tall pine stared down at him, then flew away as if alarmed by the sight. The squirrels playing nearby scurried away. For the first time in thirty years, since the death of the mare named Sabrina, Connor McCall cried. It was a muffled requiem, a quiet dirge of despair.

That night it snowed. The next morning, Connor packed up his camp, and at four a.m., he walked to Archer's house to retrieve Millie, hoping Hadley wouldn't bark. He couldn't face Archer and her rejection of their chance at happiness together.

Hadley didn't bark, and Millie came along easily. Connor tacked her up by the remaining moonlight; she seemed hesitant but accepting. The several inches of snow formed good footing for their walk down the mountain to the trailer, to begin the long trip home. Alice followed closely behind, a solemn shadow.

Archer awoke early that morning. She had slept poorly. When she saw that it was five thirty, she got up and quickly put on the coffee. She had made a mistake—she felt it. She wasn't helping Annie; she was just beating herself up pointlessly. Pulling on her jeans, a sweatshirt, and insulated Wellington boots, she grabbed the lantern.

"Hadley, come on," she called. They ran down the logging path. Archer anticipated Connor's delight. He might laugh and say, "I knew you'd change your mind. A woman's prerogative. I waited for you to come." He might. It could be a Hollywood ending.

The sun was just starting to come up. She needed the lantern for only a few minutes, and then it was light enough to see. She jogged steadily, with each steamy breath vowing, *I'll explain, make it right.*

She turned the bend, and the campsite came into view. She stopped dead in her tracks. The tent and equipment were gone. All that was left was a barren patch where the tent had been, and the outlines of tent pegs.

Archer drooped. It couldn't be. But it was. It just wasn't meant to be—that's what it meant. She looked down the path that led to the road, but saw only Millie's hoofprints in the snow…leaving. This was the Berkshires, not Hollywood. No happy ending to this little drama.

"Godspeed, Connor," she whispered, turning away. "Have a good life."

# CHAPTER
# 27

Despite Archer's personal gloom, March blew in, blooming, blustering, and lovely. The weather was warmer than normal, and trees were already budding, nature's contrast with her mood feeling somehow almost mocking. Archer went to her job on her committed days, and the work was a saving grace.

*I lived before him,* she thought, *and I'll live after him.* She continued to go to the movies on Wednesdays, but the enjoyment was spare. The first week, when she approached the ticket booth, the cashier asked, "Oh, just one today?"

*From now through eternity, just one,* Archer thought, but aloud she said, "Yes, just one, thank you."

Several days after Connor left, Archer resumed her morning runs. For a few weeks she consciously avoided the route by his campsite, but it was the best and prettiest trail, so she began to use it again. The first day she ran by, she was stunned to see the daffodils he had planted greeting her in their bright yellow finery.

"Well, I'll be damned," was all Archer could say as she stopped to take it in. "Connor's garden."

She wanted to call him and tell him, but he wouldn't want to hear from her. When something isn't working, it's "on to the next play," he used to say. She was something that wasn't working.

That afternoon, Archer went into town to pick up her mail from her post office box. For weeks now, she had hoped for a letter from Connor. She doubted he would call, but he might send a note at least, maybe renew his invitation to join him.

But after a month of disappointments, she discarded that dream as well. Love did not conquer all, and fate would not make it all come out happy. Fate also could make things come out ugly and mean. She, of all people, should know that by now. At most, shards of happiness were what she must gather and cherish—mere shards to pick over in her dotage.

Archer waved to the postmaster, slid the little key into the slot, and pulled the door open. Inside, she saw a big manila envelope. Pulling it out, she saw Connor's name and address neatly handwritten in the upper left corner. Archer's address was written in the same neat block print, and along one side was written, "*Do not fold—Photographs.*"

After slamming her mailbox shut, Archer sprinted for her car. Hadley greeted her with a snuffle. Archer pulled the door open, got in, and grabbed her reading glasses from an inner compartment of her pocketbook; her hands shook as she put them on. Her mouth was dry. She swallowed hard, slit the sealed flap, and lifted the edge of the envelope.

*Please, please let there be a letter,* she entreated silently, eyes closed, slipping her hand into the envelope. There were three five-by-eight photographs and two four-by-sixes. She stared at each one for a long time.

The five-by-eights were in color. They were unposed, at the

restaurant in Boston. In two of them, Archer and Connor were looking toward the camera, smiling, both radiant. In the third, Archer was still smiling at the couple, but Connor was smiling at her, his eyes soft, keen, in love. How could she have missed it for so long? It pained her to look, but neither could she look away.

Finally, she turned her attention to the other set. The four-by-sixes were black and white. Had the photographer changed cameras? She hadn't noticed. Both showed Connor and Archer raising their glasses in a toast to the elderly couple at the other table. Archer caressed each photo lovingly. Connor. *Do I drive away everyone I love?*

She peered eagerly inside the manila envelope again. There *had* to be a note. There had to be. She shook it out, holding it upside down, and finally a mockingly small note fell out, a two-by-two square of bright yellow paper that said, "Ye of little faith! C."

"That's it?" she cried, staring into the envelope to make sure. "That's it? You've got to be kidding!"

But still, she had the pictures. She held all five close to her, closed her eyes, and sighed deeply. Then she put them back carefully into the envelope and laid it on the seat next to her. She sat quietly for a few moments, then started the engine and headed home.

When she got home, Archer found an old, empty photograph frame in one of the boxes in the basement, dusted it off, and meticulously cleaned the glass. Then she polished the wooden frame with lemon oil and fitted one of the pictures of her and Connor into the mahogany frame. She placed it on the kitchen counter, fussing with its position until she had it right—visible from her reading chair as well as from everywhere in the kitchen.

As for the black-and-whites, she went to her bedroom and got out her sewing box, where she kept a pair of sharp little scissors. She took them out, and with utmost care, she cut herself out of the photo, salvaging only a smiling Connor, which she cut into a smooth oval.

Archer then pulled the sterling locket that Connor had given her from inside her T-shirt, where it rested against her heart. Lifting the chain up and over her head, she opened the locket's tiny clasp and placed the trimmed photo in the empty spot, across from the picture of Annie. The two photos smiled at each other. Archer gazed at them for a long time—regrets enough to go around here, too. Then, with a firm snap, she shut the locket and tucked it back inside her shirt.

It was April 30. Archer sat on the front porch of the cabin, feeling the warm sun on her face and sipping her first cup of coffee of the day Hadley lay sleeping beside her. In two weeks, it would have been Annie's eighteenth birthday. *That should be recognized, at least by me,* Archer thought—*and by Adam.* At least by the two of them—her parents.

God, how had life gotten so complicated and screwed up? When she and Adam got married, the year of their graduation from Columbia Law School, life had been so simple. Adam was her soul mate. He was maple syrup, green grass just cut, Labrador puppies, vintage Springsteen. Now he lived across the country in Colorado, with two little boys and a wife who wasn't her, and Archer had become a mountain woman with no one. Still, it would be Annie's eighteenth birthday.

After her morning run, Archer walked into the kitchen and picked up her cell phone. She then opened the little drawer where she kept her PDA. It was now nine thirty in the morning—seven thirty in Colorado. Archer still kept Adam under the heading "Family." She tapped out the number, hoping Allison wouldn't answer.

"Hello, hello, MacKenzie wesidence," squawked a child's voice.

"Uh, hi," said Archer. "Uh, is your daddy there?"

"Yes, who are you?" asked the child.

"I'm an old friend of your father's," Archer struggled. What could she say? *I'm the crazy ex-wife? You know, the one that pushed your dad into moving to Denver, marrying your mother, and having you.*

"Daddy, it's an old fend!" the child shouted.

"What, honey?"

"An old feeend!" he shrieked.

"Timmy, pipe down. I think you left out your 'r.' Could it be an old *friend*?"

Archer could hear Adam's voice getting closer, laughing. She had a strong urge to hang up, but he probably had caller ID. She would feel like an idiot and a stalker if he saw she had called and then hung up.

"Hello, Adam MacKenzie."

Adam sounded friendly, slightly hurried, as if he were putting on his tie as he talked, getting ready for work. She could see him now: tousled brown hair, hazel eyes lined from laughing and squinting at the sun, blue shirt, gray flannel suit, club tie, all crisp, stooping to take the phone from his little son…his son.

"Adam, it's Archer."

Silence.

"Adam? Are you there?"

"Uh, yeah. Sorry. I just was sort of stunned. Are you okay, Arch? How are you?" he said, slightly recovered.

"I'm okay. Better. And you?"

"Fine, thanks. I was sorry to hear about your mother. I'm sorry I couldn't make the funeral."

Archer noted that he didn't make any excuses. "It's okay."

There was an awkward silence.

"Well, uh, Adam, I'm calling just to say…uh, to say I'm having a memorial service for Annie—on her birthday—at Asylum Congregational." She was making this up as she went along. She didn't even know if the church hall was available. "I hope you can come."

"Oh, Archer, I don't know. I just…you know, I have the boys, Allison…work is busy. I can't promise. I…I just can't promise." Now he was struggling.

"Well, it's okay," Archer said quickly. "I just wanted you to know. I mean, I would hate for you to hear about the service and think that I didn't let you know."

"Oh, sure, right…" He trailed off.

More silence.

"Well, anyway, it will be at four. You know the date, of course."

"Yeah, I guess I do… Archer, I'm so sorry. I…I wish it had all turned out differently," he stammered.

"I know. Me, too," Archer said. And she quietly hung up the phone.

# CHAPTER
# 28

Lauren Giordano moved briskly around the kitchen, getting break-fast for herself and her little brother, Joey. Cereal, milk, orange juice. It was an ordinary Saturday in late winter—except that it was anything but ordinary. She was to meet her father today—her real father—and she was scared.

At nine years old, Lauren was thoughtful, serene, intelligent, and kind. She knew all about her "real" father—well, at least, as much as her mother knew. She loved Donald Giordano, and he was her daddy. But whenever a Christmas package or birthday card arrived from New York or London or Tokyo, or Jackson Hole, Wyoming, with that square, clear printing, her heart speeded up as she opened the envelope or undid the wrappings and tape. She tried to pretend she wasn't thrilled with whatever Connor had sent—the last thing she wanted was to hurt Daddy's feelings.

"That's nice, Lauren, isn't it?" her mother would say as Lauren held up a book, a DVD, or a sweater. Daddy would frown and make grumbling noises.

"It's okay," she would say to her mother, but inside, her heart was singing. She stifled her glee so Dad wouldn't decide the packages had to stop.

"Look at that," Donald would grouse, gesturing loosely. "It's *enormous*. Does he even remember how old she is?" Or "My God, look at that. It's so small. Does he think she's still a baby? Send it back."

Lauren never sent anything back. She cherished everything Connor sent, even the smallest, reserving her bottom dresser drawer to house them all. She kept the silver whistle from London, the colored map of Tokyo, the funny-looking bumper sticker in Greek lettering with no to clue what it said, and the Twin Towers snow globe from New York City, so poignant now that the real towers were gone. He never called on the phone, and he never sent any pictures. Neither did she. She had heard her daddy say once, "He doesn't deserve pictures of her if he's too damn lazy to get out here and see her himself."

The only picture she had of him was taken when Connor and her mother worked together at General Technology in Chicago. Both were pictured in the company manual: Sarah smiling broadly at the camera, Connor unsmiling, handsome, intense. Lauren had carefully cut the page from the book in her mother's bookcase and put it in the bottom of her desk drawer. Had they been in love then? Did he think about her much? Did he ever want to get to know her? His notes with the money were nice, but they didn't say much, and she had never heard his voice.

Her daddy hoped he would never visit—he never said it, but she knew. She'd heard him and her mom argue sometimes about Connor. Daddy said he was useless and they didn't need his money. Mom said there was no reason to cut Connor out, since he was doing a fine job of staying on the outside all by himself. Mom said Lauren needed to have that gap in her family history filled, and she needed at least to know that her natural father was out there and had an interest. Daddy snorted, then turned back to his newspaper.

Lauren knew that her mother had won by attrition. Daddy had just stopped talking at that point. She liked the way Connor looked in the one photo she had. She liked the way he wrote his notes to her—not like a father exactly, but like someone who, while busy in the world, still was interested in her.

But now, with him coming, would he be disappointed? Would he want a prettier or smarter daughter? Or one with dark hair instead of dirty blond? She was pretty ordinary, she thought, pretty average. She hoped he would like her and would want to come back. She thought she would like him. She *wanted* to like him.

Connor stopped at a Holiday Inn about an hour east of Chicago to shower and change. The desk clerk nodded knowingly when he said he only needed the room for a few hours. Connor had tried to take a nap but slept little. He calmed his hair, which was longer than usual, by running his hands through it with some water. He tried his hat on, then off, then back on, scowled at his reflection in the mirror, and then closed the motel door behind him, leaving the key on the bedroom side table.

He parked the truck and trailer at the saltbox home in a pretty development outside Chicago at two on a Saturday afternoon. He peered at the number on the house and, satisfied that this was it, got out. He had considered bailing out more than once. Then he'd thought of Archer and of Annie.

Connor had no idea what a nine-year-old girl liked, but he did know what a horsewoman liked. He had brought the latest issue of *Practical Horseman*, some apple treats for Lauren's favorite pony, whoever that might be, and a bright pink halter.

Trying not to betray his nervousness, he walked up the path to the house and knocked on the door. He waited. Maybe he got the date wrong and they were out. As he turned to look at the adjacent homes, the door behind him opened. Connor turned quickly. His heart jumped, and he smiled.

He was facing a small but elegant girl: long blond hair pulled back in a braid, pierced ears with a small pearl in each, almond-shaped, wide-set blue eyes, and a warm smile. *She's beautiful*, he thought as he stepped into the front hall. *She's wonderful.*

"Hi. I'm Lauren." She held out her small hand. Connor took it in his, still reeling from the thrill of it all, and shook it. *A nine-year-old who knows how to shake hands? Well done, Sarah.* He wanted to stoop down and hug her. Instead he said, "Hi, I'm Connor."

From behind Lauren, a woman hurried up, smiling broadly.

"Connor! You look wonderful! How have you been? Come on in." Sarah looked motherly in a long black corduroy jumper and gray waffled cotton shirt. A little boy peeked out from behind her leg.

"Hello, Sarah! And, Joey, look at you—a big boy already!" Connor exclaimed, giving Sarah a big hug and a kiss on the cheek. "You look great, Sarah, really great, and happy."

"Well, yeah, I guess I am," she said, laughing and smoothing her bouncy hair. "And you, you look the same except no gray pinstripe suit. The jeans and boots suit you, Connor. I mean it."

"Well, thanks."

Lauren stood shyly on Sarah's other side, curious.

"Well, Connor, I've told Lauren all about you over the years," Sarah said. "Lauren, why don't you show Connor your room, and then we can talk a while down here."

"Okay," said Lauren, smiling and motioning for him to follow her.

The stairway was lined with pictures of Sarah and Donald; Sarah, Donald, and Lauren; Lauren and her little brother, Joey; just Joey; just Lauren. At the top of the stairs, Lauren led him to a small, tidy, lilac-colored bedroom.

"This is it. Not much to it, actually."

"I think it's great," said Connor. "I see you have some blue ribbons of your own already."

"Yeah, well, they weren't really big horse shows or anything, but Mom said I could lease a horse next year, and Dad said…" Lauren stopped.

"Lauren, it's okay. Donald is your dad. I…I just want to be something. I don't know where I can fit in or if you even want me to fit in anywhere. But let's see, okay?"

"Okay," Lauren said solemnly, "but what should I call you?"

"Connor. Connor is fine."

They walked downstairs together, talking about horses and shows. The front door was still open.

"What's in your trailer, Connor?" Lauren asked, spying it curiously.

"Millie, my ranch horse."

"You mean you took her all the way to *Massachusetts* with you?" she asked in amazement.

"Sure did. And my dog's out there, too—right there in the front seat."

As if on cue, Alice sat up in the front seat and turned her woolly head toward the house.

"What's that?" asked Lauren.

"That's Alice, my dog, although she's more than that. I think she takes great offense when I call her my *dog* instead of my best friend."

Lauren laughed. "Mommy! Connor has a horse and a dog out there. They came east all the way from Wyoming, and now they're going back. Can I go out and see them?"

"Why not?" said Sarah, smiling.

Connor noted that Donald was nowhere to be seen, but he didn't have time to worry about it, for Lauren was already out the door and heading for the trailer, with Joey trying to keep up.

Connor headed out, laughing to himself. He was sure Millie would become the talk of the street for a week or so after this little circus. He hoisted Lauren up on Millie's bare back, but not before putting a serious bit in her mouth in case Millie got the idea to head into Chicago for a little shopping. Millie was a great horse, but even she knew when she could play a little joke.

A crowd of kids gathered around Lauren and the sturdy mare. Joey followed Alice, who was just about his height, sometimes grabbing her collar and being pulled along by her heft. This parade went up and down the block. Other kids got to ride after Lauren, and the children seemed to be multiplying, Connor noticed. Millie became the center of attention, taking over the entire visit. Connor breathed a sigh of relief as he led another youngster up the street. It made for a simple, easy way for him to get to know this girl. He'd been right—she was a horsewoman. The afternoon ended gaily with promises of future visits.

Before he left, he bent down and gave the little girl a big hug. She hugged him back fiercely. Though he hated letting go, he finally did. He held her at arm's length and looked at her. *I may not deserve her,* he thought, *but I'm going to try to be worthy.*

Connor's last view of Lauren was of her waving wildly, surrounded by the other kids. Sarah's arm was over her shoulder, and she, too, was waving—less wildly and with an uncertain smile on her face.

*I can't expect more than that,* he thought.

# CHAPTER

# 29

May 15 was a gorgeous spring day. Archer woke early and felt rest-less. The preparations for the service had been fairly simple. She had spoken to the Reverend Stone and explained her thoughts to him: some music that Annie liked, some daisy and mum bouquets on the altar, a few words of remembrance, and that was it.

The Reverend Stone checked the schedule and told Archer that the main sanctuary was available and the smaller chapel was also free. Archer chose the chapel—small, intimate, old, granite. There would be few people, and the gathering would look puny and sad in the vast main sanctuary with its vaulted ceiling. Archer had told her family, Annie's old friend Sophie, and a few colleagues. She expected perhaps nine or ten people at most.

Archer dressed with much forethought. Annie had always liked red, so she wore a black sleeveless sheath with a red sweater. She began the drive into Hartford at about two o'clock, using the back roads instead of the highway.

She arrived at the church on Asylum Avenue at three twenty—too early for her nerves to cope with that much downtime. So she drove into West Hartford Center, where she was surprised to see so many restaurants, cafés, and boutiques. Much had changed in six years. She made a quick tour around the business block but avoided their old house.

Getting back to the church with a much more bearable five minutes to spare, she locked the Jeep and walked hurriedly to the side door that led directly into the front end of the chapel. There she pulled the door handle and stepped inside.

She felt weak at the sight. The chapel was nearly full. In the front two rows, she saw Sharon, Ted, Julie, David, Rachel Cohen, and nine or ten lawyers who were friends or colleagues. Behind them she saw not just Sophie but much, if not most, of Annie's class—or what would have been her class. Sophie's work.

Sophie smiled and waved, and Archer felt a lump in her throat. Tears formed as she looked at all the eighteen-year-olds, here to remember Annie, their bright faces serious and intense.

A quick scan also told her that Adam was not here. She bit down hard on her lip, surprised at how much she had counted on him to show up. Adam was the only person in the world who had loved Annie as intensely as she; it was the first time he had ever let her down.

Stepping to the front row, Archer sat down next to Sharon just as the first sweet notes of Enya's "Wild Child" came wafting through, ethereal and angelic, the strings clear and delicate. From the time she was little, Annie had called Enya the "angel music."

Sharon took Archer's hand and gave it a squeeze. Julie wept silently against her mother. Archer knew that the child could have little independent memory of Annie, yet she understood her sadness. The harp's notes were heartbreaking.

Just then, there was a stir at the back of the chapel. Archer turned, and there he was, herding two little boys into the back pew. Adam's boys were in suits, their blond hair carefully combed into place. They looked awed by the music and solemnity.

A tall blond woman in a smart black suit—Allison, she presumed—

followed Adam into the chapel. Stepping aside to let her into the pew ahead of him, he bent over to whisper something in her ear. She nodded, hesitantly at first, then more vigorously. Adam kissed her cheek and walked to the front of the chapel. He nodded to Archer and slipped into the front pew to stand beside her, tall and handsome.

Archer looked at him and smiled. "Adam…thank you," she whispered. "Thank you so much."

"Yes, Arch. I'm here. Wouldn't have missed this for the world. Annie never let me down." He took her hand, then added, "And you never did, either, Arch. Never. My two girls never let me down." Archer looked down, eyes brimming, and then turned her attention to the service.

She listened to recollections of Annie's friends—a few sad, but most funny. Sophie, now a student at Hartt School of Music in Hartford, was especially touching when she belted out, to organ accompaniment, "This Old Heart of Mine," a Motown favorite of her and Annie. It was a surprising, light touch, the words suiting a situation for which they were never intended. Then Archer went up to the pulpit. She started.

"Sophie, thank you so much for the reminder that we are here for a celebration, not a dirge. Annie would have loved it." She paused a second to wipe away a tear. "You know, an old friend once told me not just to grieve Annie, but to honor her. So today, on her eighteenth birthday, I want to honor her memory, rejoice in her life, and remember only the good and happy things about the past. To be sad would be so ungrateful, and I am nothing if not grateful for every moment I had Annie. As Hemingway said, 'They are not dead, those whom we love…'"

From then on, it was easy. After all, she was talking about her favorite subject in the world. When Enya sang "Adios" at the end, Archer felt she had honored her only child as she deserved to be honored on this, her eighteenth birthday.

# CHAPTER
# 30

Connor paused to gaze out the open barn door toward the horizon. The sunset shone in blue, pink, and orange fire. He shook his head, sighed, and hoisted the last bale of hay up to Felix in the loft.

"That's it, boss. Can't fit any more."

"Well, that's handy, because that's the last bale," replied Connor.

It was early June, hot, and the end of a rugged three months. After his detour to see Lauren, Connor had returned from the Berkshires to find the ranch plodding along in maintenance mode. Ordinarily, he would have been peeved that none of the big projects had advanced in his absence, but now he blessed the abundance of work. The last thing he wanted was time to think.

Shearing had to start as soon as he arrived, certainly before lambing took over. Without the bulk of the extra winter-grown fleece, lambing was easier on the ewes. With the ewes shorn, the barn was substantially roomier—and warmer, too, since their body heat was no longer held in by the wool. Nursing the newborns was easier, too, and the ewes could fit into smaller lambing pens.

For two months after his return, Connor and his crew sheared virtually around the clock—work that would determine the ranch revenues for the year. And the new lambs would guarantee the future. Most days, Connor got up before dawn and worked until dark, ate on the porch, and fell into bed for, at most, six hours of sleep.

He was heartbroken, but self-pity was not in his makeup. Although raised Catholic, he was a Calvinist through and through—work first, grieve later. Life would go on. As much as he understood that Archer's rejection of him was not for lack of love, his pain was depthless. Still, one didn't really *die* of a broken heart. *More's the pity,* he thought.

Jordan Hayes, Connor's pal and the ranch vet, had shown up shortly after his return, to tend to an ailing pregnant ewe. After giving her a shot and a friendly pat, Jordan smiled and said: "She'll be fine."

Connor nodded. "Thanks, Jordan. Felix, put Jezebel out with the rest, would you? Thanks a lot." Felix, breathing easier for the first time since he had found the sheep bleating in distress this morning, herded her out the barn door.

Jordan Hayes was a big, freckled, red-headed man in his mid-forties. His uniform was black jeans, a blue striped shirt, and a flat tweed cap, even in the summer. Born and raised in small-town western Wyoming, he had married a local girl when he was twenty-three. Now he had four daughters, ranging from eight to twenty years old. He called them "the Hayes quartet."

His wife, Lydia, was a tomboy who, often as not, could be found riding horses in the mountains with the older girls or playing hopscotch in the driveway with the younger ones. Domesticity was "not her thing," she had told Jordan straight out before they married. Jordan had just laughed. Most mornings, he threw in a load of laundry, ran the vacuum over the downstairs carpets, and set out lunches for the girls with no complaint before starting his rounds at the neighboring ranches. He was a good talker and an even better listener.

Jordan wiped his hands on a clean white cotton rag, then held out a callused hand to Connor, who responded with a strong shake and then a bear hug.

"I really missed you, Doc. It's tough to find anyone in Massachusetts who knows what to do when the sheep stampede."

"What can I say?" Jordan teased, returning the hug. "It's a dying art. Good to have you back in town, old man. Thought you'd left us for good—the seductiveness of civilization, and all that. Heard you had courting on your mind."

"Yeah, well, reports of my courting are greatly exaggerated," replied Connor. He hesitated, then said, "It actually was a pretty painful stretch. I thought I really found someone who...well, I thought I really found someone. It was magical, but..."

Jordan waited. Connor led the way to his office in the back corner of the barn. Once there, he collapsed into his desk chair while Jordan sank heavily onto the green leather sofa.

"Archer—that's her name—is complicated. Somehow it all worked, at least for a while, but I guess we couldn't translate what we had up there in isolation into everyday living." Connor gave a sad smile.

"Anything I can do, Mac? Much as I sometimes gripe about Lydia and the girls, they keep me centered, you know? It's the best thing in the world to find a true partner for life—makes all this craziness seem like it's worthwhile. How are you holding up?"

Connor shrugged. "Oh, I don't know, Jordan. I'm working hard, trying not to dwell on it. It was a blow, though. I never felt so helpless in my life, like I couldn't go forward but couldn't go backward, either. Mostly, I felt tpretty sad—still do."

"Sounds like depression to me. Seein' anyone for that?"

"No, but if you vets have any remedies for a lovesick ram, let me know," Connor joked. "Look, I'll get over it. It takes some time. It's just that I was happier than I've ever been in my life, and that affected everything I did. I smiled all the time, if you can believe that. I thanked people for selling me a newspaper, getting me a coffee. I loved grocery shopping, for God's sake, because it meant dinner with *her*. And now, it's just...well, real empty."

"Jeez, Mac. I'm really sorry." Jordan pushed back into the sofa. After a few moments of thought, he said, "Okay, here it is, best advice

I can give you: don't let a true love go without a fight. I don't know how it ended between you and her, but *the one* doesn't happen twice. Forget that 'other fish in the sea' crap. There's the *one*, and when she crosses your path, you better grab on and hold her. Lydia's family was dead set against our marriage, but we knew. We eloped and never looked back. If you know, don't accept less—fight for it."

Connor looked down, studying his hands.

"Yeah, well, it's not that simple with Archer. She has issues."

"All that means is she's a woman. Hey, come to dinner tonight, why don't you? I picked up some steaks in town this morning. Lydia's looking at colleges in Montana with Karen. We can throw back a few and catch up."

"Thanks, Jordan. Some other time."

Felix and the hands noticed the change in their boss. He was quieter and often seemed lost in thought. On the few occasions they could convince him to join them after work at the Hangout, he spoke little, had just a beer or two, and excused himself early.

One of the waitresses, Charlotte, was sweet on him, and he used to joke with her regularly and raucously when she flirted. Pre-Archer, he had taken Charlotte to the movies a few times and, after a rather drunken New Year's Eve party, had slept with her. Now he barely noticed her playful suggestions.

In their way, the hands were alarmed. They counted on Connor's demanding perfectionism, and now he sometimes let things slide. They shook their heads and mumbled, confused. It was as if their exacting teacher now accepted mediocrity without a wince. And then that photograph showed up.

The envelope arrived in his big mailbox at the end of the half-mile driveway in late April. Connor had just finished a dinner of scrambled eggs, bacon, and toast, with Alice eating half the toast. In the off-season, he would have tacked up Millie and ridden out for the mail. In season, horse and man got more than enough saddle time, so he and Alice took the pickup for the mail.

The evening sky was deep cerulean blue with a scattering of puffy clouds. Connor stopped the truck at the driveway's end and got out slowly, stiffly, to open the box. He expected the usual bills, advertisements, and bank statements, and the usual was there all right, but sticking out prominently was a large yellow envelope, stiff and unbending.

He pulled out the mail all at once, and the large envelope slipped from his grasp and hit the ground. Stooping to pick it up, he saw that it had been forwarded from his post office box in Lenox. He read the upper left-hand corner:

ROBERT BIONDI
Photography Studios
363 Commonwealth Avenue
Boston, Massachusetts 23464

Connor stared at the packet for a moment, then chuckled ruefully to himself. "Beautiful timing…just beautiful."

Connor threw the mail on the floor in front of the passenger's seat and drove back to the house. Dropping the bundle on the front hall table, he hung up his hat, then picked up the pile of mail again, pawing through it to remove any bills. Stepping over to the trash bin in the kitchen, he tossed the rest and climbed the stairs to bed, Alice following closely behind.

Connor's alarm clock rang at 4:30 a. m. For the hundredth time he wished he had gotten one of those CD alarm clocks—at least then he could wake up to Ella Fitzgerald, Vivaldi, or Sinatra. He folded the blankets back and ruffled the curly fur on Alice's thick neck.

"Come on, old girl," he said. "Another day."

He threw on his jeans, a warm turtleneck sweater, and a fleece jacket and headed down the stairs. Alice, not wanting to miss a thing, got up with a grunt and ambled down after him. In the kitchen, Connor opened the cupboard and took out his favorite mug, the ceramic one with a blue cow on it and "The End" written on the inside bottom, and filled it with coffee, thanking God for timers on coffeepots. Then he took his mug, grabbed a woolen throw for his shoulders, and went out to sit on the porch rocker. It was still dark outside and darn cold, but he took pleasure in looking out on his own land, which extended as far as he could see in every direction.

In an hour, it would be light enough to work. He rocked, sipped his coffee, and wondered what Archer was doing now. It was already almost seven at the cabin. Maybe she missed him. He had hoped she would call, maybe write. But nothing. Then he knew, it was over. At the end of his life, in a little compartment, would be his six months with Archer. No more, no less. Just six months, in a box all by itself.

Connor stood up and stalked back into the kitchen. He opened the cupboard under the sink, pulled the yellow envelope out of the trash bin, and brought it back out to the porch. He should at least look at the pictures. After all, the photographer *had* sent them as promised, much to his surprise.

He turned the packet over and peeled up the flap. It tore, and he ripped the top open. Inside was a small stack of photos.

"Alice, if you could only get my glasses for me," he commented to the black, hairy hulk lying at his feet. Alice looked up at him and wagged her stump at the sound of her name.

He got up and went into the front hall to get his glasses, then came back out and sat down. The first set of photos was in color. There were three poses. The first showed him and Archer raising their glasses to the anniversary couple. God, she was beautiful!

Connor sighed and shuffled on to the next photo. It was similar to the first, but their smiles were wider, more vibrant, more full-faced.

He flipped to the third pose and stopped breathing for an instant. Jesus! Was he that transparent? In that view, Archer was still facing forward, looking at the elderly couple, but he was looking at her. His eyes were soft, bright, totally in love. No mistake. Did one person *always* love the other more in a relationship? Was it ever equal? He wondered. Talk about capturing a moment in time!

He flipped to the next set of photos: two poses in black and white. Both were full-front views, less candid, with both him and Archer aware of the camera and playing to it. They looked happy. He sighed. She was something.

Connor put the photos back in the envelope and let it rest in his lap. Did he need this memory? He leaned back in the rocker and closed his eyes. Maybe he should return east and pick up where he left off. But he had a business, with others depending on him. And even if he could get away, Archer was still haunted—nothing had changed. She would resent his interfering with her warped idea of penance, which would doom their love. It would be unbearable to have things turn ugly, to turn something beautiful, though fleeting, into something tortured and ugly. *That* he couldn't survive.

Connor was never one to force a situation. But was Jordan right? Should he fight for her? *No*, he thought, *you can't make someone see things they don't want to see. It's doomed before it begins.* It was all impossible, and it always would be.

Connor got up and took the package inside. He took one copy of the photo of him looking at Archer and returned the others to the envelope. *My finest hour—hah!* he thought. A toast to a feeling as old as civilization—being in love. A cliché. But when it happened to you, it didn't feel like such a cliché anymore. It felt sacred, startling, and brand-spanking-new, all at once. *And it also hurts,* he thought, *and I don't have time for this.* He went upstairs to shower and dress for another day of haying.

The farmhands had assembled at the main barn, ready to work in one of the flat fields to the north. Before his trip east, Connor had always been there first, checking equipment and moving everyone else faster than they wanted to go. Since his return, more times than not, the men were there before him, leaning on the walls, scuffing their shoes, smoking a last cigarette if they thought they could get away with it before Connor arrived. Cigarettes were absolutely forbidden anywhere on the ranch.

"So, what do you make of it, Felix?" asked Jake, a nineteen-year-old with a long blond ponytail halfway down his back. "You know him best. Don't you think he's really weird since he got back? What'd he say to you?"

"Nothing. He just stares a lot and looks kind of dreamy. And then, he has that picture of him and that woman, the one who answered the phone out there. He's all dressed up in the picture—hardly looks like him, but it is. Sometimes when I'm coming up to the office I'll look in and see him just staring at it. Then he sighs and shakes his head, and that's it—nothing else."

"Did he say anything about her? I mean, any fool can see he's hurting. Anyone know a good therapist? When I lived in L.A., they were on every corner. Maybe we could do like…you know, an intervention kind of thing. Make him get some help."

In unison, every head turned to look incredulously at Jake for a second—eyes narrowed, heads shaking, no words necessary—then back at Felix.

Felix continued. "I asked him once who she was, and you know what he said? He said, 'A dream. She was a dream.' Then he just went back to work. Nothing else. Isn't that weird? A *dream*? She's right there in the picture! I mean, yeah, he just meant she's dreamy or something like that, but sometimes he talks in riddles, you know? He's always been strange, but not this strange. I thought maybe he'd perk up after a while, but it's been months."

"Hey, shut up, here he comes," someone said.

Connor's truck pulled up to the barn. He clattered to a dusty stop, opened his door, and stepped out. "Hey, let's go, ladies. What is this, a coffee klatch? We've got to finish that field and get everything up in the loft today. Rain's coming tomorrow...let's move it. John, Caleb, Bob, Tony, Big John, George, Josh, Kit, you go with Felix. Joe, Cal, Gregorio, Todd, and Edwardo, you come with me. Let's hit it."

# CHAPTER
# 31

Connor sat on an airplane on his way to Edinburgh, Scotland. It was July. Shearing and lambing had been over for several months. Sales and contracts had to be firmed up and business expanded, if possible. He was thinking of hiring a farm manager—something he wouldn't have dreamed of a year ago. He'd been a control freak all his life. Now...well, he still cared, but it was different. Sure, the guys noticed, and he knew it bothered them, but he couldn't help it.

Then there was the photo. They couldn't seem to keep their hands and eyes off that photo.

Connor had positioned it on his desk, tucked discreetly behind his phone, with piles of books and papers obscuring it. These guys, who wouldn't have noticed an eight-foot grandfather clock with neon hands and a fifty-decibel gong, suddenly had acquired the most acute powers of observation. They had noticed the photo in no time and couldn't seem to get enough of it. It wasn't enough that they looked at it; there usually was some running commentary accompanying the viewing.

"Nice tie, Mac."

"Now, where was this taken, Mac?"

"Is that a tuxedo or a dinner jacket, Mac?"

"That your girlfriend, Mac?"

"How'd you meet her, Mac?

"Why didn't she come back here with you?"

"Did she dump you, Mac?"

Some would actually pick up the photo, turning it this way and that, going to the window to view it in better light, until Connor would finally grab it back.

"Her name's Archer, and she lives back East in the Berkshires."

When the man would look blank, Connor would say, "Massachusetts. You know, where Boston is? Celtics? Patriots? Red Sox?"

"Oh, yeah, sure, I know Massachusetts, Mac. I'm not ignorant, you know. It's near New Jersey, right?"

"Not really," Connor would mutter under his breath.

After two months, everyone in the county knew that Connor had a photo of a woman named Archer in his office, and half of them had found an excuse to stop in and see it. The other half got a full report on it; then they talked more. Though Connor saw through the pretense, he figured it was part of small-town life.

"She looks pretty nice, don't you think?" said Ray, who ran the feed store.

"Yeah, and Connor looks gone on her," replied Charlotte, working the lunch shift at the diner.

"Yeah, but where is she? Why didn't she come back out here with him?"

"Maybe she didn't want to live on a ranch. Some women don't."

"I think there's some secret, Felix said to anyone who would listen. "Something happened, and Mac's not inclined to talk about it."

Connor landed in Edinburgh on a Monday and found the city bustling. It was odd doing business on the Fourth of July, a day he associated with barbecues, picnics, and swim parties. He had a room at Gleneagles in Perthshire. He had stayed there before and liked it well enough, though he usually found that a simple B and B met his needs just fine.

Gleneagles was in a beautiful rural setting, with four restaurants, shops on the premises, several world-class golf courses, and stables. Although Connor played no golf and cared little for shopping, a few days of anonymity with some pampering at this full-service resort trumped the cozy but chatty ambience of a bed and breakfast.

After checking in, he changed into jeans and headed down to the barns. They were clean and professionally managed. Connor hoped a few riders were still in the arena, working their horses.

As he entered the lobby, a young woman called out in a heavy Scottish brogue, "Sir, are you a guest of the hotel?"

"Ah, yes, I am," said Connor, digging into his pocket for his key and approaching the counter. He showed it to the woman—Jane, according to her name tag—and she noted it on her pad.

Smiling, she nodded. "Go right in, sir. Have a nice stay."

Connor pushed open one of the stable doors and ambled down the concrete aisle. Horses nickered, and some hung their heads out to sniff at him. He stopped to pat one on the nose.

In the indoor arena, he leaned forward against the half-wall separating spectators from riders and took off his Stetson, resting it on the ledge as he watched. There were only three riders, but they were impressive. One young man took several four-foot jumps with ease and grace. A teenage girl skillfully managed a feisty thoroughbred that tried twice to run off with her. Last was a blond woman in her thirties—tall, willowy, lovely, on a sleek chestnut warmblood—prancing in an extended trot to Beethoven's Fifth Symphony on the speakers. All went beautifully until one of the barn workers dashed across the ring to get a shovel, and the chestnut spooked and bolted across the arena. Its rider cursed loudly but stayed on. Catching Connor's look of amusement, she laughed and walked the nervous horse over, holding out her hand.

"So glad you got to see that. Hi, I'm Fiona Ferguson. Please tell me you're the new trainer," she said, leaning forward to shake his hand. Her blond hair curled out from the bottom of her riding helmet, and her blue-green eyes crinkled as she smiled.

Connor shook her hand. "Hi. Connor McCall," he replied. "And no, I'm truly sorry to say I am not your new trainer, ma'am."

"Well, you are clearly not a Scot" Fiona noted, leaving it unclear whether that was a good or a bad thing.

"I'm from Boston, Massachusetts, in the States…well, actually I'm now from Wyoming, out west. Are you a guest here, too?"

"God, no. I train here, you know, with Mark Phillips. He's not here too much, but he's the best, so…it's my last chance to try for the British Olympic team, so here I am for my second year. This fall is the tryout, so we'll see. I live in a cottage down the road."

"Ambitious goal," Connor commented. "Is that the horse you'll be entering?"

"Oh, God, no! This is a green prospect for next year or the year after. Good horse—just needs some mileage and seasoning. She's still skittish at loud sounds, sudden movements—as you saw—but she's a good girl." Fiona patted the mare on her neck. "Do you like horses?"

"Oh, yes."

Connor and Fiona had dinner that night at one of the restaurants in the hotel. It was fun, and Connor felt good talking, laughing, preening a bit for the beautiful woman sitting across from him. At the end of the evening, he drove her home to her cottage, escorted her to the door, and kissed her cheek, thanking her for a lovely evening.

Fiona smiled up at him quizzically and said, "Well, Boston, do call me or catch me at the barn tomorrow, or I really shall be positively heartbroken."

She went in, and Connor walked back to his car, buoyed by the lovely evening, and drove back to the hotel, where he slept well.

The next day, he drove out to St. Andrews to meet with one of his best clients and discuss the next year's order. The meeting went well, and Connor was pleased, though eager to getting back to Gleneagles.

Arriving there, he changed and hurried down to the barn, where he saw Fiona riding a gray horse. When she spotted him, she waved and cantered over.

"You gave me a moment of insecurity, you know, Boston. Thought I'd lost all my charm," she said, walking the big gray gelding up to the railing. "I've been riding 'round and 'round all day, you see, hoping you'd stop in. Old Gray Ghost here is positively dizzy. He gave up on you hours ago, but then, I'm more determined. See if *he* makes it to the World Trials."

Connor smiled. "Had to do some business first, unfortunately. Dinner?"

Fiona turned her horse away and squeezed, and as he broke into a canter, she called over her shoulder, "Okay. My house, eight."

Dinner was splendid. Fiona was a good cook. In his honor, she had made roast beef, baked potatoes, and salad.

"Isn't that what you Yanks are always eating in the movies?" she asked with a wink.

Connor smiled. "Only in Hollywood. In real life, we survive on burgers and pizza."

He returned to Gleneagles at midnight, whistling.

The next day, they went to St. Andrews together. Fiona showed Connor where Prince William supposedly roomed, then took him to a small tea shop on a side street for tea and clotted cream with scones. They caught a production of *Hamlet* performed by a university theater group, then drove back to Perthshire singing Scottish ditties.

Connor parked his rented car in front of Fiona's cottage and turned to her. In the moonlight, she looked fresh and pretty. "My dear

Fiona, I have to leave tomorrow for London, then back to Wyoming.
The past few days have been great. I…I've really loved having your
company."

Fiona looked down at her hands for a moment without speaking,
then looked up, black curling eyelashes framing green eyes.

"Will I ever see you again, Connor? Great men who are straight,
available, employed, and love horses are not so very common around
here." The lightness in her voice had a serious edge.

"Sure, you will. I'm in Scotland a couple times a year, and I'll be
watching for you in the Olympics—and, of course, we'll always have
St. Andrews," he quipped.

Fiona looked at him, questioning, head cocked.

"Well, you know how, in *Casablanca*…" but he stopped when he
saw she didn't have a clue what he was talking about. "It's just a little joke.
Forget it. Look, Fiona, you are absolutely terrific. But my life is unset-
tled right now, and I wouldn't want to mislead you, and I just—"

"It's that woman you told me about, isn't it?" Fiona interrupted.

Connor hesitated, then said, "Maybe, in a way. I mean, I haven't
even talked to her in over five months, and I don't think I'll ever see
her again, but…"

"She's in your soul, though."

He looked up from studying his own hands and said, "No, she's
not in my soul. She *has* my soul. I have nothing to give anyone else
until I get my heart and soul back from Archer. That's just the way it
is for right now."

"It's always timing, isn't it?" lamented Fiona, shaking her head.
"Why are the good ones always taken, even when they're not? Anyway,
if you get your soul back, do come looking for me, darling. You know
where to find me, Boston. At the big barn, attached to a big horse."

"You bet I will," said Connor, hugging her good night.

# CHAPTER
# 32

Archer sat on the porch with Hadley. It was the Fourth of July. The morning couldn't have been more beautiful, and her preferred fireworks—fireflies, lots of them—would be out tonight. She held a mug of strong coffee and was rocking slowly in her chair. She and Hadley had arrived home yesterday evening from a few days with Gavin in Boston.

It had been perfect—at least for Archer's purposes. Gavin was relaxed and happy to have her with him. She wanted to chat, catch up on local gossip, and get his feedback on anything and everything. They caught up on shoptalk first.

"So, how's business?" Archer asked as they settled into a corner booth at a local pub, around the corner from Gavin's nineteenth-century condominium in Beacon Hill.

"Architecture is fine and booming. And our…um, other business is clipping along as usual. I was in San Antonio myself three weeks ago. I rarely do jobs anymore, but this one called for my particular talents. After reviewing the file, I decided to take care of it myself." Gavin took a sip of his beer. "You heard about Barry?"

"Yeah," said Archer, sipping her glass of Scotch. "I heard he'd gone somewhat berserk and wanted to do every job you would assign him. Where is he now?"

"We sent him for R and R to the Jennings Institute in Hartford. We have two good contacts there—one who heads intake and one who'll be his therapist. When Barry's released, we'll have to make him an inactive."

"Will he accept that?"

"Yes, he will. He has no choice. We'll have to sit down with him and get him some ongoing help, but he's a good man—just heart-broken. He'll be okay in administration but not in the field…not anymore."

Archer nodded.

"So, what happened to you and Connor? Not that it's any of my business, but, well…what are friends for?" he added a little apologetically.

"Long story, but if you want the *Reader's Digest* version, his life is in Wyoming and mine is here."

"I see," said Gavin, sipping his beer and nodding. "But just for a moment, playing devil's advocate—and not that I want you to move any farther from me—what is so great for you about being here? I mean, they have phones in Wyoming, and they have courts of law in Wyoming, so what's the draw here?"

Archer looked startled. He, of all people, should know. He, of all people, should understand. "*Annie* is here. I have a life at all only because everything about her is here."

Gavin nodded, looking down at the table and fingering the yellow paper napkin under his drink. "You know, Arch, I understand all of it. But, since all of us are in this great waiting room on earth until we can find peace, it's not a betrayal of the cause to get some joy where you can find it." He paused and seemed to aim for a tease, saying lightly, "And Annie's not really just in the Berkshires, you know."

"I know, but…" She stopped, trying to find words, and finally just held her hands up in resignation. "It just plain seems wrong to be happy when Annie is dead and I'm not."

Her hands dropped to her side, and her face fell, beseeching Gavin for an answer that she knew didn't exist.

"Archer," he said, "Annie's death isn't made any less heinous because you survived and find that you can sometimes actually laugh. We don't forget what happened; we just know we have to go on. And since there's no great honor in killing ourselves, we go on. Think about this. Why do you do this thing that we do? Have you ever asked yourself that? Do you do it for vengeance?"

Archer thought for a moment, then said, "At first I did, but not now. Now I do it because I think it's right. I feel sad every time I do a job, but I also feel like someone who is totally innocent may get some closure and a piece of life back because of what I did."

"Yeah, I know what you mean," said Gavin, looking thoughtful. "But, Archer, even though you know I wish it could be with me, life does go on, and love makes it tolerable. It's the *only* thing that makes it tolerable. To throw away a real shot at love seems…oh, I don't know, *arrogant* maybe. Or wasteful. I don't know, but it's just not something to squander. At least, that's how I see it."

Archer nodded slightly, head cocked to one side, but felt unconvinced. She remained silent as she took another sip of her drink.

"Look, Arch, we do this because we believe there are failures in the justice system, right? That justice wasn't done. But we have our *own* failures. I'm not so blinded that I don't see that piece of it. Barry's situation isn't common, but it's pretty predictable, wouldn't you say? For someone whose grief has exploded all bounds and has no other outlet? And our work didn't spare Katharine from killing herself. To dull the pain is one thing, but you've got to have some positive counterbalance in your life. You've got to give yourself permission to look at the other side, even though in some ways it feels disloyal. If you don't, it's all negative and you can never heal."

They both sat in silence for a moment.

"And what do *you* have, Gavin? What's your counterbalance?"

He took a sip of beer, wiped his mouth with the napkin, and

grinned. "Hey, I have you. You give me faith, Arch, that there's still beauty and goodness out there."

Archer looked at him, then laughed. Gavin took her hand, kissed it lightly, and then motioned to the waiter to bring the check. "Hey," he said, "let's take Hadley for a walk before catching that movie, okay?"

"Great," she said, standing up and leaving her glass half full. "I'm doing a job in New York in two days, so I'll need to leave kind of early this afternoon—have to review the particulars when I get back."

"No problem."

They had had a lighthearted break, for the most part. Good food, good conversation, lots of laughter. It was so weirdly sad. Both of them had been parents; both had once been part of a couple, part of a family. Now she and Gavin were singles—unwilling, childless singles rattling around the world, clanking against each other, hoping to find something to fill the void until their own deaths. Did that mean they believed in God, in some concept of heaven? That they would see their loved ones someday bursting through St. Peter's gate?

Archer shook her head at that one but was unwilling to reject the notion out of hand. Still, she didn't want to count on God to carry out justice. She laughed ruefully at herself. She'd never been good at delegating, even to God, but it was the height of arrogance to think she and the Group could balance the scales better than God.

The Group—it had been her salvation, her god, for the past six years. She had thought long and hard before becoming involved—after all, it was hardly like joining the PTA or the Smith Alumnae Club. Though not an irreversible choice, it was certainly a life-altering one.

Outsiders would call them vigilantes—or worse—and Archer had long since stopped being defensive about it in her own mind. It had helped her to recover somewhat; indeed, it was the *only* thing that had helped. Not the Valium, not the Zoloft, not the shrinks, not even the group therapy. The Group alone had helped. After her first job, she had stopped cutting herself.

Still, Gavin was right. Katharine and Barry hadn't been cured by Old Testament justice. Their losses hadn't been lessened, or their burden lifted; they had self-destructed. Maybe she could find something else. Or could she?

# CHAPTER
# 33

A rcher had reviewed her instructions before leaving the cabin. She had the essentials memorized. The job was straightforward. She didn't need a hotel room; she was driving down and back in a rental car and taking her equipment with her. She did take the precaution of a disguise, however. Even in New York, a hospitable domain, she could take no chances.

At ten a.m., she set out for Springfield, Massachusetts, to pick up a rental car. She left the Jeep at the cabin and got a ride to the bus station from Jenny, explaining that the Jeep needed new brakes and that she was meeting a friend for lunch in Springfield. If something happened to her, she didn't want her car found at the bus station.

When Jenny dropped Archer off at the bus station in Lenox, she didn't see Archer slip into the ladies' room, and she certainly didn't see her emerge as an attractive Eurasian woman with straight black hair, dark eyes by virtue of colored contact lenses, pale skin made paler with the help of ivory make-up, and clear red lipstick. She wore fashionably narrow black pants, high patent leather heels, and a black cotton long-sleeved T-shirt. A shiny silver necklace held a modern free-form medallion close to her neck.

In Springfield, under the name of Lily Takata of Burlington, Vermont, Archer rented a Ford Taurus from a Hertz agency next to the train station. She drove to New York, reviewing her assignment in her head. The specifics were as bad as any crime she'd ever heard of—actually worse than most.

Gerald Jerome had been arrested two years ago, along with his wife, Antoinette, for torturing their two adopted children, leaving one dead and the other severely retarded from chronic malnutrition and physical abuse. The Jeromes were upper-middle-class professionals; he was a criminal defense lawyer, and Antoinette had worked in an advertising agency.

The problem was that Antoinette, known to her friends as Toni, was the primary witness against her husband. She was implicated as a coconspirator but also clearly had suffered his abuse herself. The broken bones and the bruises on her legs and back all bore witness to her own victim status. However, Toni had hanged herself in her jail cell a year after the arrests. Once she was dead, Gerald pointed the finger at Toni, claiming it was all her doing—that he was at worst a passive participant and that Toni had been the evil mastermind.

While Toni had written a detailed statement before her death, detailing Gerald's abuse of Lee, their little girl, Gerald's lawyer had successfully suppressed the statement's admissibility, arguing that he could not cross-examine a dead woman. He argued that Toni's statement, now incapable of being properly challenged, was so prejudicial to Gerald's right to a fair trial that it had to be thrown out. While corroborating evidence from neighbors and teachers noted Lee's bruises, without Toni the other statements were only thin suggestions of wrongdoing, with little clear connection to Jerome. The meat of the case was gone, and with Lee and Toni both dead, so was the case. Without more evidence, the judge said he had no choice but to set Jerome free. Several days later, to great public outcry, he walked down the courthouse steps, a scowl on his pudgy face, but a free man all the same.

Archer had scouted the site a few weeks earlier and quickly concluded that her preferred long-distance shot was not in the cards this time. Gerald Jerome lived in a brownstone on the Upper East Side, with no yard, no public hallways, and no easy access except directly from the street. He worked in a high-security high-rise on Broadway with just one way in and out. There was no patio that he routinely lounged on; he took cabs from his front door, not subways; there was no vacant building nearby. This would have to be a close-up.

Archer studied the photo of Jerome one last time. At fifty-three years old, he was bald and clean-shaven, had large, bulging dark eyes, and was build like a fire hydrant. Archer smiled slightly to herself. Finally, Mr. Jerome would have the opportunity to pick on someone his own size.

Archer sat in Starbuck's, nursing a cappuccino. Looking at her watch, she took the last swallow and headed out into the street, hoisting her duffel over her shoulder as a middle-aged couple strode past, arm in arm. Today she was an employee of United Parcel Services, still Eurasian but dressed in dark brown. Her other clothes were a few blocks away, in the trunk of the rental car.

Archer walked the two blocks to East Eighty-third Street, between Second and Third Avenues. It was quiet, pretty, and tree-lined. She strode down the sidewalk, passing Jerome's brownstone on her left as she waited for a man in a Mercedes to pick up his dinner date at the next building over. When the Mercedes pulled away, she turned back and walked toward the Jerome brownstone, a small empty package under her arm. She climbed the steps, her heart speeding. *Okay, focus,* she reminded herself. *It's just another job. Think of those kids.*

At the door, she glanced at the name plate: *Gerald and Antoinette Jerome*. She knocked heavily on the door. Within a second, a raspy voice called out.

"Who's there?"

"UPS package for Gerald Jerome."

"Leave it at the door. I'm just out of the shower."

"Sorry, can't do that, sir. I need a signature."

The voice turned nasty. "Oh, for Christ's sake, all right. I'll be right there."

Archer set the empty package aside and waited a moment. Then, as she heard the lock on the door click, she coiled, ready to spring. As soon as the door cracked, she cocked her leg and thrust with all her might, slamming the door's edge into Jerome's forehead. His eyes opened wide, and he gazed at Archer for a split second, total under-standing in his eyes, before teetering crazily back on his heels. He careened backward, slamming into a wall, then bounced forward. With effort, he steadied himself.

Archer then made a fatal mistake. She looked at Jerome, one hand in the pocket of his white terry robe, bulging eyes wild. She hesitated for just an instant, but it was all the time he needed. Lurching forward, he pulled a small handgun from his robe pocket and fired twice. At the same instant, Archer dove to the floor in an aikido roll, which turned her around to face him. A quarter second later, she had taken a two-handed aim and fired one shot back, into the center of his forehead.

Jerome wavered for a moment, grabbed the end of a table, overturning it, and toppled heavily forward. He grunted, then was still. Archer allowed herself perhaps a second to rest, then moved to her knees, crawling to him, knowing he was dead but needing to be certain. She reached for his wrist, turned it over, and felt for a pulse. Nothing. She pressed a finger to his neck. No pulse.

Then, for the first time, she was aware of the pain in her side, and the growing maroon stain on the brown UPS shirt. She had been hit by at least one of Jerome's bullets. *Okay, focus*, she commanded herself, already feeling her strength begin to ebb. She looked around the room. If she were going to die, it wasn't going to be in this place of perversion, where children had been fodder for a monster's sick fantasies. *God damn it, get up!* She righted herself unsteadily, feeling faint, and grabbed the back of the sofa to lean on. She had to get out of here with some passing resemblance to a UPS delivery person.

She could hear neighbors' voices and doors opening. She had a suppressor on her gun, but Jerome hadn't—the sound must have carried to every apartment in the building.

Archer scanned the room…no prints—she still had her gloves on. No hairs—the wig took care of that. No hand-to-hand struggle, so nothing of her under Jerome's nails. Blood? She inspected the room at a glance. Only Jerome's—hers was confined to shirt and glove. She had to move *now*. Stumbling to the door, she turned the knob, nudged her head out, and looked both ways. She took a tentative step. A few people were beginning to poke out of doors and windows. It took every ounce of her strength to straighten, stand tall, and move out the front door, doing her level best to assume a normal gait.

Grasping the handrail, Archer edged down the steps and onto the sidewalk. She steadied herself, turned right at the sidewalk, and walked stiffly toward Third Avenue, holding herself together by a thread. At the first opportunity, she staggered into an alley. It was narrow, barely wide enough for a car to pass, and dark. Doubled over, she stumbled as far back as she could into the darkness. As she moved, she peeled off the gloves, tore them to bits, and scattered them while lurching deeper into the gloom.

Archer knew she should keep moving—get as far from this crime scene as she could, move back up to Lexington Avenue, and get to her car—but she didn't have the will. It was that simple. She had reached empty. Instead, she limped to a deep doorway, where she finally was free to tumble to her knees, then eased down onto her side, which was steadily seeping blood. She was having trouble getting her breath. A fatal bullet wound, she knew—just a matter of time now.

She ran down her checklist again. No ID on her. The rental car was in the name of Lily Takata. Dead-end trail there. Her personal car was safely at home. No hotel room to trace. Her revolver had no serial number and was untraceable. All cul-de-sacs. They would eventually discover she was Archer Loh, but nothing would tie her to the Group. It would remain in the clear, its identity safe.

As Archer slumped over to the ground, any pretense at normality gone, she thought she saw a figure in dark blue approach from the street at a walk, then break into a run, and finally stoop beside her. A cool hand gently brushed her brow. It was over for her, she knew, vaguely amused at the cosmic humor—a target enabling her to fulfill her preferred destiny.

Just before she lost consciousness, Archer thought, *Thank God…at last. Merciful God, at last, at last. My turn.*

The NYPD arrived at the scene within seconds. The assistant chief of police, Charlie Caruso, had been heading to a testimonial for a retiring captain when the call came in. Charlie was a popular veteran with twenty-five years on the force, still handsome with black curly hair and pale blue eyes, a born and bred New Yorker from the lower West Side. His car was a block away from the crime scene.

"Hey, Jimmy," he said, "I haven't been to an actual crime scene in over a year. Let's go take a look and show 'em how it's done."

"Sure thing, boss." Jimmy put on the lights, hitting the siren and the gas. Within a minute, they were on East Eighty-third, pulling up in front of the brownstone. It was chaos, with the street blocked off at both ends, with police cruisers and an ambulance crowding the curb. The paramedics were already inside the brownstone, checking the condition of the victim. Neighbors milled about in the street, chatting on the sidewalk: young women with crying babies; men with their hands in their pockets, chatting in low tones; old women clucking and shaking their heads.

One cop called to the crowd in general, "Anyone see a woman leaving this building?"

"Yeah!" yelled an old man leaning on a cane and gesturing in the opposite direction from where Archer had gone. "She went that way." He then turned to the woman standing next to him. "Whoever killed him should get a goddamn medal. I hope they *never* catch her." He crossed himself. "She's a goddamned hero in my book."

The woman nodded grimly and said, "I just hope the sick bastard *did* know what hit him. Anything less is too good for him."

Assistant Chief Charlie Caruso surveyed the scene for a moment. He knew this building for some reason. He checked the address on his car computer and then understood why. Within seconds, he knew that the house belonged to Gerald Jerome, the scumbag child abuser who got off scot-free after killing his daughter and turning his son into a traumatized, severely retarded ward of the state. Not just *killing* his daughter, Charlie recalled. She had been beaten daily for years, tied to a chair for four days once for spilling her milk, burned with cigarettes on her arms and back, left on the kitchen floor with broken bones while Jerome went out for dinner, and finally was found dead after one beating too many. Poor little Lee Jerome. And the little boy hadn't fared much better. Charlie had heard that the poor kid was institutionalized, with a kidney that no longer worked after repeated kicks to the back, and emotional problems.

Suddenly, Charlie blinked, remembering the confidential message on his personal e-mail last night.

"Hey, Charlie, want me to start scouting the neighborhood for the perp?" asked one of the patrolmen, leaning into the car and interrupting his train of thought. "Lady over there seems to think an Asian woman working for UPS ran out of the building around the time shots were heard."

Charlie looked up, then shook his head. "No. Thanks, Scott, but I think I'll take a look around myself. You go in and see if there's any evidence in there. Forensics should be along any minute." He didn't add his customary warning not to touch anything.

"Okay, boss." The officer turned and headed back to the brown-stone.

Charlie stepped out of the squad car, looked right, then left, and headed down the street, flashlight in hand. He noted the three squad cars lining the street, lights flashing. At least three more were on the way. Soon Jerome's apartment and the quiet East Side neighborhood would be crawling with black-and-whites.

Charlie strolled west up East Eighty-third. When he came to an alley, he hesitated, then continued past it, then stepped back and peered into the dusky gloom. He thought he saw a faint shadow near the back of the alley. Drawing his pistol, he headed down the narrow way.

He found her at the alley's dead end—a woman bleeding heavily from her side, apparently from a close-range gunshot wound. Charlie shoved the gun in his shoulder holster, then stooped, and felt her pulse. Dead, he thought at first…but no, there was a faint heartbeat. He rummaged through her pockets. No ID, no wallet. Nothing. She sure as hell had on a brown UPS uniform, though.

He studied the face more closely. She looked Asian, but that could be the eye makeup. As he lifted her body to check for other wounds, the black wig slid, revealing a beige skullcap. He recalled the e-mail again, and finally it added up.

He whipped out his cell phone and speed-dialed a number.

"Gavin? Charlie Caruso here. You have an operative on the East Side tonight?"

"Yeah, I do. One of my best."

Pause. "Well, I think I have her. She's been hit, Gavin—hit really bad—and this place is swarming. She was seen, and someone may be able to ID her."

There was silence for a moment; then Gavin said, "You've got to move her, Charlie. You've got to get her out of there. She can't be taken, not this one. And she can't die." Gavin took a breath, then continued more slowly, "Please, Charlie, I can't lose her. Not this one. I…can't lose her… Okay, here's what I'd like you to do…"

He gave Charlie a contact phone number, which Charlie wrote down on a pad and pen pulled from his inner coat pocket.

"Charlie, she's really special. I…I can't do without her," Gavin said simply.

"I'll *say*, she's special. She eliminated this town's number one slimeball and got out of there with a slug—maybe—two, in her, to boot. By rights, she should be dead on the floor next to Jerome… I'll do everything I can, but I gotta be honest. This is a bad hit. Really bad. I'll keep you posted." He paused. "I'm sorry, Gavin. I really am."

Charlie hung up and dialed another number. "This is Assistant Chief Caruso. I need an ambulance at East Eighty-third yesterday. Gunshot wound. This one has to go to Columbia-Presbyterian."

"Mount Sinai's closer, Chief."

"Well, thank you so much for the geography lesson—me being new in town and all. I know where Mt. Sinai is and where a Hundred and Sixty-eighth is. And I still want Columbia-Presbyterian—you hearin' me okay?" Charlie gave her the number of the building next to the alley.

"Fine. Columbia-Presbyterian," the dispatcher replied, adding under her breath, "dumb, though."

"I heard that. And make it fast."

Finally, he dialed the number Gavin had given him. The line was answered on the first ring. "Hello."

"Dr. Chang? Dr. John Chang?"

"Yes, this is Dr. Chang."

"Sorry to bother you at home, Doctor. This is Charlie Caruso, NYPD. Gavin Kennelly gave me your number. We need you now, Doc, at Columbia-Presbyterian. Gunshot wound to a female operative. It's bad."

"I'm on my way."

# CHAPTER
# 34

For eleven days, Archer drifted in and out of consciousness. Sometimes she dreamed of galloping through the Connecticut woods on Clique, jumping over logs and splashing through brooks. Once she saw Adam waving at her, Annie in his arms, as she arrived home from the office; and once she was back in Syracuse, putting her rifle together blindfolded while someone played Christmas carols on a honky-tonk piano. On the eleventh day, Annie came to her.

"Mommy? Are you okay?"

Archer raised her head a little and opened her eyes. And there she was, poised on the edge of the chair, twelve years old, slim and coltish, wearing faded blue jeans and a dark-green Dartmouth sweatshirt, dark hair pulled back in a ponytail, blue eyes bright, looking just as Archer remembered her.

"Annie…?"

She nodded.

"How…? Are we in heaven?" Archer asked anxiously, trying to blink away the fog.

"I am; you're not. It's not your time, Mommy," she added dismissively. "It wasn't your fault, you know. And he only touched me on the outside, not where it counts. And…don't get mad, Mommy, but don't do that stuff for me. Don't do it in my name. It doesn't help me."

Just as Archer reached out her arm to try to hold Annie, her daughter began to fade, and in her place was Peter Bennett, sitting at his desk. Instead of his usual mug of coffee by his side, he had an enormous martini, which he was stirring with his glasses. He looked up just then and smiled sadly at her, shaking his head.

"Archer, Archer, my dear girl. Did I teach you *nothing* about courage? You gave her life, and you cannot go on regretting that. You've done your part, my dear. Now, let go. It's enough. It's *more* than enough. Let it go."

Dr. Chang had been as good as his word, thought Charlie Caruso. He was standing at the ER entrance, already dressed for surgery, when Charlie arrived in the ambulance. Archer, unconscious, was wearing a large NYPD T-shirt as a minidress, her face devoid of makeup, her thick brown hair pulled back in a ponytail. Dr. Chang did the intake and handled the case personally.

Charlie circulated the story that the lady's father was an old friend of Dr. Chang's, and so he had taken on the case as a favor. Since all gunshot wounds had to be reported, Dr. Chang advised Charlie that based on the trajectory, gun powder patterns, and caliber of bullet, it appeared to be a self-inflicted accidental shot. The story was that the high-strung woman from Westchester had shot herself when she panicked at the approach of a local panhandler. Charlie wrote up his report and closed the case.

Twelve days after Archer's admission to the hospital, she regained consciousness. Sharon arrived with flowers the next morning.

"Arch, you're awake!"

"Yeah, thanks, Shar. I'm feeling okay, actually." Archer looked around furtively. "Shar," she whispered. "I saw her."

"Saw who?" asked Sharon, getting a vase from a cupboard for the flowers.

"Annie. She came here to me last night."

Sharon turned around with her vase of flowers and placed them on the table next to Archer's bed. She smoothed Archer's hair back from her eyes and spoke soothingly, as if to a young child.

"Arch, you've been delirious for days. I'm sure it seemed real to you at the time, but you were just having a dream. You know how real dreams can seem sometimes."

"No, Shar, no. It was Annie. She came and talked to me. I'm serious. It wasn't a dream. She was as real as you are," Archer insisted.

"What did she say?" asked Sharon.

"She said it's okay and she's happy. That I have to go on with my life."

"Hey, see? Now, isn't that just what I've been telling you?"

"Yeah, I know. But it's such a cliché—that life-is-for-the-living stuff and all that. But she looked happy. She really did, Shar. And she was the same funny, caring kid. She said he only touched her on the outside, the part that doesn't matter."

The two sisters sat silently for a few minutes until Sharon broke the silence. "Arch, I know something happened between you and Connor after Christmas, but I still think he'd like to know that you're sick. I'd like to call him."

"I'm not sick. I got shot. There's a difference. But anyway, no. We haven't been in touch at all since he left, and I...I don't want him to come here because he feels sorry for me, or something like that."

"Well, Archer, as I understood the chain of events, *you* rejected *his* offer. In my book, it's your place to contact him."

"Yeah, well, I need to think. I need to rest and think." Archer rubbed her head.

Silence.

"Do you really think you talked to Annie?"

"There's no 'think' about it."

That evening, Sharon got Connor's phone number from information and called Three Chimneys. One of the ranch hands answered and said Connor was away in Scotland. Sharon left her name and number, though she wasn't confident it would reach him anytime soon.

The day Sharon drove her home from Columbia Presbyterian, Archer had asked lightly, "So, Shar, did you ever try Connor's phone number?"

"I did, but he was away on business."

"Oh," was all Archer said.

As August passed, she was able to do a little more each day. She could walk a little farther, carry a few more groceries, survive with fewer naps, and since she had no work, she had a lot of time to think.

She thought about Annie, of course, but now more of her thoughts were good thoughts, happy memories. She thought of Connor, too—how she met him, the fall and winter with him, all they had shared. She ached to pick up the phone and call him, but she was afraid. One thing had changed, though: she wanted to live.

Connor returned to Three Chimneys with orders that would take the ranch through another two years of solid business, with capital to expand the operation. He had stopped in Chicago for a week on the way home. Lauren was on summer vacation, and they had carefully planned some time using e-mails back and forth. Connor had spent three days in Chicago, going to her riding lessons and meeting her friends. For the next four days, he drove with Lauren to a resort for families farther up on Lake Michigan.

They canoed, ate trout cooked on an outdoor grill, and rode bikes along the lakeshore. They also had long talks at dinner about what each of them liked to do on vacation, foods that delighted them, and foods that disgusted them. They talked about favorite colors, a boy Lauren liked, and why girls Lauren's age were sometimes mean. They saw three movies and chatted for hours about what they had seen, what they each thought, and quotes that stuck with them. It was the best trip Connor could have imagined for a man who hadn't met his only child until she was nine.

He thought, as he did often, about Archer. He wondered how she would react to a phone call, but the thought made him sick to his stomach. He had told her that if she didn't come with him, he wouldn't haunt her. She had never asked him to stay in her life on any level. He sighed. Whenever he thought about Archer, he went around the same well-traveled circle. There was no future of any kind. She had made that clear.

When Jake answered the ranch phone, the phone message from Sharon had gone into his head, and he had every intention of writing it down. But then another call had come in, and then a man was at the door saying something about one of the dogs needing to go to the vet, and ten minutes later, Jake looked at the pen in his hand and couldn't recall why it was there.

# CHAPTER

# 35

It was September 5, Archer's birthday. She was forty-four. For her, the fall, not New Year's Day, was the time for organizing and fresh beginnings.

She started to clean the basement. As she did, she found that many things could be thrown out, and began making piles. Definite saves, definite toss-outs, definite maybes. She worked steadily for two days, and after seven trips to the town dump with the definite toss-outs, she started in on the maybes and eliminated half that pile. She hesitated for a moment at the box with the unmarked training manuals from the Group. It was moved to the maybes. After three days of sorting, Archer realized she was packing—packing to leave.

The next week, she called Rachel Cohen to submit her resignation.

"Oh, Archer, do you have to go? You've been a godsend. Is it the money? I can ask for a salary for you. The Center's board meets next month."

"No, Rae, it's not money," said Archer, smiling through the phone line. "The Center gave me more than I gave it. No, I'm going to get him back somehow."

Rachel sucked in her breath. "Oh, my God, you're going to get back your cowboy! Like Scarlett O'Hara. Wow! If anyone can, you can, Arch. Go for it, girl; you go for it."

"Thanks. Wish me luck, and I absolutely will stay in touch. You are the best, Rae." Archer hung up, and as she did, Hartford faded away.

The last card from Peter Bennett arrived two weeks after Archer's forty-fourth birthday. She chuckled when she pulled it from her P.O. box, recognizing Peter's distinctive script.

Old Peter must be slipping, she mused as she climbed into the Jeep next to Hadley. He was never late with anything. He must be, oh, God, about seventy-eight—and she had thought him ancient when she met him twenty-two years ago. *The arrogance of youth,* she chided herself. But the guy never gave up. She would have to give him her new address—when she got one."

She put on her reading glasses and opened the envelope, looking forward to Peter's dry wit. The clipping fell out first. Odd—Peter never sent extras. It was from the *Washington Post,* a few weeks ago. She read:

> *Peter Bennett, 79, of Silver Springs, Maryland, beloved husband of Claire Burnham Bennett, died Friday in a car accident in Cairo, Egypt, where he was working as a consultant for the U.S. Government. Devoted father of Samuel Bennett of Denver, Colorado, and John Bennett of Ames, Iowa, Peter was a loyal civil servant, avid kayaker, and world traveler. Peter will be missed by all who knew him. Donations may be made in his memory to Magdalen College, Oxford University, Oxford, UK.*

Archer refolded the clipping and laid it on the dashboard. She leaned her head back on the headrest and swallowed hard as sorrow and loss washed over her in strengthening waves. Her more recent contacts with Peter had been limited, but they had given her security, continuity, and solace. They made her feel that some things never changed, and could be counted on to be there always. Archer hadn't known that Peter had a wife and sons—he'd never mentioned them. She sat lost in thought for several minutes, then forced herself to go on. She unfolded the note with apprehension. It was handwritten, dated three days ago.

*Dear Archer:*

*It's been a while. I'm sorry to be the one to tell you that Peter died in a "car accident" while in Cairo. I enclose the obit. Peter worked right up to the end. He went the way he wanted to go, boots on.*

*I found this card on top of his desk, ready to go when I cleaned out his belongings, and wanted you to get it. He must have planned to mail it as soon as he got back.*

*I also wanted you to know, Archer, that he never stopped thinking about and caring about you. He once told me if he'd ever had a daughter, he'd want her to be like you. But he said he'd never want her in the business. Too risky. He understood. He really did. But he couldn't help wanting you for us—you were that good.*

*You also should know that Peter followed your career—in all its aspects—and I think, in his way, he was pleased that his assessment of you was right. You WERE his finest shooter—and for the good guys.*

*Archer, take care of yourself and make it work for you.*

*Warmest regards,*
*Gen. Harrison Dobbs, U.S. Army*
*Vice Chairman of the Joint Chiefs of Staff*

Archer closed the note and let it drop into her lap. She leaned her head back again and sat without moving. So, Dobbs went all the way. *Bravo, Dobbs, bravo!*

Cars around her came and went, and Archer barely noticed. Finally, she picked up the card. On the cover was a simple picture of wildflowers in a pitcher, on a table on an old-fashioned porch. She opened the card, and inside it said, "Congratulations, Birthday Girl." Handwritten in a loose scrawl at the bottom, Peter had put, "Dearest girl, should I stop waiting? —Peter".

Then the tears flowed. She cried for Peter Bennett, who, in his strength and conviction, had been her mentor. Whenever she had thought she couldn't cope, she remembered his words. *Goddamn it, Archer,* he would bellow at her when she shook, *choke down that fear. Choke down that loathing, and courage will come. It's in you, girl. It's in you. Just tap into it. Do it—now!* And it had come. The courage had come. The courage to do things she didn't want to do, things she cringed at doing, things that left nightmares as their legacy, things that made her tremble in the replaying. *Courage is grace under pressure,* Hemingway said. *Courage is being scared to death—but saddling up anyway,* John Wayne said. Peter had taught her that she could go on automatic pilot if the cause was just, and the job would get done. He had taught her that not feeling was, in certain circumstances, a virtue—it kept the horror from becoming paralysis.

His kind of certainty must be comforting, Archer reflected as the tears fell. *You know, Archer,* he would say to her, *contrary to popular belief, not everything in life is relative. Some things actually are just plain right or just plain wrong.* Strangely, the man who had handpicked her as an assassin was, in a way, her moral compass. He had taught her that you always had choices: to kill or be killed, to believe in something enough to die for it or live a mediocre life in which nothing is worth dying for, to surrender or fight. *That way,* he said, *even if you lose, you win.* She had refused to work for his causes, for someone else's agenda, but used everything he had taught her on an agenda she understood and embraced. Sitting slumped in her Jeep in the post office parking lot, Archer cried softly for Peter Bennett, a man she truly loved and admired.

Archer called Gavin to tell him she was leaving for Wyoming at the end of the week. He sounded delighted.

"Boy," he said, "when you decide something, you move fast. That's my star. What do you think Connor will do when you tell him?"

"I don't know, and it doesn't matter. We were meant to be together," she said lightly. "I think—I hope—he'll act like he was expecting me."

"And when will *I* see you again?"

"This Thanksgiving. You're coming to Wyoming, and we'll come back east at Christmas to see you," said Archer, with more assurance than she felt.

"You're sure?"

"I'm sure."

She paused, then said, "Gavin, you've been my rock for years. You know that, don't you? And you know I'll always be here for you if you ever need me, but I'm retiring."

"I know, love, I know. It's okay… It's okay, Archer," he repeated. And she could feel his smile.

Next, she called Sharon.

"But, Archer, what's your plan? Did you call Connor to be sure he's not already married or something?"

Archer sagged for a moment. She had never thought of that possibility. "Gee, thanks, Shar. Give me a little credit. My charms *have* to have lasted at least six months," she sniffed, hoping it was true. "He can't have gotten over me that fast…can he? Anyway, I'm going to get him back. Unquestionably."

Archer hesitated a second, then said, "You know, Shar, for all the tragedy I've had in my life, I've also been blessed. I was blessed with Annie for as long as I had her, and I've been blessed with only wonderful men passing through my life. Not a pig or a bounder among them. Men who believed in me when I didn't believe in myself. From Daddy to Adam to Gavin." She wanted to add Peter Bennett and her training cohorts from Syracuse, but she kept those to herself. "Connor is the last in the line of wonderful men who supported me when I couldn't support myself. I'm going to do everything in my power to make things right with him. I'm going to Wyoming, and if it's too late, at least I'll know I tried."

Sharon smiled. "Are you selling the cabin?"

"Not yet, but I spoke to the realtor who had the listing when I bought it. She thinks it would sell fast. She said Boston and New York people are always looking for summer retreats up here."

"Are you at least going to call first? I mean, it'll be something of a shock to just show up, won't it?"

"No call," said Archer. "I don't want to give him time to think about it. I need the element of surprise on my side. And Hadley. He loves Hadley, and more importantly, Alice loves Hadley. Connor would never turn Hadley away."

"But, when will I see you again? When are you going? Are you flying?"

"Nope, driving. I'm leaving Friday. I just have one more loose end to tie up."

# CHAPTER
# 36

Archer and Hadley drove to East Haven the next day. It was pouring rain, but Archer still hopped in and out of at least ten different models of two-horse trailers. As the rain hit her face and the wind whipped the brim of her rain hat back and forth, she meticulously checked trailer specifications, weights, towing requirements, and safety features. She had to be sure the Jeep could safely tow whatever she chose.

Finally, she decided on a Featherlite two-horse with a dressing room. It was available immediately, and it met her needs. She watched as the salesman hitched it to the Jeep. Hadley stared suspiciously at it, her tail motionless. For Archer, this was old home week. She loved nothing better than taking her show on the road.

As she pulled out into traffic, the rain stopped. She felt light, young, and hopeful. New beginnings—a redo. Maybe it was possible to have one after all.

The next morning, she loaded the Jeep. Her dark auburn hair was pulled back by a big tortoiseshell barrette, and she wore jeans, a navy crewneck sweater, and a light blue fleece. As she slammed the back car door, Archer turned to look at her cabin, maybe for the last time. She gazed at it steadily. Plain and unassuming, it had done its job well, keeping her safe as she mended.

The tapestry of early fall color swished in the breeze, treetops sweeping blue sky. "Oh, don't tempt me, you Berkshire Circe," she whispered, tears forming in her gray-green eyes. "Don't tempt me into staying. I need to go."

And with one last fond look back, she turned away and opened the car door.

"Let's go, girl," she said, and the lab trotted around the side of the cabin and hopped into the backseat.

They drove slowly on narrow country roads, snaking along creeks and around hills to Mad River Farm in Simsbury, Connecticut. Archer had called Jane Russo two days ago to tell her she was coming for Allegra. Jane had been flabbergasted. After six years of no contact except for payments, Archer was taking the horse.

"Is there a problem, Archer?" Jane had asked.

"No, not at all," Archer said. "I'm moving out West, and…and I want Allegra with me."

"Oh, well, that's fine. That's just fine." She recalled the hesitation in Jane's voice. "Are you all right, Archer?"

"Fine, just fine. And thank you—really, thank you for asking."

Around midmorning, Archer pulled into the dirt driveway at Mad River Farm. It had been almost seven years. For the three years before that, it had been her and Annie's home away from home. She had been here twice a day, six days a week—even more often when there were horse shows—sometimes bringing work to do in the car or the bleachers.

Driving up the familiar dirt road, Archer watched the horses, turned out in their paddocks on both sides of the driveway. Several trotted up to the fence, whinnying loudly as she passed. The rhodo-dendron bushes lining the entrance were bigger than she remembered them, and a new indoor arena stood behind the original one. Other-wise, the farm looked well kept, recently painted, and as good as ever.

Archer parked, opened the car door, and slipped on her old brown leather paddock boots and her dark green nylon riding jacket.

She stopped for a minute and remembered. Annie would always hop out of the car, skip to the barn door, turn, and give a single side-to-side wave, then disappear into the barn. Sometimes on a Friday evening, she might turn and dramatically blow a kiss to her mother. *Au revoir, ma petite Maman,* she would call out her grade school French, before opening the barn door and disappearing inside. After-ward she would chatter excitedly about the horses, how her riding had gone, what the other girls did, how their horses had done, and what was planned for the next day.

She paused at the top of the line of stalls, hesitant. A door behind her opened, and Jane Russo came out of the office, smiling, hand extended.

"Archer, how are you? It's so good to see you looking so well."

"Thanks so much, Jane. I *am* well. How is Allegra doing?"

Jane hesitated for a moment, looked down, hands in the pockets of her jacket, then looked up at Archer again.

"She's pretty good, actually." She paused. "For the past six months, I've let a nice, sharp little thirteen-year-old girl ride her occasionally—just to give her a bit of exercise, you know."

When Archer expressed no upset, she went on. "Carrie rides very nicely and can't afford her own horse. She's learned all she can from our school horses and has real talent. She's done some low jumps on Allegra, and I swear, Archer, that horse takes care of that child, moving right or left to keep her balanced, like she wants to make sure she doesn't fall off. Never saw anything quite like it…uh, anyway, I know you didn't want to sell or lease her, but I didn't think you'd mind a girl using her lightly. I hope it was okay."

"That's fine, Jane. I'm glad you were kinder than I was. Thanks." Archer paused. "Is she in the same stall?"

"No, we moved her to the next aisle over. Just go around the corner at the end of the row, to the right. She's in the second stall on the left. Go on down, why don't you? It's quiet here this time of day."

Archer walked down the aisle, speaking softly to the horses as they poked their noses out for a pat. "Hello, you fine fellow...How are you today?...And you?...Yes, and you, too, silly."

At the end of the aisle, she turned to the right and started up the next row. And as she rounded the corner, she saw a dark bay head with a sharp white heart in the middle of its forehead. Turning fluidly toward Archer, full-faced, Allegra looked steadily at her. Archer stopped dead in the aisle, staring at the animal that had been the object of Annie's love and obsession. Beautiful Allegra, possessor of Annie's soul. "Forgive me, dear one," she breathed.

Archer walked the length of a stall and drew the glove off her right hand. Allegra's head hung out over the stall door, and she reached out to touch the soft, downy nose. Allegra looked at her, then nodded and nuzzled her cupped hand. After a second, the mare pulled back her nose, and Archer slid the stall door open and stepped into the space of fresh shavings and sweet mounded hay.

Archer swallowed hard and began to cry softly, hugging tightly the only great love Annie would ever have. She took the worn leather halter, engraved with a small brass plate that read, "Allegra—Owner, Annie MacKenzie," and slipped it over Allegra's ears. She fastened the throat latch but did not move to leave, instead caressing the smooth, dark neck and bringing her face close to breathe in the warm, sweet, earthy scent. Archer wept into the mare's neck while the mare stood patiently, quietly alert.

"I'm sorry, Allegra. I'm sorry it's me and not her," Archer said over and over.

Allegra bobbed her head a few times as if to say, *Well, here you are now. It's time. You've finally come for me. I've been waiting for you.*

Alone amid the fragrant hay and September warmth, clean bedding, and cool scent of leather, Archer dreamed of riding with Annie in England, in Vermont, in Wyoming. She dreamed of Annie graduating from college, and a wedding, and grandchildren. She dreamed of celebrating Christmas with Adam and Annie and Annie's children in the house in West Hartford. She dreamed of teaching her grandchildren, alongside Annie, to ride and ride well. Then she sobbed into the mare's neck until she had no more tears. She shook her head hard and straightened up. It was a wonderful dream, but a dream nonetheless.

Archer dried her tears on the backs of her gloves and put a lead rope on Allegra's halter. Patting the mare's neck, she murmured, "Let's go, Allegra," and slid open the stall door. She stepped out, and the horse followed her down the aisle and outside to the waiting trailer. Allegra went up the ramp of the trailer without hesitating, as if this were all exactly as she had expected. She stood patiently as Archer fastened the trailer hitches on either side of her nose, latched the padded safety bar behind her rump, lifted the ramp into its locked position, and closed the door behind her.

"Now I'm ready, Allegra," Archer said as she shut the trailer door. "Ready to see if we have any life left in us.

# CHAPTER
# 37

Eight days after picking up Allegra, Archer arrived in Little Tempest, Wyoming. She liked it immediately. The main street was wide, and the buildings were log structures. A covered board sidewalk ran in front of the line of shops on each side, and a crossroads bisected the street with a single traffic light.

Archer stopped at the light. Stores selling cameras, jewelry, and outdoor equipment lined one side, and a leather store occupied most of the block across from them. A pretty bar/restaurant/cafe called the Hangout stood on the corner. Plants dangled from the café's outdoor porch, where four tables were set for early dinner customers. The sun hung low in the west. In another hour, they would need blankets to dine outside, Archer thought.

As she pulled into the parking area of a small gas station to check her map, she was struck by the chrome blue sky and the fresh, brisk breeze. Late September was cool here. She pulled a spruce-green fleece from the backseat of the Jeep and put it on, then pulled her reading glasses from her pocketbook, spread the map out on the hood of her car, and looked at it carefully. Yes, this was it, but where was Three Chimneys?

Archer was scanning the map again for some clue to where Connor's ranch might be, when she realized she was not alone. She looked up to see three men staring at her with friendly curiosity.

"Hi, there, ma'am. Need any help?" asked the eldest. He was tall, sturdy, about sixty, wearing jeans and a black cowboy hat. He tipped his hat to her. "I couldn't help noticing the Massachusetts plates on your car."

She smiled, squinting at the sun in her eyes, and lifted her left hand to shade them. "Well, yes, thanks. I'm looking for Connor McCall's place, Three Chimneys. Do you happen to know how to get there?"

The older man nodded and smiled. He moved closer to look at Archer's map, when one of the younger men, who wore stovepipe boots, said, "Hey, isn't that the girl from the picture?"

The third man, with a black ponytail to his shoulders, looked over at Archer with new interest. "By God, I think it is!"

They all turned toward her as if choreographed, and the one who had spoken first actually reached into his inner jacket pocket to put on glasses. They examined Archer like an unusual biological specimen. She flushed.

"Yup, that's her," said the first man, taking his glasses off and replacing them in his pocket.

"Hey, look! She has a horse back here," said Ponytail. Allegra stared out through her barred window.

"Um, gentlemen, can you help me with this?" asked Archer, interrupting their examination of her and her horse.

Ponytail poked a finger into the trailer's open window, petting Allegra's smooth nose. The horse accommodated him, thrusting her nose out through the opening in the bars. "Oh, yeah, this is a nice mare. She just needs a little legging up. Muscles a little slack, but she'll work up real good," he declared with authority, still petting Allegra and peering into the trailer to look at her feet.

Archer glanced at the two younger men. The one in stovepipe boots was now petting Hadley, who by now had her head out the driver's side window, while the other was still gauging the roping and ranching potential of Allegra, equine star of the 1993 Bridgehampton Classic, and Reserve Champion in Amateur Hunters on the East Coast in 1994.

The older man turned back to Archer. "Well, ma'am, yes, I sure can direct you there. It's not too far. You go back out the road you came in on." He paused and tipped his head back. "Let's see, I want to take you as direct as I can. Take the wrong road, and over the mountain you go. Okay, go back the way you came, for, oh, I'd say about seven, no, eight miles. Then turn at John's ranch here, where I'm puttin' an X, and go right."

"No, Joe, I'd take her around Tupper Lake. It's longer but it's marked better. The way you're taking her, one mistake and she'll go over the mountain," piped up Boots.

"You're crazy, Jimmy. That's five miles out of the way. She's smart. Anyway, after that right, just keep going until you see Three Chimneys' gate. It'll probably be open, but if it's not, just drive around it and back onto the driveway. Connor won't mind. He's…well, you'll see how he is. He may be out on the range at this hour, or putting up hay. Probably hay. It's pretty late in the day to still be out in the hills."

"Well, thanks a lot," said Archer. "You've been very kind,"

"No problem, ma'am," said Joe, tipping his hat. "Nice horse you got there. Hope to see you again."

Archer smiled and got back in the Jeep. And after taking another look at the little map, she pulled out, going back the way she had come. The three men stood smiling and waving. As soon as she was gone, she was sure they went into the Hangout to report that Connor McCall's New England woman was in town.

Archer drove along the empty road. It took her almost an hour to get to the arched wooden gate reading THREE CHIMNEYS RANCH. Underneath, in smaller letters, was carved "Ramboulliet Sheep

World's Finest Fleece." Archer had, in fact, taken a wrong turn and gone "over the mountain."

The gate was open. She drove a few hundred feet, then stopped. Sky and hills spread in every direction; it wasn't quite like Joan Fontaine on the driveway to Manderlay, but just as breathtaking— and as nerve-racking.

The driveway stretched up a slight incline, and the hills rolled away yellow-green to the horizon. Archer could not see a house, barn, or any other structure. Now she was scared. What if Connor told her to leave? What if he hated her? Worse, what if he had someone else, someone less neurotic and less troubled than she—someone who made him happy? Hadley looked at Archer, tongue lolling, and shook her head. "I'm not ready, Hadley."

She backed out of the driveway, and headed back into town, such as it was. Back at the gas station, she asked about local lodging.

"No motels within twenty miles, ma'am," said the young man at the counter. "We don't get many visitors, but Mrs. Winslow takes in people all the time. Just six miles south, direction you just came from. Can't miss it. 'Circle J Ranch' on the gate. Just tell Dolly Winslow I sent you."

"Shouldn't I call first?" asked Archer.

"Naw, that'd just confuse things. She'll take care of your horse, too."

Archer got into the Jeep heading south and found the Circle J easily. Once on the front porch, she knocked on the open screen door. "Hello? Anyone home?" she called.

"Just a minute. I'll be right there," a woman's pleasant voice called back.

As Archer surveyed the farm—or "ranch," as they called it out here—a plump, elderly, smiling woman, her long gray hair tied up in a bun, bustled up to the door. She had to be at least seventy-five, though she moved briskly.

"Well, hello there. Can I help you?" she said, opening the screen door. "Come on in, dear. It's getting cool out there. My, what a lovely fall we've been having. Come on in. I almost have my piecrust done, so forgive the flour on my hands."

She looked at Archer expectantly.

"I was sent by…" And Archer realized she had not gotten the name of the young man at the gas station. "Well, I wondered if you had a room I could rent for a few days. I have a dog and horse, too. I'm sorry; I didn't realize I would need to stop somewhere out here, but…" Her voice trailed off.

"Well, of course I do, dear. I'm Dolly Winslow, and I have a room at the top of the stairs you can use. I assume your dog can stay with you, and your horse can go into the little paddock out front. Just turn him out there and let him romp, why don't you? I've been a widow for almost eight years now, and I like the company. No bellhops here or room service, but I think you'll be comfortable." Dolly turned to go back in the kitchen.

"Oh, thank you so much," said Archer. "I'll just turn Allegra—my horse—out, and then I'll be in with my bags."

"Fine, dear. Just show yourself up. Dinner's at six if you don't want to go to the Hangout. I'm afraid that's the only place open at night for twenty miles. If you want a real dinner, sorry to say, you have to go the forty-five minutes into Jackson."

"Oh, dinner here will be lovely. Thank you again."

"You're entirely welcome, dear," said Dolly, with a wave of her floured hands.

# CHAPTER
# 38

Dinner was a wonderful concoction of chicken in a crust with celery, potatoes, and onions. Dolly kept up a stream of talk, especially when she learned that Archer knew Connor McCall, her neighbor just over the hill.

"Oh, Connor. What a nice young man he is! Just needs to meet the right woman. I thought he was sweet on Charlotte, you know, from the Hangout. Beautiful girl, lovely figure. In my day, she'd have been snapped up years ago. But the young people these days—"Can't commit," they tell me. In my day, you saw someone you liked, you got married, you had kids, and that was that. No thinking it over for years.

"Oh, my, yes. Connor came here seven years ago. Almost lost his shirt, he did. Ha! But then he got the hang of things and is doing right well. Everyone is real happy for him. The ranchers like him. He employs a good number of the boys and treats 'em well, so I hear.

"He'd be a catch, I'd say. Good-looking, clean, makes a good living—oh, dear, listen to me, going on and on. Now, how do you come to know Connor, dear?"

Archer looked up from her cherry pie, still mulling over this woman named Charlotte.

"Oh, he inherited some land next to mine in Massachusetts. Our paths quite literally crossed out there. He's from Boston originally, you know."

"Oh, yes. I did hear he was from the East. My eldest son, William, lives back there in Providence, Rhode Island. Loves it there. And my little one, Taylor, is out in Hawaii. Can you imagine? Can't keep them home, much as you'd like to," Dolly said, chuckling. "Now, do you have any children yourself, dear?"

Archer hesitated, on the brink of saying "no", then put down her own cup of coffee and said, "Yes, I do, Dolly. Thank you for asking. I have a daughter who died several years ago but she was the most wonderful child any mother could have asked for."

Then Archer talked about Annie while Dolly Winslow listened.

The next morning, Archer woke to the sound of a milk truck pulling up to the Winslow front door.

"Tommy, I'll take two extra quarts today and another dozen eggs—I have a guest staying," Dolly called out the front door, a touch of pride in her voice.

Archer rolled over and stretched on the clean white sheets, opening her eyes. Looking up from the soft, plump pillow, she studied the yellow and purple flowers on the ceiling wallpaper, which covered her like a sheltering canopy. She turned onto her side and squinted at the clock: 8:34. With a yawn, she slipped out of bed and pulled on a flannel plaid nightshirt before walking over to the window. She pushed her long hair behind her ears and gazed out at the ranch, arms crossed, hugging herself.

From the window, she could see that the fields were no longer green but not yet brown. In the near pasture, Allegra lay in the sun.

She must be at peace, Archer thought, knowing horses were ever ready to flee on the smallest whim, and lay down only if they felt safe. Clique almost never lay down, nervous Nelly that he was, eyes darting, ears forward, tail high. He was always busy looking for the next fence to jump, the next troll to stomp. Ah, but he flew, galloping steady as the rain, pounding rhythmically, gaining pace and volume, greedily gobbling up the ground beneath them, and finally stopping in a lather, full of glee and good intentions. Clique. Truest of friends, fearless collaborator, keeper of secrets, soaring partner, his hoofbeats now silent. *Rest in peace, dear one.*

Pulling herself back from her reverie, Archer showered, got dressed, and went out to the corral to saddle Allegra for her first time in over six years. Dolly had nodded and smiled when she saw Archer dressed to ride, as though it was the most normal thing in the world for someone to drive across the country with a dog and a horse, park in her yard, and then go out for a ride on the horse she had dragged along.

Archer approached the paddock where the horse had spent the night. Allegra was alone in the field but for a lone cow, short and black, mechanically chewing its cud. At the gate, Archer stopped and watched the mare graze. Every so often, her tail would flick lazily, and, she would trot forward to a new patch of grass. For Archer, it never got old: the thrill of seeing a raised head, a flicking tail, and a horse taking off at a dead run. *My addiction,* she had always called it.

After a few minutes, she approached Allegra with halter in hand. The mare raised her head as Archer got closer, but made no move to bolt. Archer stretched out her hand, and the horse took a step toward her, then another. Carefully lifting the halter up, Archer gently wrapped it around Allegra's head, buckled it snugly, lead rope attached, and walked her to the barn.

The mare stood in the cross ties while Archer picked out her feet. Then, selecting a coarse, stubby brush from the tack box, she loosened the dirt and grass from the horse's coat. With short, brisk strokes, Archer whisked away dust and debris, talking softly all the while. Then she completed the grooming with a soft finish brush that made Allegra's coat positively glow.

Archer put her old Smith-Worthington saddle on the little mare and tightened the girth as securely as she could. She had forgotten how slim Allegra was, compared to Clique. She would need to pick up a smaller girth for future rides, she realized as she fastened the last hole in the girth's leather strap.

From a battered canvas bag, Archer pulled out three bits: a snaffle, a rubber pelham, and a gag. She chose the least severe, the snaffle, and hoped Allegra would respect it. If not, they were in for quite a ride.

"Okay, we're ready, aren't we, Allegra? Let's go, my movable feast," she whispered.

After leading the mare out to the yard, she put on her helmet and mounted her with no mounting block. Allegra moved forward, head bobbing, at a steady trot. Archer smiled unconsciously, posting easily, feeling pleasure and satisfaction.

After about ten minutes, they slowed to a walk. Stroking Allegra's neck frequently, Archer observed the vastness around her. Sage covered much of the landscape, and yellow and purple prairie flowers still bloomed in infrequent but merry clusters.

After a half hour, Archer squeezed lightly, asking for a canter, and Allegra willingly obliged, her pace steady and even, feeling like a comfortable rocking horse. Speed was Archer's own vice, and she would have loved nothing more than to tear up the hill at a full gallop on Annie's horse. But she didn't want to overdo it on a horse that was not fit yet. She slowed, and for the first time since Annie died, she felt something close to serenity, some vague acceptance that what was, was.

At the top of a hill, Archer stopped and drew in a breath at the sight. She gazed at the valley below. That was it—she knew it from Connor's description. Three Chimneys. She closed her eyes and remembered everything he had ever told her about its layout. Two thousand acres, log cabin with a big front porch facing the rising sun, a porch that wrapped around two sides. Two big barns. A pond behind the house. And sheep everywhere dotting the hills, the paddocks, the side fields. She opened her eyes, taking it all in. This was it.

Archer strained to see if she could spot Connor. She saw no one, not even ranch hands. After a few minutes, she slowly turned Allegra back toward the Winslow place. How had she gotten herself into this ridiculous position? And what the hell was she doing in Little Tempest, Wyoming, unless it was to burst in on Connor? That was the point, wasn't it? It was her turn to take the risk. He had done it in the Berkshires and been crushed for it.

Still, he survived. But what if he had survived *happily*?

She needed to summon up the courage to tell him she had been wrong. If he turned his back on her, well, she would just have to live with that. "The choices we make dictate the life we live"—Danny DeVito in *Renaissance Man. Jesus, Loh, get a grip.*

# CHAPTER
# 39

L ate that Sunday afternoon, Archer sat in a rocking chair in the corner of her room in the Winslow house. Hadley lapped at her water, then turned around twice and flopped onto the floor with a thud. Within a minute, she was snoring. Outside, Allegra grazed in the near pasture, against a backdrop of snow-dusted mountains.

It had been three days since Archer arrived, and she knew that it was now time to stop being a spectator. She suspected that news of her arrival had reached Connor, yet he hadn't shown up on her doorstep. This gave her pause.

Twenty minutes later, she woke Hadley. She had already packed, and now she wrote a check for Dolly Winslow. "Dolly, my plans are a bit uncertain," she said. "Can I return tonight if...things don't work out?"

"Oh, my dear, of course. You and that horse of yours and that pretty brown dog are always welcome."

Archer smiled. Her confidence in her reception at Three Chimneys was shaky at best. She hugged Dolly, then loaded Allegra into the trailer, put her bags in the rear of the Jeep, and cajoled Hadley into the backseat. *Okay, let's try this again. I'm as ready as I'll ever be.*

At the entrance to three Chimneys, Archer pulled in, and this time she kept driving. Cresting the top of the hill, all she could see was open sky, and for a moment it seemed that she, Hadley, and Allegra were suspended, able to fly if even the slightest breeze should blow beneath them.

Then the homestead she had seen from afar on horseback sprawled into view: log farmhouse and pretty lawns in a tidy green valley. Fluffy beige sheep were everywhere. To the rear of the house was a large pond, and to the left, a barn complex of four or five buildings.

There were big old cottonwoods around the house, and a huge front porch that wrapped around the right side. A circular driveway drifted off to the right, leading to the front of the house. Archer followed the road to the right and parked in front. She sat still for a moment, looking around. There was no one in the yard; in fact, no one was visible at all.

She opened the Jeep door and stepped out, still hearing nothing. Everything was so serene here. Hadley jumped out behind her, and she shut the door quietly, went back to the trailer, and opened the side window.

Allegra stretched her neck out the opening and inhaled the air, and Archer pulled a molasses treat from her pocket and fed it to her.

She looked around, trying to decide what to do next. The main barn stood to the left of the house, its wide sliding doors open. She and Hadley headed toward it, Hadley ten feet ahead of her. Then she saw him. Unconsciously, she stopped, moistened her lips, and unclenched her fists. Her heart leaped.

Connor stood in front of alfalfa bales stacked high and deep against the back wall of the barn. He was calculating how much hay he would need for his own farm this winter and how much he could afford to sell to the neighboring cattle ranchers and "hobby" horse people. It fetched a good price in the spring, when many ranchers had run out and were more than willing to pay five or six dollars a bale.

Connor estimated he would have at least five thousand bales to sell. He figured how many more would fit in this space before he would have to start filling the back barn. It was a big, airy structure— a good storage space as long as the hay had dried fully in the windrows before it was baled. That was the trick to producing mold-free hay— it was all in the drying weather, and this year had been good.

Connor sighed. He was tired. The day had begun at five in the morning, and he hadn't stopped since. After spending four hours in the hills with five of his men, checking the young sheep born in the spring, he, Felix, and a new hand had worked on loose fencing for the rest of the day while the other men worked on preparing the barns for winter.

Connor had just put Millie away after cooling her out and brushing her down. Now he was tidying up the barn. It gave him satisfaction as one of the few things he could control. A messy, unkempt barn was a depressing sight first thing in the morning. He stopped for a minute, put his elbow up on the end of a haystack, and rested his forehead on his arm, thinking, *Is this all there is?*

His back was almost fully turned to Archer. From a distance, he looked older and bone tired. His hat was on top of the haystack, his jeans were dusty from a day's work, and his denim shirt was soft from many washings. He had a rake leaning against the hay.

She heard him sigh heavily as he reached for the rake and began to gather the last few bits of straw. Alice lay nearby in a sunny patch just outside the barn door.

As Archer approached, she heard sheep mutterings from the pastures behind the barn. Through the open door in the back of the barn, she could see four enormous white dogs milling among the sheep: the City Girls.

Hadley had less self-control. Seeing Connor, she yelped and bounded toward him. He looked up, startled. Alice raised her head, and her little stump of a tail became a propeller as she spied Archer, got up, and trotted toward her. Archer stooped and brushed the black fur back so she could see those round brown eyes.

"You're still so beautiful, Alice," she murmured. "I missed you, and so did Hadley."

"H-Hadley?" Connor stammered. He looked up at the barn door opening. "My God, Archer? Is it really you?" he said, squinting in disbelief. "What…what are you *doing* here? I…I heard from at least twenty people that my 'lady from Massachusetts' was in town, but— I mean, I didn't hear from you and I thought maybe you decided to move on, if it was even you to begin with…"

Connor took a step forward. He started to smile but didn't finish. He shuffled, looked down a second, then shoved a hand into a pocket of his jeans, then took it back out. He looked at Archer hesitantly, as if he didn't want to play the fool again by assuming she had come all this way for him.

Archer glanced around the barn uncertainly. This wasn't going as she had hoped. Connor wasn't exactly jumping for joy. Then he spied the trailer and Jeep. At that moment, Allegra hung her head out the trailer window, snorted, and whinnied.

Connor calmed. "Well, I'd know *you* anywhere, girl. You're Annie's girl. I couldn't be more pleased to see you again."

Archer had lost any ability to be clever or witty. She had thought of at least three or four entrance lines. *Is that a gun in your pocket, or are you just powerfully glad to see me?* Or *Where have you been all my life, doll?* Or…Now they all seemed trite. "I came to find you," she said. "I hope it's not too late."

Connor stared at her for a moment. The pieces were there, but they still didn't fit. He reached down, petted Hadley gently behind her ears, then slowly straightened up and took a step back. He turned to face Archer.

"I'm not your consolation prize, Archer," he said, looking her in the eye.

Her shoulders fell. Her head bowed. There was silence. Then, after another moment, she lifted her head and said defiantly, "*When Harry Met Sally*—Sally, to Harry, when she's hurt and feels rejected by him."

Connor stared at her as if she had a second head.

Archer stared back and then said deliberately, "Am I right?"

Connor looked down at the toe of his boot for a moment, stuck both hands in the pockets of his jeans, and shook his head. Finally, he began to laugh.

"Damn. I have to hand it to you, Archer. Even at the pinnacle of our own personal high drama, you are the quickest thinker I've ever met. Well, yeah, sure, of course that's it. You got me. Hell, I figured I couldn't use 'Quite frankly, my dear, I don't give a damn.' Way too obvious—and somewhat overused, in my humble opinion."

After a pause, Connor looked up, leaned back against the stack of bales, and said, "Arch, I'm not sure I'm ready for you. You *broke* my heart, Arch. I never understood what that meant when other people said it, but I sure do now."

Archer, who had thought Connor was in her corner when he'd laughed, wasn't sure now. She looked at him, eyebrow raised.

He shook his head but continued. "Do you know what that's like? To have your heart broken? *Do you really know what that's like?* Let me tell you, Arch. It's when it actually *hurts* every time you take a deep breath—really, physically hurts in the very middle of your chest. It's when…when every time you try to enjoy something you love—like a nice movie, good food, a walk in the woods—you ache because you remember it with her, and suddenly the enjoyment is sucked dry. It's when, just when you think you're over it, it comes back in this massive flood of torment, as fresh and cutting as the day it happened. But you know what's worst of all? What's worst of all is that everything reminds you of her. Everything. The sunrise, the weather forecast, the toaster— yeah, the damn *toaster*—so first you get this rush, remembering the splendor of it all, and then an even bigger wave of despair, because you'll never have it again.

"I know why you did it, Archer, I do, but don't forget, I ended up on the mountain, waiting with a goddamn bottle of champagne."

Archer stood staring, then finally said, "I know, but I…I guess I just needed to sink as low as you can get—without dying—to understand."

Then she added softly, "I've had my heart broken, too, you know. I do know what it's like, but I felt I had no choice."

"You always have a choice, Archer," he said. "And I'm sorry. Of *course* you, of all people, know what it's like to be brokenhearted."

In the silence she heard the echo of Peter Bennett's voice: *You always have a choice, Archer.* Then she asked, "Did you see Lauren?"

Connor smiled. "Yeah. Twice, actually, and as usual, you were right. She's fabulous, and I'll never not be in her life again…if she lets me. I don't want to stir up old Donald, I really don't. The last thing I want to do is cause any discord in that household, but Lauren mentioned wanting to visit me out here next summer, so we'll see."

"I'm happy for you, Connor. You'll be a wonderful friend and father to her."

Again they were silent for a moment.

"Why didn't you call me?" Connor asked.

"Why didn't *you* call *me*?" Archer realized instantly how childish it sounded. "Besides, I did call—or Sharon did. I had a close encounter with a bullet. She wanted you to know."

"You tried to kill yourself?" he asked, shocked.

"No, no. Long story, occupational hazard."

"Ah, right. I never got the message. I would have been there, Archer; I would have. You must know that."

She nodded.

Connor lifted a hay pull from the wall and used it to pull down two bales. Archer immediately sank onto one, and Connor sat on the other. He held his head down in his hands for a moment, then looked up.

"Shot…If I'd only known." He shook his head. "Arch, I couldn't call. I didn't want to crowd you. I wanted you to be with me for just one reason: because it was the choice you made freely out of love—no force, no pressure, no guilt." He paused, then smiled a crooked little smile. "Don't laugh, but I became painfully philosophical about the whole thing. After watching *The English Patient,* which, by the way, definitely does *not* have a happy ending, I actually convinced myself that just because two people don't end up together doesn't mean it wasn't still the best thing that ever happened to them. That's how I willed myself to feel about us. That's how I got through the day. But there wasn't a day, Arch, that I didn't grieve—not a day. There wasn't a day I didn't relive some part of our time and suffer the pain all over again."

Connor paused for a second, but Archer sensed he wasn't done. She remained silent.

"I've been alone my whole life," he continued. "I'm not afraid of it. What I'm afraid of is living a life with no connections, where no one mourns my passing, because I've touched no one, where I'm not missed, because I wasn't really there. I don't want that life anymore."

Archer nodded and leaned forward. "I know. I don't know if I can explain, but I want to try… When I lost Annie, I lost hope. Isn't that really what a child is? The belief that tomorrow will come and be better, that life is worth living even when it doesn't seem like it, that we still believe spring will come even as we see deterioration and decline all around us?

"When Annie died, I lost my hope. I had all these ties that gave me a place in my world. I was Adam's wife; I was Annie's mother; I was a respected lawyer. I had an orbit fixed by all these things that defined me. I lost all those markers at the same time, and I couldn't cope. But the loss of Annie was like someone came along and erased the future. Nothing mattered anymore.

"When I met you, I felt like maybe I could set out one little marker again, maybe rejoin the human race. But I got scared. Having some hope again felt like abandoning Annie. I wasn't supposed to have hope without my child—at least, that's what I thought. Now I know I had it backwards. Only by my keeping hope can Annie remain here in spirit, be with me in my daily life.

"I love you, Connor. I should have called you and I should have come earlier. I've been a blind fool. *You* are the knight I've been waiting for my whole life—not to rescue me but to love me."

Connor listened intently to every word, nodded at points, and then replied, "I do understand, and I'm not trying to exact some price because you did what you needed to do then. But I've regrouped, Archer. I can't go through that again. I need to know you're sure this is what you want. Not Wyoming—I don't give a damn about Wyoming; we can go anywhere—but *me...us*. I just can't trust you—or her," he said, pointing at Hadley, "or her," he said, pointing at Allegra. "Will you all be here next month, or will you have packed up and decided it was a big mistake to come out here? I need to sleep on this, Arch. You've been thinking about it for a while, but I'm still shell-shocked just to see you. I need some time."

Archer looked down at her hands, discouraged.

"So you're going to make me wait for an answer?"

"Just till tomorrow. Give me that, Archer."

She bent her head and shook it slowly. Then she looked at him and nodded.

"Okay, I'll give you that."

Archer turned to go back to Dolly's ranch for the night, but Connor caught her arm. "Stay. There's no need to leave now. I have three empty bedrooms. Just pick one, and I'll go put Allegra in an extra stall."

Archer nodded slowly. She selected a room in the back of the house, overlooking the pond and the distant peaks. She watched from the window as Connor took Allegra from the trailer and led her to the barn. Then he pulled away in his truck to pick up some sandwich fixings for an early dinner. They ate together in silence.

As soon as cleanup was done, Archer turned to go to her room. Before leaving, she said, "McCall, please do me a favor—for old times' sake?"

Connor looked at her, eyebrow raised in question.

"Don't break my heart slow."

Archer slept fitfully in the guest room across the hall from Connor, Hadley at the foot of the bed. At four a.m., she got up and pulled on her jeans and T-shirt and zippered fleece. She crept down the stairs and tiptoed into the kitchen to put on some coffee.

To her surprise, it was already brewed, and Connor was sipping a cup as he stood at the counter looking out the back window. He was already dressed. Alice lay at his feet. He looked up as she entered, and smiled.

"Hey, didn't sleep too well?"

"Couldn't. Decided I might as well get up. What are you doing up this early?"

"I couldn't sleep, either," he said, reaching for a cup from the cabinet and pouring some coffee for her.

"Thanks," she said, and took the steaming mug. She looked at him expectantly. "It's tomorrow."

"Yeah, so it is." Silence. Archer tilted her head, then motioned for him to continue. Connor looked down, scuffed a foot against the floor, then looked directly at her. "Okay, well, I did some thinking last night about all this. And you know, I thought about the Berkshires and how we met, and I wondered what we should do today. And then I thought about what the weather would be, and that maybe I should just do my normal rounds and we could talk later, and then, well . . ."

Archer put her mug down, frustration mounting. She turned away to gaze out the window at the green fields as far as she could see. Then she crossed her arms across her chest and, turning back to face him, said very softly, "Connor, just tell me. I'm a big girl; I can take it."

"Well, the thing is, I mean, do I have to build a fancy box stall for that Eastern show horse you brought out here, or what? I mean, we're simple folk out here, and I hope she'll take to the West after the show circuit and all," he said, taking a sip of his coffee.

Archer stood still just long enough for him to put his cup down, then jumped into his arms. He pulled her into a tight hug, lifting her off the ground.

"I'm a pushover, aren't I? But, *damn,* you feel good," he said, burying his face in her hair and kissing her neck. "Should I have held out until dinner?"

"No, no, no," Archer replied, flooded with relief. "I was afraid you wouldn't want to take a chance on me again."

"Surely you jest. You're a one-of-a-kind, once-in-a-lifetime find, Archer Loh. Like I'm going to throw you back into the sea for some other guy to find?"

She laughed and hugged him tighter.

"Come on, let's take a little walk. It's just starting to get light, and someday all this will be yours."

Archer laughed again, grabbed her coat, and put her arm through his. He opened the back door, called the dogs, and headed out. Without looking at her as they walked, Connor said, "And how do we get past it, Arch?"

She turned and looked at him questioningly.

"Your side job—it *is* the elephant in the parlor, you know."

Archer looked down, then back up, and said jauntily, "We can talk about it later. Yes, it is the elephant in the parlor, but we Hemingway aficionados can handle big game, you know."

"It's serious, Archer, and I am, too. I can live with ghosts. Heck, I even *like* some ghosts, but I can't compete with them, and I sure as hell need to know them, because I don't want to run into them some night by accident."

Archer looked down, hands fidgeting.

"Didn't you ever wonder why I never said anything, Arch? I didn't know if you worked alone or were part of a bigger group—still don't know—and I didn't know how you learned to do what you do, but I knew you were fighting for your life. And I was too afraid of doing anything that might threaten our being together. But I've had time to think. I don't want to watch you hurt yourself again and again. I love you too much."

"I know. It's over for me, McCall. No regrets, but it's over for me. We'll talk tomorrow."

Connor cocked his head but nodded, appearing to accept that answer for now. He shook his head and said, "Fine, Scarlett."

He opened his arms, and she turned into them. He kissed her hard before tucking her head into the hollow of his shoulder and holding it there. They stood together in a tight embrace for a long time, with little movement or conversation. Archer turned her head up to him, and he kissed her, this time lightly, barely brushing her lips.

He released her gently, and they turned in unison toward the open field next to the house. They walked holding hands just as four enormous white dogs pranced over, wiggling, never taking their eyes off the herd.

"So these are the City Girls," said Archer, delighted.

"Yep, that's them. I'm actually thinking of adding Chicago and L.A., given the production of this spring's breeding program."

In the September sunrise, he held her close and said, "God, Archer, I thought I'd lost you forever, but you made me stop being afraid to love. And that helped me find my daughter. As they say, 'To fear love is to fear life.'"

Archer looked at him quizzically.

"Not a movie," he said. "A philosopher—Bertrand Russell."

"Deep, McCall, very deep. How long have you been saving that quote to pull out at just the right moment?" she teased back.

"There's a lot you still don't know about me. I'm full of mysteries that will take you years to unravel—*years,* I tell you, woman."

Silence. Then Archer looked up at Connor and asked, "So, McCall, where *does* one go to see a movie out here in lovely Little Tempest? And I do mean *little.*"

"Just a ways into Jackson, about forty-five minutes from here. Little Tempest isn't the end of the earth, you know. And—here's the thing—they have matinees on Wednesdays, kid. How's that for deluxe living?"

Archer threw back her head and laughed. "Oh, boy, maybe *The African Queen* will be playing next week"

They continued to walk toward the pond behind the house and barn. "So, is this fate, Connor? Was your mother right after all?"

Connor shook his head but said, "I don't know, but what do you put on the odds of two people like us meeting on that beautiful mountain, no one for miles, at that particular moment in time? I put my money on my mother and your father setting us up. They probably figured that unless they did something soon, we were both too stubborn to get out of our own way." He paused and turned to her. "This is it, by the way."

Archer looked up at him. "This is what?"

"My one spectacular moment. When you jumped into my arms, and I knew I really was your choice, *that* was the moment I'll never lose. Now I get it. I know what you were talking about."

Archer smiled and nodded.

Connor took her by the shoulders and held her at arm's length. He gazed at her steadily.

"Archer Loh," he said, "there is little in this life I'm sure of, and I seem to know less and less as each year passes. But this much I do know. I'm in love for the first time in my life, and it's forever."

Archer looked back at him, smiling.

"And I'm in love, too…for the last time in my life."

*Murphy's Romance.*